Alan R Cable was a transport consultant for one of the world's largest IT companies, Hewlett Packard, from 1995 to 2000. He was not aware that when he took on this consultancy, this was going to be the key factor for 'Aid into Africa' being launched. Aid into Africa delivered, over the years, 350 tonnes of educational and medical aid into East Africa. It was in 2008 after some 38 flights into Africa that retirement beckoned.

It was his grandson, Rue Cable, back in 2012 who encouraged him to attempt to write a book. In 2015 thanks to his son, Rob, and his wife, Michelle, they managed to get *Rob Hat* published as a Christmas gift. With further three books on the back burner, Austin Macauley Publishers have taken on *Hoodwink* for him.

To my two grandchildren,
Rue Cable and Grace Turvey.

In memory of my late father, Bob Cable, who has been gone now for 51 years, but I still carry him in my heart.

Alan R Cable

HOODWINK

AUSTIN MACAULEY PUBLISHERS™
LONDON • CAMBRIDGE • NEW YORK • SHARJAH

A CIP catalogue record for this title is available from the British Library.

ISBN 9781528950589 (Paperback)
ISBN 9781528951432 (Hardback)
ISBN 9781528974738 (ePub e-book)

www.austinmacauley.com

First Published (2021)
Austin Macauley Publishers Ltd
25 Canada Square
Canary Wharf
London
E14 5LQ

Thanks to my son-in-law, Paul Turvey, our daughter, Sarah, and not forgetting our granddaughter, Grace, for their support over the past 7 years. I am confident this support will continue. Thank you!

A special thanks to my wife, Yvonne, for our fast-approaching 53 years of dedication to each other.

You can fool all the people some of the time, and some of the people all the time, but you cannot fool all the people all the time.

Abraham Lincoln
16th US President 1809–1865
Year 2015

Even today Mr Lincoln's quote still rings true in today's society, and it would take a very foolish person to contradict the 16th US President.

We are all possible of being lied to, deceived, duped, and tricked along with those who would hoodwink us to gain a substantial benefit and, of course, not forgetting those that play lip service to the truth.

The following narrative will illustrate that you can hoodwink the people some of the time, and some of the people all the time, but you cannot hoodwink all the people all the time.

Prologue

March 2015, with Prime Minister Simon Davis for the Peoples Unite Party, the PM will do whatever it takes to see that The Peoples Unite Party gain the keys to 10 Downing Street again. With the election due on the 7th of May, he was feeling confident that he and his party would once again be walking inside the number 10 black door.

Simon Davis's feeling of confidence was about to be kicked into the long grass when he and his Chancellor of the Exchequer, Graham Johnson, boarded the train at Southampton Airport Parkway Railway Station to Waterloo Station.

Elsewhere, Trevor Charles Baines, one of London's most wanted notorious professional criminals from South East London was being put to rest at Honour Oak Cemetery. Trevor Charles Baines from South East London—who was always one step ahead from being caught by the law—was being put to rest.

With the Metropolitan Police Force, none the wiser to where his millions of ill-gotten gains are, the newly promoted DI Judy Reynolds, along with her DS Jones from the Reading Police station, was in attendance. Granted, the detectives were standing back to show respect to his wife Glenda and his 30-year-old son Charlie Baines who did not deserve any respect as they say 'like father, like son.' The sole purpose of their attendance was to observe the last burial of the day for this renowned low life of a human being put beneath into a six-foot hole.

It was in April at the reception of the Tato Hotel. On the mountain slopes of Mount Kilimanjaro was Peter Goodman. He was waiting for Kibo Safaris for his ride to the Machame Gate to assemble with further climbers from Africa Tours to get underway for their trek up to the Roof of Africa.

Part 1

Chapter 1
Sister-in-Law

It was a beautiful sunny and warm day of March; Grace and Rob had just completed the cleaning of their last car at Premier Supreme Private Car Hire Company operating from Ladbroke Grove London.

"Rob, could you pull my wellingtons off for me?" Grace asked, unzipping her waterproof coat and plonking herself down on the bench in their cabin.

Just then, Dave Smith—the owner of the company—walked into their arch where they were working. He entered into their cabin that doubled their office and had to laugh seeing Rob struggling to get Grace's wellingtons off.

"Rob, I see you have reported to Morris Van that you feel the clutch is slipping and might be in need of a new clutch, in which case you can leave the van here tonight. It should be fixed for your return on Monday when one of my drivers will pick you up at Saints House around 8 am." Dave Smith said knowing fully well that Rob was going to ask about getting into Premier this Saturday.

"What? Are we walking here from the Kings George Estate tomorrow?"

"Call it a bonus. See, I am giving you both Saturdays off besides all my cars out this Saturday; hence your services will not be required. Enjoy your weekend!" the MD said walking out of their cabin. Just as he was leaving, he turned. "My daughter Linda, and now your sister-in-law, along with your brother Tony will be here shortly to take you both home," he said closing their cabin door behind him.

"I thought they were not due home from their honeymoon until Saturday," Grace said, still waiting to get her wellingtons pulled off.

"Sod it, Grace. I was taking Rosie's clothes to Southampton and to pick her dirty washing up that Pauline, her friend, will be washing and ironing after we finished here Saturday. Now it seems I am going to have to get the train out of Waterloo." Rob was saying, at last, getting her right wellington boot off.

"It's a shame her mobility scooter is not back from the garage after its repair; you could have used it for your trip to Southampton," she said trying to keep a straight face watching Linda and Tony reversing their Mini Cooper into their arch.

"You two are looking well, so how was your honeymoon in Kenya?" Grace asked waiting in the back of her car. Rob had dashed across the parking area with the keys for their arch to the enormous terrapin being the office for Premier.

"Fantastic, the Leopard Beach Hotel on the white sands of Diani Beach," Linda said looking in her interior mirror where Grace could see her nose was peeling. "Here you go, Grace. I hope you like it," she said handing her a box containing a bottle of Jimmy Choo perfume.

"Thank you," said Grace.

Tony was outside the Mini waiting for Rob to return. "Sorry to keep you waiting," said Rob.

"Get your arse in, Rob."

As he clambered into the back, Linda hand him a box that held a large bottle of Armani aftershave and said, "Now you can smell nice."

"Thank you, sis, that sounds so good now saying sister-in-law; your nose is peeling," Rob said with Grace giving him a dig in his side.

"She doesn't need you to remind her."

"Rob, would you believe that our Uncle Alan and Aunty Yvonne drove from Machame Tanzania and paid us a visit at our hotel in South Mombasa. They booked in for the night."

"Now tell them the funny bit Tony that had us in hysterics," Linda said starting to laugh before Tony informed them.

"They brought Alan's friend Bernie, the pig, and smuggled him into their room, which was a bloody nightmare. Our uncle had to give the housemaid a few Kenya Shillings to not to say anything and to keep her from screaming seeing Bernie took a fancy to her white plimsolls." Tony told them with Linda laughing; mind you, the laughing soon stopped when she hit the traffic jam at Marble Arch.

"We got home early Thursday morning, and waiting at our door was my mum and dad, who had yet to see our house since we had decorated and moved in. This was when he mentioned about giving you two a lift home this evening seeing they needed to work on your Morris Van." Linda told them.

"Besides, we also need to see our folks at Saints House; we have a few gifts for them," Tony said.

"Anyway, so how is your house at 7 Orchard Drive?"

"We are so happy there, Rob. We now only need to decorate our spare room, so when Grace and you wish to stay over, you both be comfortable." Linda said noticing Grace blushing up from her vision from her interior mirror.

"Yes, bro, thanks to you that we own this house with no mortgage to worry about," his brother said noticing Rob was also blushing while holding Grace's hand.

"Rob, if your ears ever start burning late at night, it will because of the ambulances with their sirens blaring out going into St Thomas' Hospital, and as you know, the hospital is only a stone's throw from Orchard Drive and your brother is for everlasting cursing you for buying us this house," Linda said clipping her husband round the ear.

Chapter 2
Morality

"I got your text Rob about our 80-year-old friend Rosie having an accident with her mobility scooter and that she was stopping with her son in Southampton so he can keep an eye on her. So where in the hell is she now?" Tony asked.

"Well, first she's okay—a broken leg and a few bruises—but well shaken up. She now knows not to drive on the main road again after she decided to overtake the number one bus down New Kent Road. The driver never saw her as he pulled out from the bus stop with Rosie and her scooter thrown to the other side of the road. She was fined £50 for reckless driving; I guess to deter her from driving her scooter on the main roads." Rob said but failed to inform his brother where she is currently.

"Peter, her son, was called away on business for a week and she is unable to travel; hence, he's put her into a rest home for the elderly and believe me, she is one unhappy bunny. So, Rob is visiting her tomorrow Saturday. Pauline Shaw, her friend, is dropping off some further clothes and items from her flat and leaving them with your mother, Tony," Grace had butted in and told him what he was also asking.

"Shit Rob, why did you buy her that mobility scooter? We have all seen her whizzing around the Elephant and Castle with no consideration for any bugger," Tony said noticing his brother grinning.

"It's not bloody funny." Rob decided not to defend himself; he just sat there looking out of the window at the traffic that was not moving down Park Lane.

"Wow, calm down lads. Rosie would bang your heads together if she knew you two were arguing about her bad driving habits," Linda kind of shouted to the brothers. Not another word was spoken until they reached Buckingham Palace on their right. While heading towards Westminster Bridge, they saw hundreds of tourists clicking away with their cameras at the palace along with the Queen's Guards in their red uniform and Busbies.

"Rob, how you two coping with morality?" Linda asked.

"Meaning?" Rob asked looking puzzled at Grace who simply shrugged her shoulders much as to say, 'I don't know what she means.'

"You two are kidding me, let me see," she said stroking her chin. Though Linda was thinking what she wanted to say to highlight the past three years of their lives that was not the norm. She could have simply said, 'how you coping living a normal life,' which no doubt both of them would have understood far better.

"It was in June 2012. For your 17th birthday gift, I managed to purchase Tony and you a pair of tickets for Ascot Races. Earlier in June, there was a bank robbery at the National Bank at Clinton Green, which was close to Reading. With the criminal's gang leader, Jim Stone, still at large and wanted by the Metropolitan Police who believed he still had over a million pounds and a vast amount of highly valuable jewellery in his possession. Unbeknown to you Rob, the criminal Jim Stone was heading to Waterloo Station and was going to be arrested on his arrival by the Borough Police Force.

"Your brother took a tumble at the race track and had to spend the night in Heatherwood Hospital, leaving you to travel home alone.

"Once again, you never knew that you shared the carriage with Jim Stone who was holding on tight to a very large suitcase containing his share of the bank robbery. Once your train arrived at Waterloo Station, he was off seeing our boys in blue. He set off so fast even the Jamaican athlete Bolt would have been impressed. Rob, you sat there staring at his large suitcase that, for an obvious reason, he failed to take with him.

"To cut a long story short, yes, thanks to you! You helped a great many good causes with this stolen cash. You concentrated on helping good causes that our PM Simon Davis had betrayed by cancelling their government's funding. I think it's fair to say that our PM never sent you a message of thanks."

With Linda highlighting just how his brother managed to help thousands of the less fortunate, it made Tony feel extremely proud that he's of the same blood. "Love you, Rob," Tony stuttered getting the words out. Rob sat there holding Grace's and remained silent.

"Then it was back in October 2013, you and Grace visited your uncle and aunt in Tanzania. Whilst you guys were in Machame on the foothills on Mount Kilimanjaro—that you both managed to climb—you two were helping your uncle with his charity aid into Africa. Meanwhile, in Machame, an audacious diamond robbery had taken place in Mwanza Northern Tanzania where Johnson Diamond and Tetra Diamonds had millions of pounds worth of diamonds stolen.

"It was after you guys visited Zanzibar and on your return, you took a flight from Dar-as-Salaam to Kilimanjaro International Airport. Anna Kajeme was dragged off your flight but managed to push under the seat in front of her children's large pink plastic bag that turned out to have 750 diamonds glued on. As you are fully aware, Anna Kajeme is still out there, and I am sure she's got no love for you having her large heist of diamonds. Yes, you benefited to the sum of 2.5 million pounds. Yes, Rob, she will no doubt want to seek her revenge.

"To cut your adventure in East Africa short, you received your 50% share of the reward paid by Lloyds to Johnson Diamond Mind and Tetra Diamonds.

"With this money, you helped an orphanage in Moshi Town, Treasures of Africa." Whilst in a traffic jam at Westminster Bridge, Linda turned in her seat and looked directly at Grace.

"This orphanage had a baby dumped at its door that you Grace fell in love with. You found out that the baby needed a heart operation and once again, that reward money helped with the cost involved at Machame Hospital in Tanzania.

Rob and Tony's uncle and aunt, eventually, adopted the baby also now named Grace Hat. Yes, you two in the back of my Mini Cooper are her Godparents.

"Baby Grace aside Rob, you helped your uncle with his 'Climbing for a Brighter Future' project where he helps to feed the orphans and street children in Moshi and Arusha. Various other good causes gained a benefit here in the UK."

Tony interrupted, "Drive on, Linda, we are starting to move again."

Driving past Waterloo Station, Linda went on to say, "Rob, thanks to you, we now own our own home. Once again, thanks to you, you also bought your parent's home—Saints House from the Walworth Council—along with Grace's mum's flat on the 4th floor of Saints House for Jean Long and Grace's two younger sisters.

"Rob, I am so proud to be your sister-in-law, and as Tony said, I do love you and, of course, your wife to be, Grace."

Tony turned to face his brother and Grace and asked: "Now do you understand what Linda was saying? Are you coping with morality?" Rob never said anything; he simply nodded.

"Rob, you're fast approaching 20, and your adventures from 2012 until 2014 are enough to last you a lifetime."

"Rob, I am pleased you are now embracing morality and hopefully enjoying life," Linda said as they pulled into the King George Estate at the Elephant and Castle. Then, they drove into the first block of Saints House and parked in front of Grace's mum's garage.

"Linda and you, bro, I have not done anything wrong, and I am not guilty of sod at all," Rob said giving Grace a kiss on her cheek.

"Just be aware, Rob. They say things happen in three's, so just be careful. Your third adventure might be around the corner," Linda said getting out of the car and lifting her seat for Grace to get out.

But she heard Grace say, "Rob, two's enough. No more."

Once out of the car, Linda lifted her boot and Tony lifted a carving of an elephant in Ebony wood, which had half-filled the boot along with a carrier that possibly contained a gift for their mum. "Dad's going to love it; you might not because our lift's been out of order all week, and that looks bloody heavy." With Rob saying that they were all laughing. If not all of them, Linda, Grace and Rob had a good chuckle at his brother's expense seeing he had got five flights of stairs to walk up.

Linda and Tony went on their way up to the 5th floor, leaving behind Grace and Rob by her car who talked about what Linda was going on about.

Just then, Pauline Shaw—Rosie's friend and neighbour who also lived on the ground floor—called out from her front door. "Here you go, Rob, you being here saves me having to troop up to the 5th floor. Anyway, you need to take this case and a few personal belongings to Rosie on Saturday," she said walking towards them.

Rob turned to Grace, "Look at the size of her tatty case." Grace wanted to laugh as she watched Pauline approaching them, handing Rob the case. "Shall do, Pauline," he said smiling as he noticed all the stickers advertising where Rosie had spent her holidays.

"Give her my love."

"Shall do."

"Rob, before you go home, Rosie called me earlier. It seems her son could be away for longer than a week, and my friend is very low; I had a struggle understanding what she was saying as she was crying down the phone. If possible, could you arrange to have her sent home to Saints House? I will look after her in my flat."

"First, let me visit her, and I will see if it's possible," he said heading for the stairs.

"Rob, judging by all those stickers on her ancient case, it seems our Rosie has visited a great many places in the UK," she said walking behind Rob up the stairs, still trying not to laugh.

One hour later, Linda and Tony were headed home. Rob's dad Jim was polishing his massive elephant while his mother Julie was taking all the family's fruit from their old glass bowl and transferring the fruit into her new carved bowl that Linda and Tony had bought her.

Grace was sitting in the corner counting all the stickers on Rosie's old case. "Rob, there are 35 stickers on her case, some going back to the 50s. I love this one, Butlins Skegness Holiday Camp 1958. Wow, it's even got a photo of Billy Butlin on the sticker."

Rob gave her daggers, "Sod you, people are going to laugh at me on the train to Central Southampton tomorrow."

Chapter 3
No Tears

"Rob, before you shoot off to Southampton, look at this on the BBC News." Jim Hat called out and then paused the TV and waited for his son to come into their living room. One minute later, Rob appeared struggling to put his coat on whilst struggling with Rosie's large case at the same time and came close to tripping over the large elephant that his dad had left by their coffee table.

"Press play, Dad."

"Over to the Honour Oak Cemetery in South East London where we can all witness the burial of the notorious most wanted UK criminal, Trevor Charles Baines, the most unexpected death at the age of 60," the news reporter said on the BBC1 News.

"Dad, the police had pulled Baines in for that National Bank robbery at Clinton Green, and I of people knew he was not guilty." His father never made any comments to Rob's remark; he simply raised his eyebrows much as to say, 'let's not talk about that bank robbery that you got yourself involved with.'

"It seems Mr Baines is being put to rest at the perimeter of the cemetery with the woods directly behind him," the onsite young lady reporter said into the camera.

"Bloody right, he's now out of sight, out of mind."

To date, the only crime Trevor Charles Bain's been found guilty of was driving without road tax and insurance. The late Baines was the criminal that controlled South East London. He was said to be worth millions, and the Metropolitan Police are still none the wiser to where this stolen cash is.

"There is a large turnout for this burial at Honour Oak that could consist of many criminals associated with Trevor Baines." Once again, the young reporter said looking straight into the BBC camera.

"Dad, look to the far right there's DS Jones, the 7-foot copper, and is standing beside to the newly promoted DI Judy Reynolds. I bet they are saying goodbye to bad rubbish."

"I heard on Radio 4, there are large rewards being offered to the whereabouts of this stolen cash that he's accumulated since the 90s," his dad was saying walking out to the kitchen.

"Do you want a cup of tea before you dash off?"

"No, I am fine, Dad," Rob said as he continued to watch the news where he could see Baines' son Charlie with his arm around his mother Glenda as they were watching the coffin being lowered into his grave.

"Other than the Baines family, there will be no tears in South East London to see the back of this low life, Trevor Charles Baines," the newsreader said handing back to the studio.

Then the BBC flashed a photograph of Mr Baines holding a large cigar in his right hand about to smoke, displaying the large tattoo on the back of his right-hand TCB.

"Other News…" Rob paused the TV.

"Look at his hairstyle, Dad." Rob's dad came back in their lounge with his tea.

"I guess, Son, he modelled his hairstyle on Brian May from the pop group Queen."

"My money says he can't play the guitar," Rob said getting up ready to leave.

Chapter 4
Age Is Just a Number

Saturday at 10:30 am, the youngster on the 53-bus heading towards Waterloo Station was amused seeing he was sitting on the bus with Rosie's old suitcase on Rob's lap with part of it resting on the young boy's lap sitting by the window. "Mister, you have a lot of holidays; you must be very rich?" the young lad of around six said and, just like Grace, he was attempting to count the stickers he could see.

"If only I were, young man," Rob told him.

Once on the train to Southampton Central, he was glad it was a Saturday seeing there was a choice of seats hence he shared two seats with his suitcase as his fellow passenger.

Stopping at Southampton Airport Parkway Station only around 100 footsteps from the Airport, he noticed on the platform—going east to possibly Waterloo Station—they were putting out three large blue flower pots containing an array of flowers. There were also a couple of guys painting the walls as though the station was having a spring clean. Perhaps they were going to do the platform going west a little later, Rob thought as he looked out his window seeing there were no such activities going on.

Getting out at Southampton Central, he took out a crumbled-up piece of paper from his pocket that he had written down Saint Josephs' Care Home for the Elderly. Not having the foggiest idea how to get there, he approached the first taxi in the rank. The cabbie got out of his Mondeo trying to keep a straight face as he put the suitcase in the boot.

"Where to son?"

"Saint Joseph's Care Home for the Elderly, please." Once in the taxi, the driver went to his metre. After a simple tap on the metre, it read £5 and he pulled away. He turned immediately left and drove 50 yards without getting out of first gear; he pulled up outside Saint Joseph's Care Home.

"There you go, son," he said, got out the car and took the suitcase from the boot. Before Rob got out of the car, he looked at his metre that still read £5.

"Hope you don't think that you're getting a tip," Rob said knowing he had just been ripped off.

"Anyway, hope you have a great holiday," he said shoving the £5 in his pocket and handing Rob his suitcase. As he got back in his car, and before closing the door, he called out: "Nice case, son." Rob never turned around; he just gave the taxi driver the finger and entered into the care home.

Rob's first impression at St Joseph's Care Home was simply a terraced property; however, once he entered, he could see that the Home went back a considerable distance. The interior was looking tired that a coat of paint could brighten it up. Rob just stood there when he noticed on the table a small plaque that said 'ring for attention,' which he duly did by picking the brass bell and giving it a ring, and there he waited.

Two minutes later, an elderly lady appeared as though she had just come out of the kitchen holding a tea towel along with a spoon. "Can I help you?"

"I have come to visit Rosie." The lady never said anything; she just turned and walked down what seemed a long hallway.

It was then he heard her shout out: "I have a young gentleman asking to see a Rosie, do we have a Rosie here with us?"

Not so loud this time, he heard a woman call out: "Send him through to the conservatory."

She came back and faced Rob, "Go to the far end of the hallway where you see it opens up into a large conservatory." With this, he walked down the long corridor. On either side, there were rooms; all brown fire doors were numbered one to five on his left, so he assumed on the right would be six to ten.

Large would be an understatement as he stood looking into the conservatory and saw a dozen small armchairs placed in a circle. Around half of them were occupied by elderly people just sitting, some sleeping while others were just looking into space, not taking any notice of Rob just standing there holding Rosie's out of the ark suitcase.

Just then, a young lady in a dirty kind of uniform with cardboard named tag pinned to her blouse wheeled into the conservatory his dear friend Rosie. "Here she is; we were in the bathroom," the young girl said leaving Rosie just inside the conservatory, which could be the recreation facility, and walked away. Rosie stared at Rob, and the tears started to flow down her cheeks; she held out both her arms beckoning him to her. Rob was now kneeling at the side of her. "Wheel me to room number four," she said crying on Rob's shoulder. He now understood why she had been crying down the phone to her friend Pauline.

If he thought what he had already seen was not acceptable, he was in for a far bigger shock when he wheeled her into room four. There were two single beds with one of them having a very attractive middle-aged lady just laying on her back, staring at the ceiling, and wearing what seemed a grubby old dressing gown. "Rob, I was told her name is Barbara. From all accounts, she has dementia and that's where she has lain in the four days I have been here. The staff does come in and try to feed her and keep her clean. The smell Rob is horrendous when there are times, she would stay there for hours without being attended to."

Rob looked around, and he could see a blind that was in tatters. She had a bedside cabinet with the draws missing that was totally bare. The dim light was working but lacked a shade. The floor was missing any kind of covering; even the shelf at the side of her bed was totally empty. With that, Rob opened her case and took out photos of her son, and an old black and white photo that could be of her mother. He put these on her dressing table along with a small travel clock that once again, he placed on the dressing table. There were some clean clothes. "Where do I put these?" Rosie pointed to two carrier bags that looked stuffed with what looked like dirty washing in the far corner.

"Don't they do your washing and ironing for you?"

"Not yet, Rob. Perhaps they will later?"

Rob never questioned her further; he took half a dozen Daniel Steel books from the case, which he put on the shelf. Wrapped in tissue paper was a large photograph that I had taken last year at Xmas of all our family including Grace's family, along with Rosie and her friend Pauline Shaw taking centre stage in the photo. "Good Christmas, Rob," she said taking the picture from him and placing it on her bedside facing towards her bed.

"Rosie, I hear your son will be away on business for some time now."

"Rob, I can't stop in here much longer; this is a very sad place." Rob never said anything; he was looking at her poor face that seemed to be a massive bruise. It was only then that he noticed her right leg was in plaster.

"Darling Rosie, I have loved you all my life, and do you realise that I have never known your full name?"

Rosie started to chuckle, "You get me out of here, and I promise to tell you."

Rob looked at her, went over and gently kissed her blue cheek, "So my dear friend, you want to blackmail me?"

"Yes, if it works," she said trying to kick him with her plastered leg.

"Now you listen to me, you are 80 years old and your ailments will take far longer to heal."

"Rob, age is just a number."

Then Rob kissed her, this time on her lips, and then whispered in her ear: "Very true, but in your case darling, it's a very high number."

Just then, the lady that wheeled Rosie into the conservatory came in with a bowl of water. "Would you take Rosie into the kitchen that's at the left of the conservatory and perhaps make yourself a tea whilst I clean this poor soul up?"

"Can I ask how long this lady has been with you?"

She never answered immediately; she was counting on her fingers. "I have worked here for eight months; on my first day, this is where she was laying, and other than getting her up to change her bed linen, this is where she remains."

Rob walked over to her, leaned towards her and asked, "Barbara, would you like a cup of tea?"

All she said was, "Mummy."

It was Rosie who chirped in, "That's all she ever says."

Thirty minutes later, they were back in room four with Barbara still staring at the ceiling totally oblivious to Rosie and Rob. "That's so sad, Rosie, what a waste of a life," he said looking at this very attractive lady living in a different world than his.

Helping Rosie onto the bed, putting two pillows on the bed and lifting her right leg onto them. "I have come up by train seeing my vans in for repair. I have spoken to Pauline, and she's adamant that she wants to look after you. Today is Saturday; you are to contact your son and inform him that you're going back to Saints House, where Pauline will take care of you. Then, you tell him you are not happy here and enlighten him to the conditions here, and he's to inform the management here at this hell-hole that he's arranging to take his mother out of here. Once you have done this, you are to call me to let me know everyone is in agreement with you leaving this, in my opinion, shit-hole."

"Rosie, I promise I will pick you up Monday evening," Rob said taking all her dirty washing out of her two carrier bags and replacing her clean washing into the two Tesco's Carrier bags, then putting the dirty washing in her case.

"Nice case, don't you think?" Rosie said with a wink.

"If you say so," he said putting the clasps down on her case.

"Four days I have been here, and those days I will never forget. Thank you, rest assured I will not be crying myself to sleep tonight and Sunday night. When you get home, give your Grace a big kiss from me."

"Rob, how's your Godchild baby Grace doing? She's such a little darling."

"We plan to spend the Easter break in Tanzania, where Grace will no doubt be in her element, not forgetting she's fast approaching two years of age now."

"In a perfect world, I shall be picking you up Monday evening. In the meantime, I need to catch my train back to Waterloo with your case that is much older than me."

"My case Rob was, in fact, my parents'," she said with one of her saucy winks. Rob had to smile thinking this embarrassment belongs to the Antique Road Show.

"High number or not, I am still alive and kicking now off with you now," she said blowing him a kiss watching him banging her case on the room's fire door.

"Don't you dare scratch it, Rob." As earlier with the taxi driver, he never turned to face her; he just gave her the finger, and he could hear her chuckling and saying to her roommate, "Barbara, he has a heart of gold."

Chapter 5
With Your Support

Whilst Rob was at Saint Joseph's Home for the Elderly in Southampton helping his dear friend—and hopefully assisting her to get her back home to enable her friend Pauline to care for her—our PM Simon Davis along with his Chancellor, Graham Johnson, had been at the Southampton's largest University in the South East. He was addressing thousands of Undergraduates and Post Graduates with his endeavour to convince them that they need to vote for the Peoples Unite Party on the 7 of May.

His next arranged visit was for his Chancellor and himself to address the staff at the Southampton General Hospital making promises one after the other to persuade them to vote for him and his party. As in Southampton University, the key message was 'with your support, my promises will be kept.'

Their next scheduled meeting was arranged for a 3 pm visit at the Southampton Airport where a large hanger had been set up to address the staff. On an aeroplane, a large blue banner of the full length of the plane said: Fly with The Peoples Unite Party with Your Support We Will Win.

In front of the plane, a podium and microphones were in place for the arrival of the PM and Chancellor to convince the workforce to vote for the Peoples Unite Party.

Chapter 6
Trains Are Not for Me

This time Rob had taken the short walk to Southampton General Station; he was waiting for his train to Waterloo Station. The case he shoved under the bench seat out of sight when his mobile went off, not recognising the caller. “Hello, Rob Hat here.” He waited for the caller to identify himself.

“Hi, Rob. It’s Peter here, Rosie’s son.”

Rob was thinking, *‘Good old Rosie, you have wasted no time in calling your son.’*

“Having just coming off the telephone to my mother, I am extremely grateful that you have taken the time to visit her.”

“Peter, we have spoken a few times earlier. I trust you are well.” Peter went quiet; Rob guessed he was deciding what to say.

“I am fine, thank you; it seems my choice of a home for my mother was, without any doubt, the wrong choice.”

“With the greatest respect, Peter, St Joseph’s Care Home offers, in my opinion, very poor care for my dear friend.”

“Rob, I will be calling the owner of the home and inform Mrs Jenkins that my mother will be leaving her establishment on Monday evening.”

“Peter, you can rest assured that her closest friend Pauline will take good care of her. Please make sure that the home hands over any medication that’s been prescribed for her.”

“Shall do, and thank you once again for caring.” Then, the line went silent just as the train pulled into the station.

He was just about to enter the carriage next to the First Class when he realised that he had forgotten the case; hence, he rushed back to get the suitcase and jumped into the carriage that seemed was only carrying a few people.

“I see you’re a well-travelled for such a young man,” the elderly guy said nudging his wife beside him and pointing to Rob’s case.

It was 5 pm when the train pulled into Southampton Airport Parkway Station. Rob had to smile now knowing why the flower pots were put out, and the whole platform had had a fresh coat of paint added. The PM Simon Davis and Graham Johnson were there with PM carrying his Parliamentary Red Case. They were shaking hands with various people; Rob guessed that they were thanking people before boarding the train.

The elderly couple who had earlier had a chuckle at his expense were sitting behind Rob. "What a pair of arseholes; they should have come into our carriage, then I would have given them a mouthful," the guy said.

His wife replied, "Be quiet, Harry. You're embarrassing yourself." Rob would like to have added to the guy's comments seeing at 17 and again when he was 18, he had a run-in with Simon Davis and, in his opinion, calling him an arsehole would be an understatement, but he decided to bite his tongue.

Leaving Vauxhall Station, Rob was now the sole passenger in his carriage, and the train was picking up speed approaching Waterloo Station. He was looking forward to getting home only to get rid of this ancient suitcase. He was eager to get back home when an enormous sound of metal hit him, and he was thrown backwards over the seat behind him. With his head hitting the metal surroundings of the seat behind him, Rosie's suitcase finished up at the far end of the carriage.

He could not be certain just how long he had lain across between the seats. His head had hit with his body hanging over it looking as though he had attempted to dive into the next row of seats. Putting his hand to the top of his head, he felt as though he had a ball being blown up on his head, but was relieved that there was no sign of any blood on his hand as he took his hand away.

Getting to his feet, he realised that he must have been unconscious for a while seeing there was a commotion outside the train with injured people being stretchered across the lines where the fencing had been cut away, showing a row of ambulances waiting to take those hurt to hospital. The four doors in his carriage sliding open startled him, making him step back. Eventually, he built up the courage to put his head out of the carriage and look down the line.

"Oh my god," he said out loud seeing they have had a head-on collision with a train going west. He could see the engine and the first two carriages of both trains heading towards the sky. "You lucky sod," he said thinking just how lucky he was not to have been sitting in the first two carriages. Granted, his carriage was leaning backwards. Still looking outside to his left, he could see railway officials escorting a great number of passengers across the lines to where the cutting in the fence was.

Turning his attention once again to the front of the train, the two trains appeared to be suspended in mid-air. He was watching the ambulance crews who were handing down people from the first two carriages. Some were guided across the rail lines while others being immediately put onto stretchers. He couldn't be sure, but he thought he could see PM Simon Davis being put on a stretcher with the Chancellor limping beside his stretcher as they were heading for the opening in the fence that now had a great many trying to view what was going on.

Rob was back inside the carriage, where he noticed the joining doors to the First-Class Carriage were open. It was a struggle, but he managed to scamper up and get through to the First-Class Carriage where the floor was covered with plates and smashed glasses and on the third row down, he could see the PM's red Parliamentary red case on the floor. He managed to duck behind a seat as he noticed two guys in their high visa jackets lifting out what seemed to be a young lady who started to scream out in pain. His instinct was to take hold of the PM's red case, which he duly did, and then made his way back to his carriage and started to look around in search of Rosie's case. "There you are, my little beauty," he said out loud putting the PM's case inside and fastening it.

Now hanging outside the carriage, he calls out: "Help, please!"

Ninety minutes later, he was in St Thomas' Hospital with a great deal of commotion in the A&E. He eventually got checked out with the young nurse doing her best not to laugh at his suitcase; however, she did say, "I see you have had many holidays?" Rob decided not to make any comments. To his relief, he was able to venture home. Yes, he was fortunate not like many others, thank God there was no fatality on either train. Unfortunately, the two train drivers won't be driving trains for a long while seeing they are both in intensive care; that's what he was told by the nurse who attended him with a head that would not allow him to be wearing a baseball cap for a while.

At 7:30 pm walking out of the hospital, he was trying to decide whether to call into 7 Orchard Driver to ask his sister-in-law for a lift home or to walk to Waterloo Station and pick up a bus to get him home. Deciding on a bus, he was heading for Waterloo Station when his mobile went off. "Don't you bloody tell me you were on that effing train that crashed just passed Vauxhall Station heading to Waterloo?" Grace asked half expecting him to say that he was. Rob had to put his mobile away from his ear seeing she was going ape shit down the line. "I have only just heard about this rail crash on Channel 4 News," Grace said, who had calmed down a little at least he had answered his mobile, which meant that he was alive. "I'm okay, Grace others are not even my arch enemy the PM was stretchered off the train; yes, I am lucky and now heading from St Thomas' Hospital to get a bus from Waterloo. Listen, Grace, I promise to tell you later, but I need you to get hold of your mother's keys for her garage for me?"

Grace went silent then screamed down the phone ignoring what he had just promised: "Why?"

"I will call you when I am close to home and hope to meet you by the garage. I will tell you this much, trains are not for me." Then, he ended the call.

Chapter 7
I Did Warn You, Things Happen in 3s

Walking into the Kings Estate, taking the first on the left with Saints House immediately in front of him, he could see Grace, Tony and Linda waiting by the garage with her Mini Cooper parked in front of the garage leaving enough space to open the garage.

With them all inside Grace's mum Jean Long's garage, Rob put Rosie's case on the rickety old table that he once had in access of one million pounds on from the National Bank. "Grace, this brings back memories," Rob said lifting the lid of the very old case.

"Not all good memories," Grace said with all four of them looking at the red parliamentary case placed on top of Rosie's dirty washing.

"Hell, bro, you are a glutton for punishment; you get caught with this, you will be for the high jump," Tony said lifting the red lambs leather case out with Linda putting Rosie's case on the floor.

"Simon Davis, our PM, along with his Chancellor, was in the first-class carriage when the oncoming train hit us. The first two carriages took the brunt of the crash. I was in the third carriage and was knocked senseless," Rob said pointing to the very large bump on his head. "When I came round, I saw a great many people fleeing for safety while the authorities guided them to the edge where the fencing had been cut away with ambulances taking those being stretchered off.

"When I looked to my right, I could see where the two trains had a head-on collision with the two engines and the first two carriages on both trains heading towards the sky. This was when I thought I saw the PM being stretchered off the train with the Chancellor limping beside him," Rob said trying to explain what he saw and knew.

"I guess you must have climbed into the carriage where the PM was taken from?" his brother said.

Rob said sheepishly said, "Something like that."

"Needless to say, all the TV channels have been showing this more so seeing our PM was travelling on this train and is currently undergoing investigations for a damaged back," Linda said staring at the red case.

"Linda bloody warned you things happen in 3s," Grace said sounding very angry as to why he just had to go rummaging around carriages and picking up this red case that she couldn't take her eyes off. That could, once again, bring problems to their doors.

With Grace, Linda and Tony looking worried, they watched Rob open the case; they all had to smile when they saw a bag of jelly babies. There was a family photograph along with what seemed a possible birthday card sealed addressed to Mrs Judith Davis. Putting them aside with his mobile telephone, there were various parliamentary papers and two folders marked in red 'Private and Confidential.' The four of them stood there, and I guess they were all thinking should they view what's inside?

It was Rob that opened them; they both looked identical. Both said: Manifest 2015 to 2020 when in power once again.

Rob opened the two covers on the folders with one saying: Manifest what we must and are selling to the UK's population. "He's even highlighted the word 'must,'" Rob said, now looking at the other folder with the second folder saying: this is what we will only deliver to the residents of the UK. Both of these manifests were duly signed by Simon Davis, the PM.

"Fucking hell Rob, these folders are marked 'Private and Confidential.' What you have here is toxic. Without any doubt, these papers will bring the Peoples Unite Party out of the running for them to enter 10 Downing Street again along with the PM being prosecuted for attempting to deceive the population of the UK," Tony said, far too scared at this juncture in knowing just how our PM was going to hoodwink the public.

Both at the same time, Linda and Grace asked, "Now what are you going to do?"

"First, we do sod all for a while, and let's see just how deep Simon Davis digs to get his red case back? Then later, I will send the family photograph, his mobile and the card addressed to his wife and not forgetting his Jelly Babies to the Post Office at Portcullis House in the Commons, and I will sign it with a question mark."

Linda picked up his mobile. "Rob, he must have been on his mobile when the train crashed hence it's not locked, so there just might be information on his Samsung that once again might go to prove he's attempting to deceive the people of the UK," Linda said putting the mobile on the rickety table.

"So, Rob, you send his items back to him, and then what?" Tony asked.

"Nothing, let's let this arsehole of a PM sweat, and I believe he will sweat buckets knowing these two files are out there that could reach the tabloids." Linda stood there trying to figure out what he would do.

She then said, "He will write a further manifest making his wrongs right."

Tony smiled and then had to say, "He can write a further 100 manifests; it will not change what he was prepared and planned to do with the beauty of it they were signed by the PM."

"Rob, let me take those two manifests home along with his mobile to work out the truth from the lies he is willing to use to remain the PM?" With Rob nodding to her scenario and looking at Grace seeing if she was going to object to Linda's idea.

With Linda and Tony heading home, Grace put the red case in an old sack and put in the far corner of the garage out of sight. Grace then locked up the garage, and she carried Rosie's case to Pauline's flat with Rob giving Pauline the good news that he will be picking up Rosie Monday evening from St Joseph's Home for the Elderly and bring her back to her place to enable her to care for her friend.

"Come on, Grace, you can give me your support as my parents give me hell for not contacting them." Grace never said anything until they got to the third floor and heard the lift door opening. They both rushed into now the vacant lift.

"I love you, Rob, but you're on your own when your mum and dad give you a rollicking for not contacting them to say you were okay."

Chapter 8
That's a Mansion

DI Judy Reynolds pulled up in her old Mini behind her DS Jones, who had parked up earlier in his unmarked Ford Mondeo police car that had a good view of the late Trevor Charles Baines large property in Sandhurst Berkshire.

Jumping in beside DS Jones, "That's what you call a nice house," his DI said taking the sergeants binoculars off the dashboard to get a closer look.

"It's not a house; that's a mansion," the 7-foot copper said getting out of his car to stretch his legs. A couple of minutes later, he leaned into the open window. "Four days I have sat here seeing Charlie Baines coming to the door letting in various people who could be offering their condolences. Those visits aside, I have not seen any movements what-so-ever," he said getting back into his motor.

As they sat there some 250 yards from the property, two Mercedes shot by and they parked at the gates to the property with the first car's driver getting out of his Merc and going to the large double gates and appeared to speak into the wall. Within a minute, the gates swung open allowing the two Mercs to drive in. Glenda Baines appeared at the door and immediately walked back in with two smartly guys walking in, leaving the two drivers outside.

DS Jones was snapping away getting as many photographs as possible of the two guys entering the property. DI Reynolds was watching closely with the binoculars. She scribbled down the two cars' registration numbers and handed them to her DS and asked, "Check them out, John."

It only took a couple of minutes, the DS said. "You're not going to like this boss; those two cars belong to the Frank Frazer twins."

DI Judy Reynolds looked at her DS, "You're not telling me that those two bastards have arrived at Baines mansion to offer their condolences? Not that Met could prove anything but the Frazer crew had teamed up with the Baines mob in 2014 that from all accounts set up the jobs to pull off three bank robberies all at the same time in Scotland."

DS Jones just sat there staring at his boss and said, "Looks like the late Trevor Baines still owes the Frazer's money from that heist, and they have come to collect." Five minutes later, Charlie Baines was at the door seeing their guest out with one of the twins beckoning over their two drivers, and within seconds, poor old Charlie boy was getting the shit beaten out of him.

"Wow, I bet that hurt, and you could be right, the Baines owes those evil gits cash," DI Reynolds said then went on to say, "After all the years, the Met has been trying to nick the bastard. He always escapes under the radar; hence we are still none the wiser to where his stolen fortunes are. Judging by the beating Trevor's son just taken, the Frazer's are also none the wiser to where Baines fortune is; I guess they have walked away with sod all," DS Jones said.

Then Judy Reynolds was getting out of his car and ordered, "Keep me posted to any movements." She then walked to her Mini.

It was five minutes later that an ambulance drove past the DS and the gates to the Baines property were still open. They lifted Charlie Baines on a stretcher into the ambulance with his mother, Glenda Baines, climbing into the back to be with her son.

The DS was watching the ambulance driven by his unmarked police car and DS Jones was thinking that they could be heading to Frimley Park Hospital.

"Charlie, if you were really hurt the bells would be ringing," the DS said out loud winding his seat down and closing his eyes.

Chapter 9
Running Scared

Three weeks had passed since the train crash and Grace and Rob were sitting in their cabin at Premier Supreme Private Car getting ready to leave for the night.

"Rob, I have read that report Linda had done from the two manifests and the information she gained from the PM's mobile time and time again these past weeks. I can't believe that he is saying and promising the population things that his government has no intention of delivering."

"Grace, Simon Davis is playing lip service to the truth what Linda has highlighted, for example, he's promising that the Peoples Unite Party will put 20 billion into the NHS within the next five years. In fact, the PM Simon Davis will find a valid excuse for only handing over only 10 billion."

"What would be the government's excuse then?" Grace asked.

"Reading the correct manifesto and reading between the lines, he will be bringing private companies via the back door to run sections of the NHS.

"He promises to abolish the so-called Bedroom Tax that will not happen in the next parliament. Then he goes on to say that he intends to reduce the tax we all pay. That once again will not be in the correct manifest.

"Yes, our PM intends to hoodwink the whole population to, once again, gain the keys to 10 the black door in Downing Street."

Then, on his mobile, Linda saw a text from our Chancellor, assuming as it's signed off by GJ being Graham Johnson, and he's saying, "Are you sure that you're doing the right thing? I don't believe you should deceive the population. Anyone other than you, I would never give this scenario the time of day, GJ."

With the PM replying, "Trust me, my friend. I know what I am doing; the last thing I want to do is to jeopardise your career and betray your friendship, SD."

"Rob, as Linda said, it's criminal, but how the hell is he selling these tactics to his cabinet?"

"I don't know, Grace, but I am sure he knows perhaps he will also deceive his ministers who sit on his front benches."

"It's been a while now, and there's been a great deal said about the train crash on the TV and in the press, but there's not been a single word about the missing red parliamentary case he had left on the train," Grace said getting her coat on for their journey home.

"Grace, on Thursday the 2 of April, we will leave Heathrow to spend our Easter Holiday in Kilimanjaro. It's on our visit I will be sending Simon Davis's mobile, the family photograph along with the card addressed to his wife plus his Jelly Babies and, of course, his mobile from the Arusha Post Office to Portcullis House in the Houses of Parliament and I will sign it off by saying: 'You can fool all the people some of the time, and some of the people all the time, but you cannot fool all the people all the time (Abraham Lincoln, 16th US President 1809–1865).'

"I will set up a TZ email account should he wish to contact me. I will let my uncle monitor the account, which he can forward to me in the UK when the PM replies. I feel confident in saying our PM will be running scared."

Chapter 10
Saucy Cow

Rob and Grace—with their overnight bags packed for their night's stay at 7 Orchard Drive with Linda and Tony—were walking down the stairs of Saints House.

Just about to get into their bright red Morris Minor Van, they noticed Rosie come whizzing towards them on her repaired mobility scooter. "You're unbelievable, Rosie. Why the hell are you driving your scooter with your right leg still in plaster?" Rob asked with Grace seeing the funny side of her determination that a bit of plaster won't stop her from being Rosie.

"So, where are you two love-birds off to?" Rosie asked winking at them.

"None of your business," Rob said.

"We are spending the night with Linda and Tony," Grace said knowing full well she would push and push to find out where they were off to.

"You pair are aware that kissing on the lips can make babies?" Rosie said followed with another wink.

"Nice to see you're well again and back to being a nosey and saucy cow," Rob chirped in, giving her a wink followed by the victory sign getting into his van.

"That's what I like about you, Rob," Rosie said leaning into the now open window of the van.

"That is?" Rob asked.

"Sod all, of course, just joking," she said.

"On a serious note, Rosie, is your son back in the country?" Rob asked.

"No, he called last night and, from all accounts, he will be working out of the UK for a further year. He went on to say that he is relying on you to keep me out of trouble," she said blowing him a kiss and headed again round the car parking area at full speed.

"Grace, I have more chance of being struck by lightning than keeping her safe and sound," he said pulling out of the Kings Estate.

"But you will," Grace said leaning over kissing him on the cheek.

Knocking on the door of 7 Orchard Drive. "In you come, you're just in time to watch Coronation Street," Linda said darting into their lounge in fear of missing something.

"Rob, put your bags upstairs; hope you like it, second door on the right."

Two minutes later, Rob stood on the landing and called out: "Wow, Grace, you're going to love it and, yes, I am having the left side of the bed." He said chuckling and walking downstairs to join them. In the living room, Grace was sitting on the sofa blushing to Rob's comments.

"Take no notice of him, Grace," Tony said watching her looking uncomfortable.

After dinner, Rob explained his intentions of sending the PM's items from Tanzania. "Oh, to be a fly on the wall when Simon Davis receives his post," Linda said knowing that all hell will break loose in 10 Downing Street. With the PM's fear being that he now will be aware that his private and confidential information is out there with him, he will be dreading this info could be sent to the media that, without any doubt, would end his career.

"Rob, a great many of us have many bad habits, but in your case, you have the habit since 2012 of being in the wrong place at the wrong time," Tony was saying clearing the plates off their dining room table, but if the truth be known, he admired his brother for all the good he's done with his bad habits.

Linda left the table and shot upstairs and two minutes later came down with two cuddly toys and a couple of pretty pink and yellow dresses along with a Cadbury's Easter egg. "There you go, Grace, these are for your godchild baby, Grace."

"Linda, is the egg for me?" Linda never responded, but her look was more powerful than words.

"Thursday, I will pick you both up at 6 pm from Saints House and get you to Terminal 4 at Heathrow," Linda said, as Grace admired the dresses laid out on the coffee table.

"Thanks for these gifts. I am sure she will love them," Grace said.

Rob then added, "Don't be late, Sis." Once again, his sister-in-law gave him a dirty look.

At 11 pm, Linda and Tony said goodnight and ventured up to bed, leaving Grace and Rob looking at each other feeling awkward that they were going to be sharing a bed in Rob's brother's home. "Turn the TV off, Grace, and remember what Rosie said that kissing on the lips can make babies."

"That sounds great to me, lover boy," she said with them both tiptoeing up the stairs.

Chapter 11
I Love You

Just touching down at Kilimanjaro International Airport. "Rob, I have butterflies in my stomach knowing that baby Grace is only a few minutes away."

Getting their bags and heading towards getting the clearance from the airport officials to depart through the glass doors into Tanzania. Grace was jumping up to see if she could see his uncle and aunt and her godchild on the other side of the glass doors in the arrivals. "Rob, she's kind of walking I can see them," Grace said walking out into the area where taxi drivers were handing up their boards with names written on them to who they are waiting for.

Holding Yvonne's hand to keep baby Grace steady. "I told you she's now walking," Rob told her.

Grace swept baby Grace up into her arms, "Oh, I have missed you so much!" With hugs and kisses completed, they headed out into the warm air even though it was only 7 am.

All seated in Alan's hold jeep, they headed for Machame on the foothills of Mount Kilimanjaro.

"Rob, I have read all the information you e-mailed me so what's your plan once Simon Davis gets what you intend on sending him?" Alan Hat shouted to be heard over the noise of the engine, plus Grace had her window wide open that didn't help in having a conversation. Rob sat there looking at baby Grace, fascinated with Grace's long black hair blowing in the wind.

"If you kiss her much more, you will wash her away. Well, Uncle to be totally honest with you, I am not sure what I will be doing," he shouted out, making baby Grace jump seeing that Grace had closed the window up.

"I see your options could be to blackmail the PM, make demands that he should do what the UK needs, or my option would be to hand those two manifests over to the media, and then everyone would see the real Simon Davis who is willing to hoodwink the nation," Alan said then added. "We are going over to Zanzibar, leaving you two in charge of baby Grace and, of course, our home, and not forgetting my dear friend Bernie. If you like, I could send your package to Simon Davis from Zanzibar," he suggested.

"If you manage to lose Bernie, you would not have any complaints from me," Yvonne said ruffling her husband's hair.

"Zanzibar is fine by me; I need you to set up an email account address from the island to allow the PM to contact us on and I am asking you to manage the traffic for me. You see what I am saying when you read what I am sending. Can I use your jeep whilst you're away for the Easter holiday?"

"Sure, Rob, we fly out this evening. Besides, Rob, I have a job for you to do for me on Saturday. I will tell you more about it later."

Rob was sure Grace never heard a word of their conversation seeing she was preoccupied with baby Grace.

Alan was backing into his parking area alongside his bungalow. Even sitting inside the jeep, they could hear Bernie snorting and banging himself up against their front door trying to get out.

"I won't miss him, Rob," Yvonne said stepping over the pig trying to get in and going crazy to see Grace and Rob again. Still holding baby Grace on her knee, she opened her holdall. "Come here, Bernie, I have a great gift for you," she said pulling out a pair of large pink plastic flip-flops. Grabbing them, Bernie was off and headed into the kitchen and plonked himself under the table and started ripping them apart. "Grace, I am sure Bernie eats them seeing I never see any remains of the footwear he gets hold of," Yvonne called out with Grace putting baby Grace in her buggy that was in the hallway.

"We are off for a walk, aren't we, my little darling?" Grace said backing out the front door.

Once outside, Alan and Rob could hear Grace saying to her godchild, "I love you!"

Chapter 12
TCB

7 pm after dinner, Yvonne was busy packing what they needed for their short break on Zanzibar. "Yvonne, we need to leave here by 8 pm," Alan called out to her and, at the same time, handed Rob a sheet of paper. "Here you go, Rob, this is what I want you to do for me at 7:15 am Saturday," Alan said then walked into his office and came back with a camera that had a sticker on the back saying 'Property of Kibo Safaris' along with two metal magnetic plates advertising the companies name and handed them to his nephew. "Don't lose the camera." Rob never responded; he was busy reading what was being asked of him.

Of course, at this juncture, Alan never knew that Rob was in for one heck of shock in around 11 hours from now.

(1) Magnetic plates, one on each front door.
(2) You arrive at Tato Hotel Saturday for 7:15 am.
(3) Pick up a Peter Goodman.
(4) Take him to the Machame Gate for his climb to the Roof of Africa.
(5) Once at the Gate, meet up with Africa Tours, who have a party of five that Peter Goodman will be joining for their climb.
(6) Use the camera and take a group photograph and try to make sure Kibo Safaris's name is seen on the jeep that the company will use for future publicity.

"No problem, Uncle. I will not let Kibo Safaris or yourself down." It was his aunt standing at the door that stopped any further conversation about what Rob had to do.

"All ready to go here."

Grace was busy in their lounge playing with baby Grace. "Grace, I guess you're too busy to join us at the airport?" Rob called out.

Rob then heard Grace asking baby Grace, "Do you want to go for a ride, darling? No, Rob, she says she's too tired; see you later."

At 6 am Saturday, Rob was tiptoeing around trying not to wake up his goddaughter while getting ready for his 7:15 am appointment at the Kibo Hotel. "Grace, I should be back around lunchtime if not before," he said leaning over the bed kissing Grace when he noticed baby Grace looking straight at him smiling in the middle of their bed. "Don't tell Aunty Yvonne she shares our bed."

Grace never answered; she just put her index finger to her lips much as to say, 'Don't wake her up.'

"You should be so lucky she's wide awake."

After a shower and shave, a quick coffee along with dunking half a dozen biscuits into his drink, he was off to the Tato Hotel that was only half a mile away.

On arriving at the security gates of the Tato Hotel, the young askari (guard) must have recognised him from his visit when he was 18. He was with Grace, his uncle, and his aunt Yvonne there for dinner. That was a special day since Rob had proposed to Grace by the swimming pool with Mount Kilimanjaro as the backdrop for the occasion. "Jambo young Mr Hat karibu (welcome) once again to the Tato," and lifted the barrier to let him and his jeep into the hotel.

Parking at the reception, the Manager Mr Urio walked out. "Hi, Rob, your uncle informed me you would be covering for him today. I will call their room and let them know you have arrived," Mr Urio said and walked back inside. Rob parked up and wandered into the reception area thinking what the Manager said 'their room' and 'to let them know you are here.' He checked the instructions again his uncle had given him, and it clearly said a Peter Goodman with no mention of anyone else.

At 7:30 am, coming into the reception that Rob thought could be Peter Goodman, a guy in his fifty's or perhaps a little older giving Rob a nod of acknowledgement that he was the climber. He was dressed in the correct attire with his rucksack on his back holding a pair of walking sticks. A shaven head with a large moustache whilst he headed to the front desk, "Peter, thanks a million for waiting for me," the tall, very attractive, and smartly dressed African lady with her sunglasses on said as she entered into the reception. It never took a high IQ to realise that this lady was not going to be climbing to the Roof of Africa. Giving Peter Goodman a kiss on the cheek. "Only joking, darling," she said walking over to Rob. "Rob, can you kindly drop me in Moshi Town before you head to the Machame Gate?" Rob never answered; he was trying to figure out how she knew his name. "Forgive me, Rob, let me introduce myself. I am Anna Kajeme."

Rob stood there with his mouth wide open and stuttered out, "No, no problem."

"Of course, Rob, if I had turned around on my flight from Dar to Kili, we might have met?" She then whispered in his ear, "It's a small world, fancy meeting you here." Then she said out a bit louder hoping Peter Goodman was too busy talking to the receptionist to hear, "You fucking owe me."

"Let's make a move, darling," Peter said coming over to her and kissing her with their tongues overworking. "I am going to truly miss you; I should be back in six days," he said looking towards Rob, who simply nodded a yes to the six days for his return.

When they got to Moshi, Rob jumped out to open the rear door for Anna Kajeme with the diesel engine making enough noise, so he felt confident that Peter Goodman could not hear from the front what he was going to say to Anna

Kajeme. "You can fuck off." With that said, she gave Rob the finger and went to the front door that Goodman had opened and leaned out to wet his tongue once again.

Back on route again to the Machame Gate, they stopped in the village to allow Peter Goodman to purchase a few goodies for his trek. Thirty-five minutes later, they arrived at the gate where a great many climbers were checking all their equipment before handing all their bags to their guides for them to carry.

"I guess you're Kibo Safaris? We have been waiting for a Peter Goodman?" he said that must have been the head guide for Africa Tours.

"That us," Rob said then got out with Peter Goodman. Then jumped out and was shaking hands with the Africa Tours head guide. "Okay, if I take a photo?" Not waiting for an answer, Rob asked ushering the whole party and the guides alongside his jeep with Peter Goodman standing one from the left at the end with his arm over the young lady climber, and he took half a dozen photos of the six climbers with six guides kneeling on the floor in front of them.

"Mr Goodman, my uncle will pick you up in six days when you call him and inform that you're ready to go back to the Tato Hotel," Rob said getting back in the jeep. "Enjoy your safari," he said and pulled out and headed back to Alan's cottage.

On his way back, Rob was trying to figure out why the fuck was Anna Kajeme here with this elderly guy. He convinced himself it was just bad luck that she was in Machame still they were only here until Tuesday so, hopefully, their paths won't cross again.

On his way back, he pulled into Machame village and had a look at the photographs he had taken. The fifth photo, unbeknown to Peter Goodman, he sneaked up a close up of the guy with his right arm over the shoulder of the pretty thing at the end. He sat there and stared at the image trying to work out if he knew the face of this Goodman character. He looked familiar but was just about to dismiss the photo when he noticed Mr Goodman's right hand with the very large tattoo on the back of his right hand that clearly said TCB. "Oh, shit!" he said out loud and started up the jeep at the same time and pulled away, almost knocking the old guy over pushing his cart filled with half a dozen plastic containers that could contain five gallons of water per container.

For his short remaining journey back to his uncle's home, Rob was trying to get his head around that he saw Trevor Charles Baines coffin being lowered into his grave at the Honour Oak Cemetery, but now he's seen the late notorious criminal here in Tanzania.

"So, who the hell or what is in that coffin at Honour Oak Cemetery?" he said out loud reversing the jeep up to the garage and smiling upon hearing Bernie banging up to the front door trying to get out.

Chapter 13
Promise

"Charlie, step away from the mirror; your bruises are fading. Get the car out of the garage. I have a 10 am appointment at the doctor's, then I need to visit St Michaels Church to see Father Thomas and his brother Colin, the owner of the South East London Funeral Parlour; They are both expecting me," Glenda Baines said putting on her makeup.

She then decides to call Jimmy the Saw, who runs Designer Kitchens. "Hi, Jimmy, Glenda here. So sorry for the delay in contacting you," she said putting her lipstick on.

"No problems, Mrs Baines, you were right. The grave was not being filled in until the following morning," Tommy the Saw said then Glenda could hear him giving instructions to one of his staff, "Take that call for me."

"Were there any problems?" Glenda asked.

"In short, no problem, Mrs Baines. At 10:30 pm, under the cover of darkness it was accomplished; hence everything that you asked for was completed so you can rest assured no earth will hit the bottom," he said, and once again, she clearly heard him shout out: "Leave it in the far corner for me."

Glenda was attempting the impossible; putting her scarf on with her mobile under her chin, she said: "Thank you, Tommy, I will make sure Charlie drops off your fee in a couple of days."

"No rush, Mrs Baines. Me and your late husband go back a long way, just glad I could follow out what you were asking." Tommy the Saw ended the call and was wise enough not to ask any questions for her unusual request.

Tommy was one of her husband's minders that had done time in Wandsworth Prison when he could have shopped Trevor for his involvement in a robbery that Tommy had committed on his behalf in 2010. As a way of repaying him, Trevor had set him up in the Designer Kitchen Company. There was a plus for the Baines family seeing he had designed and fitted their kitchen for their mansion in Sandhurst.

Pulling up outside the Sandhurst Surgery. "Stay there, Son. I don't need to show off your bruises," she said picking up her handbag, and the two large M&S carrier bags her son lifted out for her. She entered the surgery, once in she tapped in her name and age on the monitor and took a seat and waited for the large screen to show her name and room number she needs to attend. Instead of putting the two large carriers with the other donations to an orphanage in Poland that

Doctor Stevens was organising, she kept the bags beside her. At 10:15 am, the screen said and showed: "Mrs Baines room 2."

Walking down the corridor and turning left, she knocked and entered room two. She left the two M&S carrier bags by the window and took a seat facing the doctor. "Good morning, Mrs Baines," Doctor Bowen, the middle-aged doctor, said.

"Doctor, I would have come last week, but getting an appointment is extremely difficult these days."

"Mrs Baines, I was getting a little concerned that you would not honour your promise," the doctor said turning his attention to the two M&S bags smiling then turning to face Mrs Baines.

"Our agreement aside, I fail to see why your child could not be treated here in the UK?" Glenda Baines said looking a little confused.

"Her treatment is not available; hence my agreement with you will allow me to take my Jenny to the US to be treated."

Once the Doctor had said that, Glenda pointed to the bags. "A promise is a promise," she said knowing he had earned the 200k for what he had done for the Baines family.

"Thank you," the Doctor said knowing what he had done could get him struck off, but to him, it was well worth the chance for his daughter's life.

Back in their top of the range Audi. "Next stop, Charlie, Father Thomas and his brother Colin at St Michaels."

Ten minutes later, they pulled into the church's car park. "Mum, they are over to the right in the cemetery." Father Thomas and Colin saw Glenda Baines getting out of their car, and they wandered over towards the Audi.

"I was getting worried until I got your call yesterday seeing you were supposed to be here last week," Father Thomas said and was looking very nervous, and it was plain to see his brother was sweating and looking uncomfortable.

"Yes, a little late, but the Baines family always keep their promises," she said taking out an envelope from her handbag and handing it over to the priest. "All the 50 photos are there; my advice to you Father and your obscene brother Colin is that you should both keep your sexual needs to adults and not children in your choir. It also disgusts me what you pair do to dead bodies before they are cremated." Glenda then spat in Colin's face with her son Charlie looking around, making sure no one could see them. Charlie stepped forward as though he was going to shake the priest's hand; instead, he punched Father Thomas in the stomach. They both watched him dropping to the ground shouting out in agony before the Baines were getting into their Audi and simply drove off.

By lunchtime, they were back home with their Audi back in the garage, so with the mother and son sitting in their lounge. "Now, what do we do?" Charlie asked.

"We wait and don't forget Son, we never use the landline seeing our line is more than likely been tapped. You must have also seen that Mondeo parked down the lane some 250 yards from here?" Of course, her son Charlie had been totally aware of the Mondeo and unbeknown to his mother, he had followed them to the doctors. It was thanks to a set of traffic lights that Mondeo never followed them to Saint Michaels Church.

"Yes, Mum, it's been there on and off since we put my dad to rest," he said smiling.

"I wonder what the Old Bill are looking for," Glenda said looking at her son with a silly grin on her face.

Of course, if Glenda Baines knew that Rob Hat had recognised her husband Trevor Charles Baines in Tanzania with his girlfriend, this would have given Glenda two creditable reasons for taking that silly grin off her face.

Chapter 14
George Almedia

With Rob clambering over Bernie to get in his uncle's bungalow, he was still trying to make up his mind as to whether he should tell Grace that Anna Kajeme is staying at the Tato Hotel with the guy going by the name of Peter Goodman.

Grace was in the lounge with baby Grace crashed out on the sofa with her cuddly toys all around her. "How did your trip to the Machame Gate go?" Rob looked at her, still trying to figure out should he tell her the truth about his unexpected surprise. "You okay? Rob, you look worried," she said walking past him going to the kitchen. "Tea, Rob?" she called out and jumped to see Rob standing behind her and putting his arms around her and kissing her neck.

"Linda was saying I should be careful; things have a habit of coming along in 3s. Well, looks like my sister-in-law got it wrong; she should have said things happen in 4s and a bit in my case."

"Hell, Rob, I thought you looked worried; spit it out," she said taking their tea back into the lounge.

With baby Grace still sound asleep. "Is she snoring?"

"Don't change the subject, what's your problem?"

Rob took out the Kibo Safaris camera from his jacket and flicked through the photos he took and got to snap number five. "What you see that's strange in this photo?" he said holding the camera towards her eyes.

"It's an old guy with his arm over the shoulder of a pretty young lady. Don't tell me this is Peter Goodman's girlfriend?"

"No, Grace, you need to look at the back of his right hand."

"Okay, a large TCB tattoo, so?"

"Think about that tattoo." Grace just shrugged her shoulder much as to say I don't know what you're going on about?

"If I say the name Trevor Charles Baines, does that ring any bells?"

Grace just looked at Rob and then splattered out, "You have got to be kidding me! That criminal died and was buried in South East London."

"Yes, Grace. It was, in fact, Honour Oak Cemetery. It was covered on the BBC News, and they showed a photo of the Baines character smoking an enormous cigar, and the photo clearly showed the tattoo on the back of his right-hand TCB."

Grace had a feeling she knew where this was going seeing like many others; she was aware large rewards were being offered by the banks to the whereabouts of their stolen millions were. It was said any crimes committed south of the Thames had to be rubber-stamped by Baines.

"Grace, who and what's in his coffin?"

Grace just stared at him and shook her head, "Don't you dare try to find out."

"Baines must have had a doctor and the church in his back pocket to have pulled this off, seeing he is alive and kicking and making his way as we speak to the Roof of Africa."

Yes, they both knew if it had not have been for the TCB tattoo, then Trevor Charles Baines could have evaporated in East Africa. "Okay, Rob, what are your intentions, please don't say you're going to dig up a coffin?" Grace of all the people knew that once he had something in his head to find out what's in that coffin, he would attempt it.

"Don't panic, Grace. I won't desecrate a grave even though it might not contain a body, but I know a person that would if there's a large reward waiting for him if that coffin is stuffed with cash and valuables." Grace just sat there racking her brains and trying to figure who he had in mind. It was then that baby Grace stirred stretching her legs out.

"Mummy," she said holding her little arms up to be lifted.

"Baby Grace must have been listening to our conversation seeing she just said money." Grace never responded; she just clipped Rob round his head then picked up her godchild.

"Your mummy will be back soon, darling."

"Okay, you tell me who would do such a thing?" Rob took out his mobile and flicked through his phone book and called who he wanted to speak to.

"Shit, it's going into his voice mail."

"George, it's Rob here. We are at my uncle's in Machame; call me at your first opportunity." It didn't take Grace long to realise he was going to get George Almedia involved.

Yes, George was a close friend who lives in Mwanza, Northern Tanzania, who had supported and helped them with 750 diamonds that were stolen from Johnson Diamond Mine and Tetra Diamonds both in Mwanza that were glued to the children's large pink bag. Lloyds Underwriters had paid Rob 2.5 million pounds for their safe return.

"Linda said things happen in 3s, but you were not satisfied. First, you gained that stolen cash from the robbery from the National Bank, granted that you helped thousands with. Next, you had taken the stolen diamonds tucked under the seat on the plane that Anna Kajeme and we were on flying from Dar-es-Salaam to Kilimanjaro when she got dragged off by the police just before take-off. Then from the train crash, you picked up the PM's red case giving you the three things. Oh, that's not good enough for Rob Hat. You have now spotted Trevor Charles Baines, one of South East London's most notorious criminals in Kilimanjaro."

Whilst Grace was letting off steam, Rob had got to the door. "Hang on, you said four and a bit, so what's the bit?" Grace said sounding a little pissed off that all these things have a habit of dropping on their laps.

“Trevor Charles Baines girlfriend is the bit on the side, Anna Kajeme is with him,” he said and immediately walked into the kitchen knowing Grace was going to blow her top.

Whilst in the kitchen, Grace raised her voice making sure Rob could hear her speaking to her godchild, not that the baby would know, care, or understand what she was talking about.

“Darling, that lady Anna Kajeme is a bad lady who had helped to steal 750 diamonds, and she wants her revenge along with the reward from Lloyds that your godfather received.”

Still in the kitchen, Rob called out: “She’s got more chance of being struck by lightning.”

Chapter 15
Take It Apart

Old man Frazer sat in his wheelchair with his oxygen tank by the side of him with its plastic mask on his lap. Seeing it was early morning with his cleaners just completed in his night club, Frazer's in Wokingham, were on their way out leaving him and his twin sons alone by the club's large bar.

Peter Frazer was making sure no one could hear him when he said, "Dad, it's nearly two years now, and it seems the old Bill has given up trying to find out if we were involved with the Dawson sisters' murder." Frank Frazer looked at his son but said nothing immediately as he knew his other son Tommy had disposed of the tools they used to chop them up. They were never found, and they would be home scot-free.

"History Pete, let's not talk about the past again. Anyway, you have a guest to meet." His father said taking a draw of his oxygen.

At 10:15 am, the twins were by the entrance greeting their visitors. By 10:30 am, the club had ten smartly dressed professional criminals' who had invested in Frank Frazer's full proof legal scam that would provide them all with a fantastic legal pension pot. The guys were now waiting in the private lounge for Frazer to make an appearance. Just then, Tommy Frazer wheeled his father to the centre of the lounge with Peter Frazer carrying Frank's oxygen tank.

Taking a few draws from his tank, he pulled out a notebook that he had wedged down the side of his wheelchair. "Yes, guys, I truly fucked up, and I put my hands up to this error of bad judgement."

The guys were talking amongst themselves when one of them stepped forward. "Frank, your mistake was a costly one, and between us, we have invested a small fortune in what you had convinced all here was a guaranteed legal project," Simon Taylor said looking at Frank taking further draws of oxygen through his face mask.

"Simon, we are all in the same boat here," Frank said opening his notebook. "Here we have invested 4.8 million pounds in Homes Association run by the late Trevor Charles Baines," he said handing Simon his notebook that had a name on each page and investment made that he then handed to the others.

"Baines idea was simplicity in itself seeing all of us here have one thing in common that is making our dirty money clean. Baines was going to buy properties with our cash through his legal company Homes Association that he had set up. These purchases will be rented out giving our syndicate clean money every month."

"For 18 months, we have been investing our cash, and to date—other than his bloody mansion in Sandhurst, that could have been bought with our cash—Homes Association has bought sod all for us," Colin Thompson called out, standing at the rear of the group. He then added, "Now he's fucking confidently dead, so where does that leave all of us now."

It was Simon who, the others had thought would be the ideal guy to speak on their behalf, stepped forward again to speak, "Fucking hell, Frazer, we would have still been in the pocket if we had handed back our loot to Barclay's, National Westminster and Lloyds Banks and taken their rewards that were on the table." The Frazer twins just looked at their father, knowing what Simon had said was bloody true, not that such a thing would happen amongst these ten high profile gangsters that operated in all parts of the UK.

"If Baines was still alive, I personally would have got out of this chair and beaten bastard to death with this fucking oxygen tank," old man Frazer said pushing over the oxygen canister in temper with his face mask leaping off of his lap.

Calming down with his oxygen canister upright again and taking a few drags of air into his lungs, he knew what he had to say next was going to go down like a tonne of bricks with his associates. "Since his death, I have found out from Company House that Homes Association does not exist, meaning all our cash found its way into Baines back pocket. Yes, I truly fucked up in trusting Baines after all said and done, we had worked on various projects from 1999 until 2010, so I had no reason not to trust Baines. In fact, out of the blue, it was only in 2014 our teams worked on bank projects in Scotland that were very rewarding. Having said that, he's yet to pay me my 50% that my twins went after our cash at Baines home but all to no avail."

Then Frank's son, Tommy Frazer, stepped forward to speak to the group, "Glenda Baines is a fucking good actress because she played dumb about any cash her late husband owed us from the three banks' heists in Scotland and she knew nothing about the Homes Association project. We had Charlie Baines in the corner looking as guilty as hell. On leaving their mansion—our boys with us who had waited outside with our cars—it was my brother Peter that ordered our boys to beat the shit out of Charlie Baines."

"It was prior to the Scotland projects getting underway, it was late in 2013 that Baines had decided that the Scotland jobs would be his last ones and he decided he would then go straight. This was when this Homes Association scenario was put forward to me that I was convinced it was a win-win; hence I put this idea to you guys," Frank Frazer said before spluttering into his mask.

"So, the bastard ripped us all off?" Tommy Frazer said out loud with his father still coughing and spluttering into his face mask to his face.

"You okay, Dad?" Tommy asked with his dad shaking his head.

With his dad struggling to get air into his lungs, it was Peter Frazer who came forward and said, "It's common knowledge to us all here that Trevor Charles Baines never used banks; he never took out loans, so his large house in Sandhurst is more than likely to be mortgage-free. With a little persuasion, we can convince

Glenda and Charlie Baines that it's in their best interest to sell their home that would go towards Baines debt he owes all of us here."

With Frank Frazer getting his breathing back under control, "Peter and you Tom, I want you to put a team together to search the whole of Baines home for our cash, yes, take it apart."

After Franks associates left his club, Tom wheeled his father to the bar area with Peter bringing along his oxygen tank. With Tommy being the barman, he started pouring out three large measures of brandy for the three of them. With Frank Frazer taking his drink, he said: "What Simon said was not all bollocks; all of us would have been far better off if we had taken the rewards offered by the banks."

Chapter 16
Treasures of Africa

With Grace moping around the bungalow totally pissed off, knowing Rob had been trying to contact George Almedia hoping to get him involved for him to discover what's in Trevor Charles Baines coffin.

"I was thinking earlier we should go to the Tato Hotel for dinner this evening, but now you're telling me that the bitch Anna Kajeme is booked in with the so-called Peter Goodman; hence the hotel doors are now shut for us," Grace said with Rob vigorously shaking his head for such a visit.

"What about I shoot into Moshi later and pick up a Chinese takeaway for us?" Rob said, hoping that would suffice.

"Whatever, I am taking baby Grace out for a bit of fresh air."

With Rob far from being happy with not being asked to join her, of course, he knew she was angry that he was waiting to hear back from his friend from Mwanza.

So, with very few words spoken between them for the remaining hours left for Saturday, they were both happy when the day came to a close.

"Rob, first thing Sunday, I want you to take me to the Treasures of Africa Orphanage. It's high time I show Sister Julia our baby Grace is developing. She will be amazed in just how that baby wrapped in sacking that was left on her doorstep that is now such a gorgeous and healthy child," she said, picking up Grace from her high chair and walked out the lounge into their bedroom.

"Okay, I will clear the table and wash up," Rob whispered, not wishing to add further fuel to the fire. It was five minutes later, Grace could hear him shouting at Bernie that brought a smile to her face. "Piss off, Bernie! You have wiped all the dishes clean; please let me put them in the dishwasher."

10 am Sunday morning with Grace and their godchild strapped into her seat, Rob called out Grace: "Give us a hand lifting up, Bernie, into the back, and then we can head for the Treasures of Africa."

Once at the orphanage situated on the outskirts of Moshi Town, Rob started to reverse in with the children rushing out to greet their visitors. "Karibu (welcome), my dear friends to Treasures of Africa," Sister Julia said, following her children in her care out. "Oh, what a sweetie," the Sister said when Grace had handed over baby Grace to her.

Once Rob and Grace had lifted out Bernie from the back, the children were all over him what Bernie seemed to love. "Karibu, Grace and Rob," she said as she opened the front door that the children had run out of a few minutes ago.

“Oh, Julia, it’s like walking into a hotel; what a difference to our last visit,” Grace said, wiping baby Grace’s chin who seemed more than happy looking at everything over the Sister’s shoulder. “I think Sister, she is still teething,” Grace said stuffing the wet tissue into her jacket.

“Come into our lounge.” Once they entered, Grace and Rob were lost for words seeing the transformation with its three leather sofas, two bookcases stuffed with children’s books, and in the far corner, there were two large trunks with the toys spilling out. In the centre of the large room, a large plasma TV was hung on the wall, and the opposite wall were some 50 of the children’s drawings and paintings that were pinned to the extremely large pegboard. “Yes, it’s all thanks to lover boy here and his uncle Alan,” Sister Julia said pretending to punch Rob’s arm.

“Julia, please can I help out here today with the children’s lunch and dinner?” Grace asked.

Sister Julia never said anything; she simply gave Grace a huge hug with her spare arm. “Here you go, sweetie. Go to your godmother; I think she needs to be changed?” Sister Julia said squeezing her nose.

“Rob, can you get my bag out of the jeep and can you pick me up at around 6 pm?” Grace asked giving him a kiss on the cheek and whispered: “I love you.” Rob never said anything he just wandered out of the orphanage to get the babies disposable nappies and bottles, feeling happy that they were back on good terms.

“Here you go, keep an eye on Bernie and I will see you later,” Rob said handing her the large holdall and kissing her and said: “Likewise.” Then he kissed Sister Julia on the cheek. Rob was sure Julia was blushing after that kiss; mind you seeing she is black, it was hard to say for certain that she was, in fact, blushing.

Chapter 17
Nothing Ventured, Nothing Gained

Rob was indicating to turn right into Machame when his mobile went off telling him he had a text. Rob cancelled the indicator and parked up by the sign indicating a right turn to the Tato Hotel and Machame. Opening his text message, "Hi, Rob, never picked up your message until 15 minutes ago. I have just flown in from Mwanza and I am in Hertz to hire a car and then I am off to Arusha. I see you're in Machame; if possible, can we meet at the Supermarket in Arusha by the clock tower for coffee at 2 pm."

Rob checked the time on his mobile. "See you there then." Rob sent the text and pulled out for his 50-minute trip to Arusha.

At 1:50 pm, Rob pulled into the supermarket's car park and was taken by a sparkling white Mercedes Benz parked up. He then walked into the Supermarket that sold everything from washing machines, televisions to flip flops and children's toys. It had the cafeteria at the rear of the store where George Almedia, the large smartly dressed six-foot African, was sitting by the entrance. He immediately got up seeing Rob and gave him a huge hug followed by a firm handshake.

"The last time we met was when I flew into Heathrow for the christening of baby Grace." With Grace's concerns, Rob was having problems telling George what he was going to ask him about that could provide them with large rewards from the banks in the UK.

"What do you want to drink, Rob?"

"Cappuccino with no chocolate would be nice, thank you."

Whilst George was queuing at the counter for their drinks, Rob was still having second thoughts then thinking perhaps, they could pull this off without Grace finding out.

With their drinks on their table, the pair of them caught up on what they had been doing the last twelve months. "Okay, Rob, what did you want to see me for?"

Rob had earlier on Saturday written down what he thought George might be interested in and slid the paper across the table. "This is assuming, George, you're not busy?"

George Almedia looked at him, "As you know, Rob, I lost my contract at Johnson Diamond Mine over them fucking diamonds and the con we pulled off with the company, so I am grateful for any work that's put my way."

George sat there and read what Rob had written, looking up and smiling when he reached the graveyard possibility. "I have not heard of this character Trevor Charles Baines; however, I will take your word that he was a professional criminal." So, he carried on reading, then all of a sudden, he started to laugh, "Are you providing the spade?"

"Rob, how the heck do you know that his coffin could be stuffed with money and not his dead body?" Rob took out the Kibos Safaris camera and showed him the photo of the guy waiting to start his trek up Mount Kilimanjaro.

"So, what am I looking for?"

"Look at his right hand."

"Got it, the tattoo TCB." Rob looked at him and started to smile knowing he and him, along with Grace, knew Peter Goodman was, in fact, Trevor Charles Baines.

"And would you believe I picked him up Saturday for my uncle Alan from the Tato Hotel and drove him to the Machame Gate for his climb up to the Roof of Africa? There might be a problem seeing Trevor Charles Baines's girlfriend is Anna Kajeme."

George had to smile knowing this lady hates Rob for taking her stolen diamonds from her flight from Dar to Kilimanjaro. "It's a small world, my Mzungu (white) friend," George said ruffling Rob's hair.

"George, you need to check it out. I am certain you can find his burial on the BBC website with the date I have given you for the burial along with the photograph they showed of him smoking a large cigar where you will see the TCB tattoo on the back of his right hand. There's a further problem, George; Grace must not know what we are doing until we have proved that I am right and that there are millions of pounds stuffed in his coffin that the banks will give us—handsome rewards to have their cash returned."

"Rob, let me check it out, and if I agree, I will book into the Castle Palace Hotel at the Elephant and Castle in SE London where I stayed and where we planned the con with those stolen diamonds from Johnson Diamond Mine. When are you flying home?"

Rob was not sure if he was flying home early Tuesday morning or the late flight from Kilimanjaro International Airport to Heathrow. "Not sure of the time, George, but sometime on Tuesday."

"Let's leave it for the moment, Rob, but I am a great believer in saying: nothing ventured, nothing gained."

"There's one other matter, George. I might need your help at some stage."

George looked at him, thinking you're one in a million. "Okay, Mzungu, spit it out." Then Rob told him about him finding the PM Simon Davis's red parliamentary case that contained material that could see him facing criminal charges for deceiving the UK's population…

Ten minutes later, Rob stopped after telling him the whole story, drinking the dregs from his cappuccino. "So, what do you think, George?"

"Give it to the media would be my advice, then step back and watch the shit hit the fan." Rob looked at his friend, hoping to hear other scenarios but suggesting what his uncle was advising. “Of course, Rob, you could blackmail the bastard? Whatever you decide on, I am here to help you; however, if you go for the latter, you might need me to watch your back.”

“Thanks, George.”

With them getting up and hugging and shaking hands again, they headed for the exit. “Remember, George, Grace does not need to know,” Rob said with his friend placing his index finger to his lips and sliding his finger across much as to say my lips are sealed. Rob had to smile watching George Almedia jumping in the new sparkling white Mercedes Benz.

Chapter 18
One Lucky Pig

Sunday with the air cleared between Grace and Rob, so the day was looking promising for the pair.

After breakfast, they were taking baby Grace in her buggy and, of course, Bernie to accompany them to Machame Hospital to show Doctor Shirley Armour just how well baby Grace is. Doctor Shirley was the doctor who cared for baby Grace after her heart operation.

With Bernie rushing on ahead, when the pig got to the junction where the sign said Machame Hospital to the left and straight ahead for Machame Village and Machame Gate, Bernie stopped and looked round to see Rob pointing to the left, so he was off to the hospital. "That's one smart piece of pork," Grace said bending down and wiping baby Grace's face seeing she was trying to decide if she liked the square of chocolate Rob had given her.

"Don't let Bernie hear you call him a piece of pork," Rob said with Grace throwing the dirty tissue at him that he caught and put in his pocket.

"Hell, Rob, you need to look at all the rubbish on the ground."

"Two wrongs don't make a right," Rob said kicking an empty can of coke into the overgrown hedge.

When they reached the hospital, Bernie was sitting outside the staff's open-air refreshment snack bar situated close to the main entrance waiting for any tit-bits to be tossed his way.

They were fortunate seeing Doctor Shirley Armour coming down the steps from the main entrance. "Oh, what a lovely surprise seeing you guys here, is everything…," the doctor stopped what she was about to ask. "Wow, that's got to be my favourite patient. Grace hand her over," she said stretching out both her arms with baby Grace doing likewise.

"Bloody hell, she remembers the doctor," Rob said.

Two coffees for the free along with a further piece of chocolate for baby Grace and Bernie, who had just woofed down half of a pork pie that a nursed had thrown out for him.

On Rob's last visit with his uncle, Bernie once again took a liking to the doctors' white plimsolls, what he wouldn't do for the opportunity to rip them to pieces. "Give me five minutes," the Doctor said rushing back into the hospital.

"What's she gone for, Rob?"

He just shrugged his shoulders, "No idea." It was only two minutes later that the Doctor jumped down the three steps from the entrance swinging a carrier bag.

"Here you go, Rob," handing him the bag, "and thank you for showing me how my beautiful patient is getting on. Don't wait so long for your next visit," the Doctor said.

It was then the Doctor went over to Rob taking out one plimsoll from the carrier bag and giving it to Bernie, who immediately grabbed it and rushed off. "Don't worry about Bernie, Doctor he will be waiting at the door when we get home," Rob said looking into the carrier bag.

"They are all old ones that doctors and nurses throw out with any half-decent ones that we give to the patients or their children."

"He's one lucky pig, there are half a dozen pairs in this bag," Rob said tying the bag to the buggy.

With kisses all round and a special one and a loving hug for baby Grace from the Doctor, the three of them headed back to the bungalow.

Strolling back, Rob's mobile goes off informing him he's got a text. Taking his mobile out of his pocket, he opens the message to read.

"Rob niko njiani (on my way)."

"Who wants you?" Rob looked at Grace, thinking it's now too late to speak the truth.

"It's only Talk, Talk telling me I can view my account online."

Chapter 19
Take Care

Monday evening, Rob had got held up on his way to Kilimanjaro International Airport to pick up his uncle and aunt from their Easter break on Zanzibar. Driving into the airport, he headed for the arrivals. He was still cursing the police for them pulling cars over for on the spot checks when he parked up behind the taxis queuing for potential fares.

Yvonne and Alan were outside the arrivals waiting when Rob ran up to them. "Sorry, police checks," he said walking back with them to where he had parked the jeep.

"We stayed at the Uroa Bay Beach Resort close the bungalow you and Grace stopped in last year," Alan said putting his seat belt on with Yvonne doing likewise in the back as Rob pulled away.

"Is everything okay back home? I bet Grace loved being mum since Friday, and did you manage to lose Bernie?" Yvonne said with Alan turning in his seat and giving his wife daggers.

"Yes, yes and no to your last question," Rob said smiling at his uncle.

"Rob, that package you had given me, I sent it to Portcullis House at the House of Commons using DHL on Zanzibar that should be in the UK this Tuesday. Knowing at some stage the UK's government would track that package back to my doorstep, I asked the manager of the resort if she would go to DHL and send it for me whilst she was taking back an orphan that was wandering around the resort to the children's Zanzibar Orphanage right next to DHL office. I still think you should hand over the PM's red case that contains those two manifests to the media."

Rob knew his uncle was talking a great deal of sense. "Not sure just yet," Rob said hoping his uncle was not going to press him further to his suggestion.

"I received, and we both read your lengthy email last night," Alan informed him.

"Rob, you seem to have a habit of being in the wrong place at the wrong time," Yvonne called out from the back over the noise of the diesel engine; of course, it didn't help matters to be heard seeing Rob had his window wound down.

Rob handed his uncle the Kibo Safaris camera. "Go to the photos I took at Machame Gate, look at the fifth snap." Rob carried on driving and waited for his uncle's response whilst he was looking, and then he handed the camera to his wife.

“Okay, Rob, even without the TCB tattoo, you only need to put grey curly hair on that photograph, and yes, you have snapped Trevor Charles Baines granted he’s aged since we lived in the UK.”

From the back of the jeep, they both heard Yvonne shouting: “Excuse me, French, but he’s one nasty fucker. If you and George Almedia are planning to find out what’s in his coffin, you bloody need to take care.”

“I don’t think it’s wise in you not telling Grace what you are doing seeing if this comes back and bites you in your arse. You are going to have one very sad and angry young lady to deal with,” Alan said with Rob just nodding in agreement to what his uncle was saying.

“I shall tell her if I can prove that the Baines coffin at Honour Oak contains stolen cash,” Rob said looking in his interior rear-view mirror seeing his aunt, who was still looking at the photograph on the Kibo Safaris camera.

“If old Frankie Frazer, one of Trevor Baines associate, gets wind of this possibility, then you will be more than happy to have George Almedia on board seeing all hell will break loose in South East London,” Alan Hat said watching Rob carefully reverse into their driveway and hearing Bernie trying to break out of their bungalow.

“Bloody pig will be the death of me,” Yvonne said getting out of the jeep and slamming the door.

Chapter 20
Reward

Reading Police Station. DI Judy Reynolds was anxiously sitting and waiting in DCI Gordon Taylor's office whilst he was on the telephone to the Mayor. "Let me assure you, Mrs Mayor, we are doing everything possible to recover the stolen cash for the banks," DCI Gordon Taylor said ending the call and staring at his DI, hoping she had some positive news.

"Okay, Reynolds, where are we with getting Trevor Charles Baines stolen cash back to its rightful owners?" DI Reynolds was fumbling and getting her notebook out of her jacket. "In your own time, DI," her boss said tapping his fingers on his desk.

With the DI flicking to the pages she needs to read from, "Here we go boss, DS Jones has been keeping tabs on the Baines home in Sandhurst and seeing people paying their respects with flowers on his funeral day. As you would have seen on the BBC News, he had a good turnout at Honour Oak Cemetery. Late into the evening, several people arrived at their home, but were only there for a few minutes."

The DI turned the page, "Three days after the funeral, the Frazer twins arrived in their two Mercedes at the Baines home and were invited in by Glenda Baines. Thirty minutes later, Charlie, the son, saw them out, and once outside, the Frazer twins' two drivers gave Charlie a good beating where he finished up being taken to Frimley Park Hospital by ambulance."

"And then what?" her boss asked drumming his fingers on his right hand on his desk again and checking the time on his left wrist.

"Nothing to report other than DS Jones following them to the Sandhurst Surgery where Glenda Baines entered carrying two large M&S carrier bags. DS Jones thought it's strange that when she came out and jumped in their Audi, she was not carrying those bags. He then followed them again but, unfortunately, he lost them on a change of traffic lights that went against him.

"DS Jones went back to the surgery, but the receptionist was not allowed to tell my DS what doctor Glenda Baines had an appointment with. It was whilst at the surgery he saw numerous bags and boxes stacked in the far corner. It turns out that a Doctor at the surgery has organised donations from all the surgeries patients to donate items for an orphanage in Poland."

DCI Gordon Taylor said, "Okay, Reynolds, if I give you DS Richardson to keep watch on the Baines home, this will allow DS Jones and yourself to lean on the Frazer family seeing I believe Charlie Baines was beaten up because the late Trevor Charles Baines owes them money."

Judy Reynolds was feeling relieved seeing she was thinking she was in for a rollicking, seeing she was no nearer to finding out where the stolen cash was. "Granted boss, it was mentioned on Radio 4 that there could be rewards given to anyone who knew the whereabouts of the cash. What if we could get the reward the banks say what they are jointly willing to give mentioned in the press seeing it might get people jumping out the woodwork to get their hands on the reward offered?"

"Okay, Reynolds, it seems a good scenario. You need to leave it with me and let me speak to the banks concerned." Then he added, "That's all for now."

Back downstairs in her office, she called DS Jones to tell him DS Philip Richardson will be relieving him later today. "How did your meeting go with our DCI?" DS Jones asked.

Judy Reynolds wanted to say he's an ignorant git but decided to bite her tongue and said, "No comment," and ended the call.

Part 2

Chapter 21

You Should Have Told Me

With a great many tears early Tuesday and with Grace washing away baby Grace with a huge number of kisses mixed with her tears, they were eventually out of the jeep and walking towards departures at Kilimanjaro International Airport.

Rob was checking their departure time to Mombasa and the connecting time of their flight to the UK.

Two hours later, they were boarding their connecting flight from Mombasa that had arrived from Dar-es-Salaam to Heathrow. "Row 10, Grace, A and B," Rob said carrying their two holdalls with Grace sliding across to the window seat, leaving Rob to put their hand luggage in the overhead locker. He was just about to take his seat when he looked down the plane and spotted George Almedia some ten rows back in the aisle seat. He wanted to wave out to him but decided on a nod of acknowledgement, watching his friend doing likewise.

Fifteen minutes later, the air stewardess was running through all the safety measures on their flight. After demonstrating the lifejacket's dos and don'ts, she pointed out that their lifejackets were under their seats. "I fail to see what's the value of those lifejackets if we have to crash land on a motorway," Grace said smiling.

"That's not at all funny, young lady," the elderly guy said sitting in the C seat, looking at the card that highlights all the safety measures on their flight.

"Granted, mate, it's not funny, but it's true," Rob said defending Grace, who was blushing and dare say wishing she had not made that comment.

Leaning across towards Grace. "My uncle reckons our PM will be receiving his jelly babies, and his mobile along with the card addressed to his wife," he said quietly in case Mr Grumpy next to him heard.

Grace was looking out the window watching the land disappear when she said, "What about this Baines character? What's happening?" Rob just sat there deciding not to answer her. Grace turned away from looking at the clouds as the plane was still climbing and said, "Rob, you should have told me seeing a few rows back of us sits George Almedia." She once again turned her attention to the clouds. Rob went to hold her hand, but she drew her hand away sharply.

For the next hour, they sat listening to the elderly guy snoring and farting in perfect rhythm; first, a snore followed by him breaking wind. "Grace, all George is going to do is check it out, and he will be staying at the Castle Palace Hotel where we all met last year. With my hand on my heart, I never knew George was going to be on this flight."

It was then that Grace grabbed hold of Rob's hand and said, "As much as I disagree in what you're up to, you still need to be upfront with me," she said leaning over and whispered in his ear: "He bloody stinks."

Rob wanted to laugh but said, "You're lucky you're not sitting next to him."

Whilst Rob went to spend a penny, Grace took the opportunity to wander back to where George Almedia was sitting in row 21 on the aisle seat kneeling down; she said, "I trust you are well, George? It's been a while since you had your Christmas dinner with both Rob's parents and mine, along with our dear friends Rosie and Pauline."

George looked at her wondering just how much she knew why he was returning again to the UK. "Yes, it was fantastic to spend my Christmas with genuine people who cared for one another. I was also very grateful that I was invited to the christening of your goddaughter, baby, Grace just before the Christmas festivities."

"Excuse me, young lady," the pretty air hostess asked pushing her trolley with an array of goodies for sale. Grace stood up and squeezed herself into row 21.

"Take care, George, and please look after my Rob," Grace said and followed the trolley that was heading to the front of the plane to commence her business with the passengers.

It was five hours later with Rob on his mobile leaving Grace waiting at the carousel number two for their small suitcase to come round. There was a tap on her shoulder, "Grace, I know Rob told me that you object to what we are doing, but please be assured you have nothing to fear," George said grabbing hold of his suitcase that appeared on the carousel whilst he was chatting.

"Grace, I have just heard from Linda that she will wait close to terminal four and will wait for my call and will pick us from the arrivals area where the buses and coaches pick up from. From all accounts, Tony can't get away from Gems; he's helping out with some sort of stock control," he said taking the small suitcase off Grace and putting it on their trolley along with their two holdalls.

"Here you go, George, put your case on here with ours and yes, you're in luck seeing we can give you a ride to the Castle Palace Hotel," Grace said and had to smile watching George giving his thumbs up to Rob.

Chapter 22
We Have a Problem

It was early evening on the Tuesday after the Easter, the PM was just about to leave parliament when a young lad from Portcullis House came over to where Simon Davis was just about to get into his chauffeur-driven car to 10 Downing Street. "Excuse me, sir. The post office thought this might be urgent," the young lad said nervously handing the PM the A4 jiffy bag along with the relevant documentation DHL had provided.

"Thank you, young man," the PM said getting in the back of the BMW and noticing the document was telling him the jiffy bag was sent from Zanzibar.

Sitting in the back of the car, he was curious about what was enclosed within the jiffy. He, of course, was fully aware that it had gone through the scanner over at Portcullis House hence making it safe to open. Taking his keyring out of his pocket and by using a key, he managed to get out the staples and started to shake the contents out onto the seat. The first two things to drop out were a mobile, that was clearly his, and the second item that followed was a half packet of jelly babies. He immediately stuffed them back into the jiffy while hoping his driver never noticed what he was looking at.

Back at 10 Downing Street with his wife at some charity function, he went straight into his office. "Tony, I don't wish to be disturbed," the PM called out to one of his staff who was heading up to their flat with an armful of clean laundry.

Now at his desk, he could feel his heart beating as though it was trying to escape his shirt. Placing the jiffy bag on his desk with his hands shaking, he pulled out his mobile along with the jelly babies. Putting his hand into the bag, he took out the birthday card that he failed to give Judith, his wife, along with a family photograph of them whilst they were on a family holiday in Devon. Shaking the bag for anything else, a note dropped out, and with his hands doing 40 to the dozen, he unfolded it and placed it on his desk to read what the printed message said:

'You can fool all the people some of the time, and some of the people all the time, but you cannot fool all the people all the time. (Abraham Lincoln, 16th US President 1809–1865)'

"Oh fuck," the PM said wiping the sweat from his brow with the palm of his right hand. Getting his new mobile from his jacket and entering contacts, he called Graham Johnson, his chancellor.

“Simon, why are you calling? It was only 30 minutes ago when we said goodbye.”

“Hi, Graham, if you’re at home, come in the back. I am in my office. We have a problem.”

In less than a minute, Graham Johnson walked into the PM’s office, “What’s the problem?” Simon never answered; he just slid the contents from the jiffy bag across his desk to where Graham had sat and started to look at the items and then read the note.

“Hell, Graham, this means some bugger has my red case that we both know contains those two bloody manifests,” Simon Davis said loosening his tie.

“We must have checked that CCTV half a dozen times after the train cash and at no time did we see your case being taken off the train,” Graham Johnson said reading the note again and checking the mobile to see if the sim was still intact. “Do you mind?” he said taking a jelly baby from the packet and then went on to ask, “Where was this jiffy sent from?” Once again, Simon Davis slid the DHL document over to his side of the desk. “Bloody hell, Zanzibar,” Graham said this time taking a handful of jelly babies and read the note yet again, only this time, he noticed in pencil at the bottom. “Here we go, Simon, in pencil at the bottom is the sender’s email address.”

“How do you know it’s come from the sender?” the PM asked. This time his chancellor slid the note back across to the PM.

“See for yourself.”

“Oh my God, 2manifests@zan.com,” the PM said wiping once again the sweat from his brow.

“Graham, you will need to get hold of the CCTV again of the rail crash and this time we look to see if we recognise anybody or we see a person carrying case or bag that could hold my red case.” Then the PM slapped his desk making the chancellor jump, “It’s slipped my mind the false manifest is being sent to the entire population.”

Graham Johnson looked at his boss in disbelief and said, “With the greatest respect, you have dug yourself one heck of a large hole.” And then said, “Put a stop to it.”

The PM looked at his chancellor while feeling such a bloody idiot, “If only I could see I had proofed it before my case was stolen and to make matters worse, my office accounts department paid upfront to speed things up.”

“Simon, we go a very long way, and over the years, we have made mistakes, but this stupid action you have taken to stay as the PM will truly take some beating,” Graham said taking the remaining two jelly babies out of the bag and walked out of his office.

Chapter 23
One Million

Wednesday at the crack of dawn at the Castle Palace Hotel, George Almedia was on his laptop once again looking at the BBC News recording of the Trevor Charles Baines funeral. He decided that the elderly woman at the grave with the smartly dressed guy who seemed to be consoling the woman must have been Glenda Baines, his wife, and her son Charlie Baines.

It struck him how odd it was that the grave was tucked away remotely from other graves with its backdrop being a wooded area. He Googled up the map using the Honour Oak Cemetery postcode Rob had given him. It was then that he could see the wooded area was fairly deep from Mason Road that was running parallel to the cemetery.

Writing down what he wanted to know regarding the layout of the cemetery and then checking with Rob's note, he wrote down the address of the Baines family.

Before going down for an early breakfast, he thought he would have a browse through the media whilst his laptop was open. It was the front page of the Daily Mirror that grabbed his attention.

Banks Are Offering a One Million Pound Reward

The National Westminster, Lloyds and Barclays Bank have agreed jointly to pay the one million pounds for the safe return of their stolen cash.

It's estimated that over the past twelve years, the banks have had in the region of seven million pounds stolen.

Although not proven, the Metropolitan Police believe that the late Trevor Charles Baines had organised and was in the main responsible for these robberies from the said banks.

The Metropolitan Police, to this day, believe the majority of this cash is still out there.

"That's good; a one-million-pound reward is good enough for me," George said out loud shutting down his laptop and was off for his early morning full English breakfast.

Chapter 24
Castle Palace Hotel

9 am at Reading Police Station, there was no such luxury of a fried breakfast for DI Judy Reynolds, DS John Jones and DS Philip Richardson; they were making do with three cups of tea and a pack of digestive biscuits that the DI took out of her desk.

"Okay, guys, listen up. DS Jones, you will be pleased to know that, thanks to our DCI Gordon Taylor, you will be with me seeing we need to put pressure on the Frazer family. Our boss believes that since DS Jones and I witnessed the Frazer twins' minders beating the crap out of Charlie Baines, the DCI reckons the Baines failed to pay Frank Frazer what he owes him from various illegal business transactions Trevor Charles Baines had organised.

"Sorry Philip, you have drawn the short straw seeing you're going to be keeping tabs on the Baines home along with following them should they leave their very large house," DI Reynolds said.

"It's not a bloody house, you know it's a mansion," DS Jones the 7-foot police officer butted in.

"So, Inspector, you're hoping that between us we could come up with the late Trevor Baines stolen cash or at least the whereabouts?" DS Richardson said looking at DS Jones rubbing his arse.

DS Richardson said, "Philip, you need to take a pillow to sit on because you could be there for a while shadowing the house and them."

DI Reynolds gave DS Richardson the address along with photographs of Glenda and Charlie Baines plus the house. "There's a lane on the left a short distance from the house that gives you a relatively good view of the property where you can park up." Then she went to her draw and pulled out a set of car keys. "Philip, there's an old grey Ford Focus down in the car park." She then tossed him the keys. "DS Jones will relieve you or me on occasions from the hours between 7 pm and midnight," DI Reynolds said looking at DS Jones, who didn't seem happy to know his evenings were still going to be shit.

"Philip, I need to go to my car. I'll let you borrow my binoculars," DS Jones said getting up to leave and beckoning him to follow.

Now alone in her office, DI Judy Reynolds was on Google to find what she could about Frank Frazer when DCI Gordon Taylor rushed into her office with the door banging behind him. "Reynolds, if I said to you George Almedia what and who would spring to mind?" her boss asked taking a seat opposite Judy; of course, she knew the guy had worked with them at the Met when she was DS Reynolds.

"Hell, boss, he was a private investigator for Johnson Diamond Mine in Mwanza and Tetra Diamonds here in the UK and Tanzania," DI Reynolds said knowing the big African was involved in tracking down Anna Kajeme, who was wanted by the law in Tanzania for her involvement in the diamond heist.

"Thought you would like to know he was spotted checking into the Castle Palace Hotel in South East London," the DCI said and got up without a 'goodbye' or 'kiss my arse' and left her alone again. Pausing Google, she was trying to figure what brings him back to the UK. For sure, it can't have anything to do with Trevor Charles Baines. A few minutes later, she dismissed the thought and went back into Google.

She was delighted to see that the banks have seen sense to highlight the million-pound reward in all the publications.

Chapter 25
BBC News

Wednesday after Prime Minister Questions, it was 6 pm at 11 Downing Street. "Simon, I have a contact at the BBC, and I managed to get a copy of the whole event of the rail crash. Yes, the BBC News coverage of the whole event from their arrival on-site at Vauxhall Station," Graham Johnson, the chancellor, said relieved that he was not asked why he needed it.

"Well done, Graham. What about the CCTV?" Simon Davis asked looking at his friend placing a copy of the CCTV on his desk.

One hour later. "There's nothing we have not seen many times before on the CCTV," Graham said putting the BBC disc into his PC and pressed play.

Twenty minutes later, after scrutinising the recording. "There's nothing so far that I can see that would say someone his carrying a case or holdall that would enable them to have my red case enclosed," the PM said taking his jacket off, throwing it on the sofa in Graham's office, and looking frustrated that they are none the wiser who had stolen his case.

"Here we go, Simon. There you are being put on the stretcher with me standing beside you before the medics started taking you across the lines to the waiting ambulances." The camera follows them halfway across the lines when the camera returns to the wreckage and chaos and focuses on many of the injured being taking to safety across the tracks by the railway officials. The camera returns to the front section of the train.

"Pause it there, Graham." They both could see a young guy standing on the side of the train's door on the third carriage next to the carriage they were travelling in. "Press play Graham, stop," the PM said immediately.

"Wow, he's got a large case by his side, and he appears to be shouting out to gain attention seeing the carriage is tilting backwards he's going to have a problem getting to the ground without help."

"Zoom in Graham on this fellow," and they both witness a young guy that might have the PM's parliamentary red case that could be in the large suitcase sitting on the edge of the carriage.

With Graham pouring them out two large measures of whiskey while the Prime Minister appearing transfixed to the frozen screen.

"Hell, Graham, I'll be dammed this young guy looks familiar if I am right; he always has a habit of turning up like a bad penny," the PM said slapping his hands on the desk knocking his glass of whiskey over.

"What you on about, Simon?" his chancellor asked with him now staring at the screen and wiping his desk with his white handkerchief from his top pocket at the same time.

"Granted, the image is blurred; however, if I said to you, Graham, the National Bank robbery in Berkshire in 2013 where a young lad managed to help a great many charities where we had stopped their governments' funding. This young lad aged 17 at the time, walked off a train at Waterloo Station with a case that contained over a million pounds plus a vast array of valuable jewellery. Unbeknown to the lad, the guy that had been involved with the bank robbery had to leave his very large case on the train whilst the Metropolitan Police chased him down," Simon Davis said helping himself to a further whiskey and drinking it down in one gulp.

Graham looked at Simon then back to the screen and back again to his PM, "Oh my God, you're saying we could have both been staring at young Robert Hat?"

"Hell, yes, but I can't be sure plus it doesn't fit seeing the items that were returned to Portcullis House came from Zanzibar?"

"Do you want me to get our contact on the 'QT Mr Fix It' at the special branch to check out this possibility?" The PM never answered; he just nodded and put his jacket back on, checked his watch and left 11 Downing Street through the back door.

Ten minutes later, he sent his friend a text and wrote, "I should have said thank you for your support, SD."

Chapter 26
Parking Ticket

George Almedia, after his early breakfast at the Castle Palace Hotel Wednesday, spent all day watching the coming and going from the late Trevor Charles Baines home in Sandhurst, not that there's been any movement. Parked up in the lane a short distance from the house he was watching. At 5 pm, an old grey Ford Focus pulled into the lane that George thought might be an unmarked police car about to do likewise watching the Baines property.

The Ford Focus must have done a 3-point turn further down the lane and came back down the lane and parked 50 yards behind his rented Honda vehicle. George got out of his car and walked back to Ford Focus with the guy inside wound down his window. This was when George Almedia immediately thought his concerns were right; he noticed and heard the police radio controller giving out instructions to another car that the guy in the Ford Focus was not quick enough to turn it off. "Excuse me, sir, but my map told me to turn right to take me to the M&S store," he said waving his map in front of the driver.

"It's okay. You need to pull out of this lane and turn right seeing, the road you drove down is a no through road; get back onto the main road, turn left and take the next on the right at the traffic lights an M&S comes up on your left-hand side, you won't miss it." George looked further into the car and could plainly see a small wad of photographs on his dashboard with the top one that was clearly a photograph of the home he had been watching since 9 am.

"Cheers, mate, I have been sitting here for a good twenty minutes trying to figure out where I had gone wrong?"

The guy in the Ford Focus put his head outside his car and said, "Enjoy your shopping trip," taking the photographs off his dashboard and tossed them to the passenger seat covered by his borrowed binoculars.

Pulling out and turning right and then left at the junction, George pulled into a bus stop and tapped the postcode for Honour Oak Cemetery into his Sat Nav.

Back in the Lane, DS Richardson took out his mobile and sent a text to DI Judy Reynolds: "So sorry for being late seeing I had to rush my good lady to the hospital that gave birth to our first son. I arrived at the Baines property a little after 5 pm; all seems very quiet."

Two hours later, the African guy from Mwanza parked up in Manor Road, and he could make out the cemetery through the wooded area. Leaving his motor, he walked into the area where he could see more clearly the many hundreds of graves with many headstones that would go back many years. He was thinking should he enter the graveyard from where he was or should he actually drive taking the next right and finding the entrance to the cemetery.

It was just then through the trees an Audi pulled into the very large parking area and parked up, and he could clearly see and recognise from the BBC website, it was Glenda holding a bunch of flowers along with a china vase and Charlie Baines getting out of the motor. They strolled over to the far corner and visited what must be Trevor Charles Baines resting place immediately on the edge of the wood area with no other graves within five yards of the late Trevor. On either side of the Baines plot, there were placards put into the ground that George thought from where he was crouching could say 'Private and Reserved' along with an 18-inch white plastic fence going around all three spaces. Totally undercover of the trees and bushes, George walked closer but still couldn't be sure what the placards said on either side of his grave. Charlie Baines left his mother at the grave that was still waiting for a headstone, and he walked into the woods with what looked like a folded bag under his left arm, and within a minute, it was though he had vanished out of sight.

Crouching lower, he saw the grey Ford Focus that was earlier parked in the lane close to the Baines property pull into the cemetery and park up around 200 yards from the Baines's Audi. He thought he could see the driver using the binoculars trying to see if he could where Glenda and Charlie Baines were. George had to smile seeing he was looking in the totally wrong area of the vast resting place of the hundreds of graves.

With Glenda kneeling by the grave out of sight, should anyone had been following them? It was all five minutes later that Charlie Baines stepped out of the woods. The only thing difference to when he walked in: he had a folded bag under his arm; when he came back into sight, he was now carrying a sports holdall looking that it could burst open any moment with whatever the contents were.

"My Mzungu friend, you just might be right," he said in a whisper and started to walk out of the woods and headed for his Honda. "Sorry young man, I got caught short," he said politely to the traffic warden.

"Be that as may, but it doesn't take 15 minutes to piss beside if you had read the notice that you parked under…," the Warden said placing his parking ticket under his windscreen wiper and pointing to the sign that clearly said, 'No Stopping Monday to Friday.'

Chapter 27
No Spade Will Be Needed

Thursday, as per the norm, Rob was up late for work at Premier Supreme Car Hire, where his workplace being at the far end of Ladbroke Grove. He had just enough time for a quick shower, and with his hair still dripping, he was dashing for their front door. “Tea, Rob?” his mum Julia Hat called out.

“If only Mum,” and then his mum heard the front door shut, and she could see him run past their kitchen window.

“Rob, the lift is working,” she shouted out and banging on the window while knowing there was not a chance in hell that he heard her.

Rob was dashing down the stairs two at a time; he always promised himself that he would one day count exactly how many steps there were from the ground to the fifth floor or the fifth floor to the ground. Next time, he told himself as he dashed to where his bright red 20-year-old company’s Morris bright red van was parked outside Grace’s mum’s garage.

“Our cornflakes have gone soggy,” Grace said sitting on the wall facing the garage holding two bowls of cereal. By the time they had got round the Elephant & Castle roundabout, Grace had finished spoon-feeding Rob.

Over Westminster Bridge, Rob’s mobile went off telling him he had a text. He took his mobile out of his pocket. “Who’s it from and what does it say?” he asked sliding his mobile across the dashboard.

“It’s from George, Rob.”

“What’s he saying, darling?” Grace glared at Rob and, if looks could kill, Rob would have died at the wheel before they reached Ladbroke Grove.

“George says, there’s a good possibility that you could be right plus I don’t believe no spade will be needed.” She then slid his mobile back across the dashboard and turned the radio on and put her feet on the dashboard, and listen to 8 am news on the Magic station.

When they drove into the company’s car park, they could see Jenny, their Line Manager, waiting by their arch. “You guys are back two days from Africa, and I have yet to ask you how baby Grace is?” Jenny asked, knowing by the time they leave this evening, she would have to view a great many photographs she knew Grace would have on here mobile.

“Oh, Jenny, she’s such a little darling, later I will show you the many photos I have.”

“Listen, you guys have half a dozen cars that have booked in for a clean from the nightshift drivers,” Jenny said handing Grace a large brown envelope with all the keys inside. She then tossed Grace the keys to the arch and a further small brown envelope she handed to her. “Inside are the keys for the two Rolls that have a wedding booked for 2 pm today, so it looks like you pair are going to be busy,” she said and walked to her office in the massive port-cabin. She only got some twenty feet when she turned around and called out to them: “Rob, your sister-in-law Linda called me earlier to say she will call in later to see you both.”

“She could have called us herself,” Grace said fumbling to find the right key for the two padlocks.

“She more than likely called to speak to our boss, her father, but got through to Jenny hence she took the message?” Rob said taking the keys from her to the arch and found the right key straight away.

Grace was looking around, “You might be right, Rob. I can’t see her dad’s BMW.”

Four hours later, with four cars cleaned along with two sparkling Rolls Royce’s that their drivers had just left the arch getting the ribbons on for their wedding at 2 pm. “Rob, get the last two cars in the arch, and let’s see if we can finish up by 3 pm.”

A little after 3 pm with Grace and Rob having a race to who could leather the last two cars the quickest, they watched Linda drive-in in her Mini Cooper and parked up and started to walk towards them. Then Rob’s mobile went off that he tosses to Linda, “Get that for me, Sis,” and he carried on trying to beat Grace in their private race.

“Beat you, darling once again,” Grace said throwing her leather at him and hitting him in the face.

“Now, you’re taking the piss because I called you darling earlier,” Rob said with Linda looking totally confused about what’s going on between her brother-in-law and Grace, who even in her wet gear, still looked gorgeous. Yes, to say Grace was not attractive would be like saying Elvis Presley is still alive and is living in the UK or Shirley Bassey can’t sing a note. She has a flawless complexion and her high pronounced cheekbones that many young ladies would envy.

“Rob, it’s from your uncle,” Linda said walking towards their cabin. “Coffee for everyone?” she called out entering their so-called office. Five minutes later, with three coffees for them on the table, Linda now struggled to pull Graces wellington boots off.

Rob took his mobile off Linda, “I have an attachment.”

“What’s he saying, Rob?” Linda asked.

“He is saying…,” then reads out, “Rob, what’s your response to the attached, Alan.” Rob opened the attachment and had to smile when he saw who it was addressed to.

“Give us the bad news, darling,” Grace said raising her eyebrows then winking at Linda.

Linda started to laugh and said, “Behave.”

“Okay, here’s what he’s saying. Dear Mr Lincoln, my job is to bring you to task for what you are looking to accomplish from what you have in your possession. You would be a very foolish person to attempt to take on such a high power in the UK.

"My advice to you would be to send the case and all its remaining contents by using the same method of transportation. By doing this, I can assure you the subject will be closed. SB."

"That's what I told you, Rob," Grace said shaking her head.

Linda asked, "Rob, what's the email address?"

"SB.government@hotmail.com."

"No value, Rob, mind you, it's signed SB and the email address once again signed by SB, so it looks like they want you to think the SB means the Special Branch is involved." Linda said and then asked, "What's going to be your reply?"

Rob looked at Linda and then at Grace, who was looking worried because she knew he believes he holds all the cards with what he has in that bloody case that's in a sack tugged away in her mother's garage. "Rob, you need to give the government something to scare the life out of them," Linda said looking at Grace, who was once again saying no with her head.

Rob took his mobile now off the table, "Here goes," and pressed reply.

"Dear Alan, thanks for your support. Please send the following attachment.

Rob

Hi SB,

I have three choices. The first being I could give those two manifests to the media with my second choice being Mr Simon Davis resigns. My last choice is that he pays my organisation 20 million that I will personally see that his cash went to those in need who were about to be hoodwinked in the next general election on the 7 of May 2015.

Your choice, AL."

Rob handed the message to Linda and Grace to gain their opinions. "What organisation?" Grace asked.

"Well, there are our good selves for one, and then we have Linda and my brother."

"True to a degree, Rob, but hell you're playing with fire," Linda said squeezing Grace's hand who continued to say no with her head.

"This should give you food for thought, Simon Davis, our PM." he then pressed send.

Chapter 28
Fly on the Wall

Early Thursday evening, DS Richardson sat in his grey Ford Focus in the lane 250 yards from the Baines large luxury property, some saying a mansion, when a Ford Transit with a tail lift passed by and drove up to the gates. Zooming in with his camera, he started snapping away as he watched the driver get out and speak to what seemed like the wall. A minute later, the two gates opened inwardly, and the van drove in.

With the front door opening, he focused his camera on Glenda Baines at the door. There was no handshake as he entered the large house. It was five minutes later, her visitor left the house without closing the door and went to the rear of the van, and DS Richards saw the tail lift going down and the van's shutter going up with half a dozen guys came dashing out the back and rushed into the Baines so-called mansion.

DS Richards checked all the photographs and decided to forward them to DI Judy Reynolds. He then sat there and wishing he was a fly on the wall to see what the hell was going on in the house.

There he sat, and two hours later, his boss DI Reynolds drove down the lane and came back parking behind his Ford Focus. Her DS got out and joined her bringing his camera and binoculars. "Those photos you sent me," she then took them out of her folder. "This one at the double gates is of Tommy Frazer. On this one, you caught his is twin brother Peter coming out of the back of the transit with the other guys. Has there been any further movement?" The moment she asked the question, not giving her DS a chance to answer, the front door opened, and all the guys come strolling out. "Get as many photos as you can," his DI said. With her DS snapping away, his DI was using the binoculars; she watched Tommy Frazer getting in the driver's seat with his twin Peter going to the back of the transit carrying a sports holdall that looked like you wouldn't get anything else in it. He then pulled down the shutter and raised the tail lift. Two minutes later, they watched the Ford Transit drive by.

"Would have loved to have been a fly on the wall in the Baines House," the DI said with her DS giving a chuckle. "What's so funny?"

"Great minds think alike, seeing I was only thinking the same myself."

Chapter 29
Three Graves

After the Frazer twins and their team left Glenda and Charlie. "Of course, we knew they were not going to find your dad's millions here, but how the hell could we stop them searching in every room for it. I don't believe there's not been anything damaged."

Charlie looked at his mother. "Bloody hell, Mother, having to sell our home to me is a great deal of damage making us having to pay Frank Frazer the money," he said sounding angry and rightly so. It was Frank Frazer that was fucking with his life; he's thinking going to the cabinet pouring out two large brandies.

"You're forgetting Peter Frazer took our holdall," Charlie said handing his mother a brandy who was on her mobile.

"Shit, no signal," Glenda said looking concerned that for the past three days, she was unable to make contact with whom she needed to speak with and gain further advice from.

"Charlie, first thing in the morning, I need to drop by Lamberts Estate Agents and, yes, once again, it looks like we have to make a further visit to Honour Oak." Charlie looked concerned at his mother and wanted to say it's best to go in the evening, seeing he believed it would be wiser, but he decided to bite his tongue.

Other than Glenda, her son and, of course, the church knew that Trevor Charles Baines had bought a piece of land at Honour Oak for his future death that was some years back. The land he bought was big enough to hold 3 graves; he managed to gain a written guarantee that the wooded land that the Church Saint Michaels also owned that other than the widening of Manor Road by 4 feet it would not be built on.

It was when the road was being widened with the commotions of the workforce in Manor Road along with having the road closed, this gave Trevor the opportunity to accomplish his goal in the woodlands.

Chapter 30
ASAP

Friday Morning, Graham Johnson, the Peoples Unite Party chancellor, was being chauffeur driven the short distance from Downing Street to parliament. Sitting back in his BMW, once again reading a speech he was going to deliver to the House of Commons, his mobile goes off saying he has a text. Opening it, he notices it was coming from the Special Branch from a friend known to Graham Johnson as Mr Fix It. Putting his speech back into his red parliamentary case, he opens the message.

"Hi George,

Your government is facing a critical situation hence we need to meet at our normal place ASAP. Please confirm.

FA."

The Chancellor sat there wondering what he had uncovered; he checked the time and worked out what time he would be leaving the Commons then pressed reply: "Shall do at 11:30 GJ."

Having waiting for the PM to conclude his speech to all parties and taking his seat next to his chancellor with the speaker of the Commons introducing the chancellor to commence his speech that was not going to please all the parties seeing further austerity measures were going to be introduced. Before getting to his feet, he leans over to his PM and whispers to him: "Tell you later, but it seems we have a problem with your missing case."

11:20, back in his chauffeur-driven car. "Sid, I need for you to drop me at the Embankment Underground Station and drive around and give me 15 minutes and return for me. I will be outside Costas." He then texts his friend at the Special Branch, "11:20 on route for our meet, GJ."

At 11:35, Graham Johnson gets out of the BMW at the pedestrian crossing at the Embankment Station and dashes up the steps into the station and out the other side where there were numerous street vendors selling an array of goods. Looking ahead to his left, there was Starbucks with outside seating and immediately to its left was Costas also with outside seating and in the far corner sat his contact, a young guy that couldn't be much older than 25 dressed in a smartly cut grey suit with his blonde hair tied back. The Chancellor being recognised by an elderly couple who insisted that they take a selfie of the three of them with Graham Johnson forcing a smile. Then he approached his contact and noticed a cappuccino was on the table for him, and he sat with his back to the crowds leaving the station.

Shaking the hand across the table with the young guy and said, "Okay, Freddie, what's so urgent?"

Freddie never said anything; he simply slid across the table a brown envelope. "You have a real problem on your hands," he said watching Graham opened the envelope and taking out a single sheet that he read.

"Hi SB,

I have three choices. The first being I could give those two manifests to the media with my second choice being Mr Simon Davis resigns. My last choice is that he pays my organisation 20 million that I will personally see that his cash goes to those in need who were about to be hoodwinked in the next general election on the 7 of May 2015.

Your choice, AL."

Graham sat there and looked at Freddie and then asked, "What about Robert Hat?"

Freddie took a further envelope from his inside jacket pocket and took out a further A4 sheet of paper. "Here you are, Graham," he said and read out from the paper he had. "It turns out that young Hat and his lady friend flew out of Heathrow the Thursday before the Easter holidays to Kilimanjaro Airport. We have no knowledge of them flying to Zanzibar," he said handing the paper to Graham.

"We both know, Freddie, that they could have driven to Dar-es-Salaam and then took the ferry over to Zanzibar," the chancellor said."

"That's true but most unlikely. Why take such a long journey to Dar from Kilimanjaro to use DHL to send a parcel on Zanzibar when a simple short flight to the island would suffice or by using the likes TNT or DHL in Arusha or even Moshi?" the guy from the Special Branch said.

Of course, neither of them knew that Robert Hat had been visiting his uncle in Machame on the mounting slopes of Kilimanjaro and had arranged that his wife and he Alan Hat was going to spend the Easter Holidays on Zanzibar. If they had known, they could have put two and two together and come up with a strong possibility.

"I gather, Graham, whatever is in the PM's briefcase is extremely important, and I have to assume you don't need the contents going to the media?" he said watching Graham putting the two sheets of paper into his inside jacket pocket.

"That's a bloody understatement," he said watching his BMW rounding the corner and parking within a few feet of the Chancellor who got up to go. "Freddie, see if you can bring AL out of the woodwork to see if we can come to an arrangement," he said with a young lad asking for his autograph that he totally ignored.

"You ignorant git," a lady called out to him that could have been the lad's mother as the Chancellor got in the back of his waiting car.

Chapter 31
Mount Kilimanjaro

Friday afternoon, Alan Hat received a phone call from Peter Goodman after his climb to the Roof of Africa asking him to pick up his lady friend Anna Kajeme at 3 pm from the Tato Hotel and then asking him to pick him up from the Machame Gate.

Waiting at the reception of the Tato Hotel and feeling anxious knowing he was waiting for his nephew's worse enemy. Two minutes later, she swayed into the reception knowing Peter had called a Mr Hat that he would be picking her up. There she was dressed to the nines in her red leather skin-tight trousers with her low-cut white blouse that was showing far too much of her black skin that Alan tried not to stare at. Leaving her keys at the reception and without saying a word to her driver, Anna Kajeme walked outside to his jeep and jumped straight into the front passenger seat.

With Alan leaving the reception and getting to his jeep and putting his seat belt on, "Please do likewise, miss," that fell on deaf ears. "We don't go anywhere until you belt up." Grudgingly, she did so.

Not a word was spoken until they reached Machame Village. "So, you're Robert Hat's uncle and, once Peter Goodman and I are back in the UK, we will be looking for him to get my revenge that you will be fully aware of," Anna Kajeme said lighting a cigarette.

"Wow, young lady, aren't you in for one heck of a surprise or should I say shock."

"What the fuck are you talking about?" Anna Kajeme asked.

"Your Peter Goodman is, in fact, Trevor Charles Baines, UK's most wanted criminal assumed dead. So there's more chance of you being struck by lightning than he would join you in the UK. Besides, Mrs Baines will not be too happy knowing you are in a relationship with her husband, who as I said, is wanted by the law in the UK."

It seemed to Alan that she was not at all aware that her boyfriend was a wanted criminal. "Turn this jeep around and take me back to the hotel, and you make sure you tell your nephew that he should watch his back."

Alan smiled and did a 3-point turn and headed back to the Tato and then asked, "What do I tell lover boy Goodman or I should have said Baines?"

She sat there and throwing her finished cigarette out of the window and lighting another, "Tell him what you like seeing by the time you get back to the hotel, I will be long gone."

"You took your time getting to me," Peter Goodman said waiting outside the Majame Gate reception where the climbers check-in and out on their return

"Sorry, sir, but the hotel couldn't find Anna Kajeme."

Peter Goodman waited all of five minutes before he said, "My money says she found a further sugar daddy whilst I was climbing Mount Kilimanjaro, bitch little does she know."

Alan Hat wanted to smile but said, "So sorry if she has left." Not another word was spoken until they got to the hotel.

"Here you go, mate," and handed him 1000 Tanzanian Shillings tip.

"Thank you, sir," Alan said handing him his climbing sticks and rucksack from the back of his jeep.

Driving out the hotel heading back home, he said out loud, "Arsehole!"

Once home, he was doing an email to Rob telling him what had just happened and that he should be careful seeing he believed Anna Kajeme could be heading his way at some stage.

"Alan, you need to take this bloody pig out of my kitchen before I cook your friend. Bugger off, Bernie, you're a real pain in the arse," Yvonne called out pushing him out of the kitchen door.

"Yvonne, I wish you wouldn't upset Bernie. Come on, my friend; I will take you for a walk. Just let me sign off this email and I will be with you."

Alan then heard his wife calling out: "Don't bring him back."

Alan sat at his desk and was smiling. "Don't you listen to Yvonne, Bernie, we both know she loves you really," Alan said out loud knowing his wife would hear him.

Chapter 32
That's Not a Crime

At the Bracknell Police Station, returning some stolen credit cards that they gained when they nicked the two-light fingered European guys in the Butt's Centre. The owners of the cards reside in Jennetts Park in Bracknell, and she agreed to deliver them back to the Bracknell.

DI Reynolds was waiting at the front desk to be seen and was looking through the daily papers and various property papers left in the station. The Sandhurst Property Paper caught her eye, and she started to look through it to see what properties were for sale in the area. "Jones, have you seen the price of the property in Sandhurst and Crowthorne?"

DS Jones looked at his boss, who was sitting opposite him, "I couldn't even afford a garage, let alone a house in those areas."

DI Reynolds turned the next page, "Jones, you need to see this." Grudgingly, her DS wandered over to her and looked over her shoulder and read.

Lamberts Estate Agent of Sandhurst is excited that possibly coming to the market is a large detached family home. "My God, boss, that photograph is of the Baines's home," he said looking at the estimated price of £2 million.

"Now we know why the Frazer team were at the Baines property; they are forcing them to sell their home, I guess to gain money they owe them," DI Reynolds said getting up and handed the desk sergeant, who had just returned to his post, an envelope with the cards inside and she showed him her warrant card. "Please see DI Thompson gets these for me; he is expecting them."

The desk sergeant scribbled the name on the envelope, "Shall do, miss."

"What you waiting for, Jones? Yesterday, none of the Frazer family were available, so let's go knocking again."

Eventually, they got through the one-way system at Wokingham and parked in Frazer's Night Clubs' car park on the outskirts of Wokingham on the Reading Road. With the door still open with its last lunchtime trade leaving, DI Reynolds and DS Jones showed their IDs and waited whilst a member of staff went to find Frank Frazer, who told them he was on the premises. "I see this is not only a night club; it also doubles as a restaurant," DS Jones said watching the person, who went to get him, pushing him out in his wheelchair with a further member of staff carrying his oxygen tank. Looking at the two coppers, he beckoned them over to a quiet corner where a waitress had just finished clearing the table.

He connected his mask piping to his tank and putting his mask to his face and took a few draws from his tank and then waved his two staff away. "Before you two ask any questions, I know why you are here," Frank Frazer said taking a further draw of air.

"Please tell me what you know, Mr Frazer?" DI Judy Reynolds asked taking a seat with DS Jones doing likewise.

"Okay, first you have been watching the Baines's property in Sandhurst with Mr Big copper here," he said pointing to DS Jones.

"Yes, in his Mondeo, and later a further detective arrived to keep an eye on the Baines's home I believe this time in an old Ford Focus," Frazer said putting his mask to his face taking in as much air as possible. He then went on to tell them, "My twin boys have not broken any law. I guess, like the Met, we were looking for what's owned to us by the bastard Trevor Charles Baines." DI Judy Reynolds got out of her seat and nodded to her DS to do the same.

"Thank you for your time, Mr Frazer. I wish you well," and they both walked out of his club and got into DS Jones Mondeo.

"Shit, Jones, we are watching the Baines's property, and the Frazer's have been watching us at the same time." DS Jones looked at his boss a little confused as they went down the Reading Road to pick up the M329 and then into their Reading Police Station. "Jones, we have nothing on them, the guy admits Trevor Baines owes him money, and that's no crime. If the Frazer's are asking the Baines to sell their home to get what they are owed once again, that's not a crime. Hell, Jones, it's only a crime if the Baines tell us they are being forced to sell their home; hence, we can't do sod all."

Still looking a little confused DS Jones asked, "Hang on a moment, boss, we both witnessed the Frazer twins getting their drivers to beat the life out of Charlie Baines. Surely that's a bloody crime that would enable us to dig further into the Frazer's business." DI Reynolds looked at his DS thinking he should know that Charlie Baines was beaten on his own land, and unless he informs us, we can do sod all to charge the Frazer twins.

"No, Jones, you should know it doesn't work like that, use your loaf and think about it."

The penny dropped for Jones to what she was saying. "Do you think our boss upstairs will at some stage kick this Baines's millions he's stolen into the long grass?"

DI Reynolds was about to call the DCI to report that she had nothing to report but stopped herself and put her mobile back in her pocket. "Good question, big guy, well unless we get a lucky break, you could be right. This case could go into the unsolved crime folder and put away for the dust to accumulate over the years."

They drove their remaining short journey in total silence.

At this juncture, DI Judy Reynolds never in a million years would have guessed that young Rob Hat just might have the key to unlock the mystery to the whereabouts of the stolen and missing millions of pounds that have eluded the Metropolitan Police force for a number of years.

Also unbeknown to DI Reynolds when she was a DS, it was DS Jones—the tallest detective in the Met—who helped Rob Hat along with George Almedia from Mwanza to get those stolen 750 diamonds that were tucked away in a security box at Waterloo Station.

The two guys, who learnt that these diamonds were out there, had been following young Hat. It was when Rob went to collect the stones from his security box to return them to Johnson Diamonds in Tanzania to collect his 50% of the generous reward being paid by Lloyds. Yes, the two guys who were looking to get their hands on the 750 diamonds, all they gained was a beating from the DS and George Almedia and were duly arrested by the Met at the Borough police station.

One other thing that was not common knowledge, DS Jones and his family spent a pleasant two weeks holiday in Tanzania; it was George Almedia's way of saying thank you to DS Jones for all his help.

Chapter 33
Looks Like It's a Go

At premier with only two more cars to clean, Grace and Rob were in their cabin still in their wet gear having a tea break. Looking out the window, they watched their Line Manager Jenny come walking into the arch, and then she entered the cabin. "Fancy a tea, Jenny?"

"Thanks, but no thanks. At the security gate, there's a coloured gentleman I saw on our CCTV that I have spoken with." She then said from a piece of paper she was holding, "Mr George Almedia wants to speak to you, Rob, can I let him in?" Grace looked at Rob and wanted Rob to say no, but she knew that was not likely to happen.

"It's okay, Jenny, he's a friend from Tanzania." She left their cabin and was heading out of the arch to the main gate.

"Grace, could you please make him a tea, four sugars?" Grace ignored him and carried on reading her OK magazine.

Rob got up and boiled the kettle watching him from the window parking a Honda in the company's car park. With Jenny pointing to where he needs to go, the big African guy came strolling through the arch towards their cabin.

"So, this is where you work from; I had only seen it from the outside when you were being followed."

Grace interrupted him, "And, yes, we both saw how you beat the life out of those two guys." George decided to let the subject drop but gave her a kiss on her cheek and shacked Rob's hand, and sat down. Rob then handed him a tea. "Thank you," he said taking a sip, "Perfect."

"Is there any news, Rob, regarding the PM's red case?" George asked watching Rob take out his mobile from his waterproof coat.

"Press the last message received and then the last message sent."

George read the messages twice and then looked at Rob and Grace, "So what do you think about this young lady?" As usual, Grace just shook her head, indicating a no, and went back to her OK magazine.

"You're playing with fire here. One thing conning the likes of Johnson Diamond, Mine but your own government? Wow, that's another league, and if that SB means the Special Branch, then you better watch your back," George said closing Rob's phone and handing it back to him.

"That's twice in a week that I have been told to watch my back. My uncle warned me that Anna Kajeme could be coming back to the UK looking for me."

George Almedia got up and put his arm around him and said, “I said from the offset, turn those manifests over to the media; you really can’t fuck with these people in high places.”

Then Grace got up throwing her magazine on the table, “Listen to him, Rob, he’s talking sense. Anyway, I am going to start on the last two cars in the arch.”

George filled the kettle up and turned it on. “Now for some good news,” George told Rob about his visit to Honour Oak Cemetery when a few minutes later whilst he was in the wooded area, he saw Charlie Baines and his mother park up their Audi and walk to the so-called Baines grave. Whilst his mother was attending to the grave with flowers she had bought with her, Charlie—with what seemed like a plastic bag under his arm—walked into the wooded area and disappeared. Not sure exactly how long, but a few minutes later, he appeared with a sports bag that looked ready to burst open. Rob sat there with his mouth open listening to every word George was saying.

“Looks like it’s a go,” Rob said and then added, “Kettles kuchemsha mate.”

(The kettle’s boiling mate).

Chapter 34
CIP

In his so-called Ivory Tower at Reading Police Station, DCI Gordon Taylor sat with his back to his DI Reynolds looking at his view of Reading town centre. He was listening to what she was saying about their visit to Frazer's night club in Wokingham. He swivelled his seat to face his DI with a glass of wine in his hand, and his telephone ranged. Picking it up and by the sound of it, he was having a one-sided conversation. "Yes, no problem, sir, shall do, sir, thank you, sir, for keeping me in the loop." Then he said, "Bloody CIP. Okay, Reynolds, where were we? Right, Reynolds, it looks like we are hitting a brick wall in getting the millions Baines has stolen as you're saying, Reynolds, Glenda Baines is looking to sell their home in Sandhurst. Perhaps selling their property to pay what her late husband owes Frank Frazer can only mean she is also none the wiser to where her husband's cash is."

He then handed her a copy of their joint bank account details that DI Judy read. "Looks like she has to use their overdraft facility," his DI said sliding the copy of the joint Baines bank account details across his desk.

"How do you fancy telling the mayor that we don't have a bloody clue to Baines's stolen fortune?" And then added, "Give it a couple of more weeks in keeping track of Glenda and Charlie Baines; we just might get lucky?" He then swivelled his seat back to his view.

"Thank you, Sir, I will keep you informed." This her boss totally ignored as she left his office.

"Prick," she said waiting for the lift to the first floor.

Back at her desk, counting to ten and trying to calm herself down from her meeting with her boss, she looked at her DS Jones who seemed to be in a deep conversation on his telephone. He took A4 sheet of paper out of his printer and changed his telephone to his left hand and scribbled down something on the sheet of paper and held it up so DI Judy Reynolds could see SPECIAL BRANCH then said to whoever he was speaking to, "Sorry, I think I have told you all I know about Mr Robert Hat. Please let me hand you over to my boss DI Reynolds who will confirm everything I had told you." He then transferred his call to his boss's telephone. Before picking it up, she indicated to DS Jones to pick up his telephone when, in fact, he had not put it back in its cradle. With his hand over the mouthpiece, he waited for his DI to pick up.

"DI Judy Reynolds here, who am I speaking to?"

"Freddie Andrews, special agent for the Special Branch, and that's all you need to know for now, miss."

She put her hand over her mouthpiece, and looking at Jones, she said: "Freddie?"

"The telephone is not the time or place. 9 am tomorrow at Gems Supermarket at the Elephant & Castle in their coffee lounge and before you ask, I have spoken to your CIP who I believe will put your DCI Taylor in the frame and he's aware that you just might be able to assist me in my investigation in recovering what I am seeking." He then ended the call.

"Jones, it looks like our friend Rob Hat has just jumped out of the woodwork once again."

Her DS looked at his boss stroking his chin, he got up and sat on the corner of the DI's desk and said, "You can't tell me for one second that Rob Hat is involved with Trevor Charles Baines?" DI Reynolds sat there and simply shrugged her shoulders.

DI Judy Reynolds said looking and sounding very angry, "Our DCI Taylor is a real and truly big arsehole. Whilst I was in his office, he took a call from the CIP hence he knew this call from the Special Branch was coming down here to us mere mortals; he could have least given us a heads up."

Getting his coat from behind his chair to make a move for home, his boss looked away from her PC and said, "Don't be late, I will see you at Gems."

Chapter 35
You Have Been a Bad Girl

Little after 11 pm, Rob had just said goodnight to Grace on the fourth floor of Saints House and headed to the fifth passing. By their kitchen window, he could hear the telephone ringing. Struggling to find the right key, he got in and dashed into the kitchen and picked the phone up. "Hello."

"Would I be speaking to Robert Hat?" the man's voice sounding official.

"Speaking."

"It's the desk sergeant for Bermondsey police station. Here we have in our custody your friend, Rosie."

"Who the hell is that on the telephone this time of night?" his dad said standing in the doorway in his pants.

Rob put his index finger to his lips, "What's she done, officer?"

"Rosie, Dad," he whispered.

"She attempted to drive her mobility scooter through Rotherhithe Tunnel, which, of course, is an offence but just to add to the lady's problems, she never had enough charge in her battery hence we had to get it taken away, so it's currently on charge at our station."

Rob looked at his dad and wasn't sure whether to laugh or cry. "Sergeant, I will be with you in about 15 minutes," he said and hung up.

"I love her, Dad, but driving her scooter through Rotherhithe Tunnel and then running out of charge is bloody stupid," he said looking for his keys.

"Did you leave them in the door when I heard you rush in?" his dad said wandering back to bed, and before he left to collect Rosie, he could hear his parents having a good laugh.

Running down to the fourth floor, he tapped on what would be Grace's bedroom. Twenty seconds later, she came out still dressed holding a hot drink. "Get your coat, we are going for a ride," he said taking her drink off her. "Only old people drink Horlicks," he said quietly in fear of waking up her younger sisters.

Thirty minutes later, he gave the desk sergeant his address so they could send the bill for getting a trailer to get her scooter out of the tunnel. "I will pick it up tomorrow evening providing I can use my company's tail-lift," he told the sergeant then they both helped Rosie down the steps of the police station.

"Open the back doors, Grace, this should be fun," as they lifted her into the back of the van and plonked her on top of the spare wheel.

"Can't I sit up front, Rob, this wheel hurts my arse."

Rob looked at Grace, and they both started to laugh. “No, you can’t. You have been a bad girl,” Rob said reversing out of the police station’s backyard noticing the cable coming out of the station charging Rosie’s mobility scooter.

Chapter 36
Whispering

Rob's brother, Tony, was late up for work at Gems Supermarket. "Tea, Tony?"

"It's okay, Linda. I will grab a tea and a slice of toast when I get in," he said and rushed out of their house.

A little after nine he was in the store's cafeteria. "Tea and two toasts, please. Pat, I will be sitting over on the right," he said taking the Daily Mirror out of the rack where the daily papers are put for their customers to read.

Five minutes later, taking a table next to his, he watched two faces he knew only too well. DS Jones nodded to Tony whilst DI Judy Reynolds was trying to figure out if she knew the person that her DS obviously knew the smartly dressed young guy.

Tony sat there wondering why they had not ordered any drinks when he noticed the young guy with blonde hair tied back in a ponytail in a nice cut grey suit with a folder under his arm. "Sorry, I am late, you guys want a coffee?" he asked.

"Tea for me," the 7-foot copper said.

A few minutes later, Pat brought over the two coffees and a tea. "Thank you, miss," Judy said looking directly at the guy in the next table. "Do you know him?" she asked her DS.

"Not now, boss," he whispered.

"Hi, Mr Andrews, please tell me why the Special Branch are involved with the millions that were stolen by the late Baines and why you need to speak to me?" the DI asked.

"Miss Reynolds, you have lost me. What the hell are you talking about?" The Inspector for the Special Branch asked stirring his coffee and then added four sachets of sugar. DS Jones sat there thinking, that's bloody Irish stirring first, then adding the sugar.

"It's a case we have been working on for many years, but all to no avail hence from my meeting with my DCI yesterday, I thought this was what the meeting was about." DI Reynolds said, feeling her cheeks had started to burn upon seeing she got the reason for this meeting totally wrong.

Tony sat there; granted he couldn't hear every word, but enough to know that their meeting was not about the cash that could be tucked away in the Baines's coffin.

"It's okay, Inspector. I guess you are busy and have a great deal going on in your office," Freddie Andrews said looking at his folder on the table. "No Miss, this has nothing to do with stolen money. This is a meeting concerning the government that has a problem," he said taking a photograph from his folder that he put face down on the table. "I have been informed that you have had dealings with young Robert Hat," he said with DS Jones looking uncomfortable as he glanced at Tony Hat, who himself was fidgeting in his seat.

"Have I had dealings with Robert Hat? That's an understatement. I will say this much young Hat is not a criminal, in fact, he's one in a million and has helped many less fortunate, but he's also been a thorn in the side of the Metropolitan Police Force in the South East these past three years," she said drinking down the last of her coffee.

"Yes, Miss, I have heard much of the same from my sources." He then flipped over the photograph, "Can either of you recognise the young gentleman standing on the edge of the train with a large suitcase by his side?" Tony sat there wishing he could also take a look at that photograph. "This was taken off the BBC News coverage," Freddie said sliding it over the table between the two detectives.

The moment DI Reynolds saw the train carriage leaning up some two feet from the ground, "Was this the train crash where this train had a head-on collision with a train coming out of Waterloo?" The guy from the Special Branch just nodded. DS Jones looked closer at the photograph.

"Isn't that the PM being stretchered off? And who's the guy walking beside him?" DS Jones asked.

"It's the Chancellor seeing they were both on the train coming from Southampton," his DI said.

"I guess the PM must have left something of value on the train; hence, you guys at the Special Branch are involved?" she asked.

"All I am asking you to see if you recognise the guy standing on the edge of the train, could that lad be Robert Hat?"

She picked it up to look at it closer. "It's blurred, plus the fellow has his hand on his head, and he's turning away from the camera as though he's watching them cart off the PM on the stretcher. Sorry, I can't say it is Robert Hat, but there again, it could possibly be him. Sorry, I can't be of any use. What do you think, Jones?"

The DS this time picked up the photo for a closer look and glanced at Rob Hat's brother and said, "He looks too tall to be young Hat, and as my boss said, it doesn't help matters being blurred along with his hand on his head. Like my DI said, I am sorry I can't be of any help." He said with his fingers crossed on his right hand under the table and rubbing his nose with his left hand making sure it was not getting any bigger.

"Can we ask what is it you're looking for perhaps we might be able to assist?" the DI asked knowing full well that seeing the so-called Freddie is working for the government at the highest level, he's not going to say.

Putting the photograph back in his folder, he got up. "Thank you for your time," and left the two detectives sitting there.

"What the hell was that all about?" the DI asked.

"Beats me, boss; it seems it was just a waste of time."

Judy Reynolds looked over to the guy reading the Daily Mirror. "Do you know him seeing you acknowledge him when we first sat down?"

"You're not going to like this, but that's Rob Hat's brother, Tony. He works in the offices here."

Walking out of Gems, "I bet this Tony Hat's ears pricked up when he heard his brother's name mentioned?" the DI said. "Let's be honest boss, our meeting was not conducted with us all whispering."

Tony eventually got in his office at 9:30 and booted up his PC and making sure no one was looking at him, he e-mails his brother knowing he will pick up the email via his mobile.

"Hi Rob,

Had my breakfast at Gems this morning, and sitting on the next table was DI Reynolds and your friend DS Jones. They were joined by a guy from the Special Branch, and he was asking them if they recognised what just might be you from a photograph of the person standing on the edge of the train that crashed leaving Vauxhall Station, which they couldn't be sure.

Now the Special Branch is involved, and as I said, when you brought that case home, it was bloody toxic.

Take care,
Tony XX"

Chapter 37
DS Jones

"Rob, when we finish here tonight, Linda is picking me up, and we are off for a meal and a little shopping down Oxford Street." Rob was not listening; he was more interested in seeing his brother parking up in the premier car park.

"Sorry, Grace, what were you saying?" Grace, like Rob, was wondering why his brother had come here in what must be his lunch break.

"Oh, yes, I am out with Linda this evening when we finish here."

"No problem, enjoy yourself," Rob told her turning the hose off and throwing his leather on top of the Audi that he was cleaning and stepped out of the arch to greet his brother.

"Did you read my email I sent you this morning?"

"No," Rob took his mobile out and went to his Gmail to read the message. "The government using Special Branch to track down the red parliamentary case can only mean our PM must now be in panic mode," Rob said reading through it once again."

"Bloody hell! Rob, how many more times do I have to tell you that red case could see you being banged up?" his brother said looking anxious about what his younger brother might do next.

"I doubt if the PM has told the Special Branch that he needs the two manifests that the UK population must never know of," Rob was saying looking at Tony without the foggiest idea what his next cause of action would be.

They were just about to enter the arch where Grace was finishing off the cleaning of the Audi when Rob looked to the right towards the large gates of Premier and saw DS Jones standing there in his car. "Looks like DS Jones did recognise me in that photograph?" Rob said walking over to the security gate that the DS wouldn't have the code for him to gain entry. Rob opened the gate to let the DS Jones drive in and park up.

With Grace looking worried and avoiding eye contact with DS Jones, not that it would be easy, she would need to stand on the table to see into his eyes. "Tea for you guys?" she said, not waiting for them to answer, she filled the kettle and turned it on. "You look like the three wise monkeys sitting there on the bench seat," she said getting the cups out of the cupboard with her hands shaking putting the milk in the cups.

"Would one of you three ugly monkeys say something? Your silence is making me so bloody nervous," Grace said putting the three teas on the table.

This is when all three of them said at the same time, "Thank you, Grace."

Rob opened his email again on his mobile and handed it to Grace and said, "Read it, love."

"Shit, Rob, Special Branch," she said and then added: "What the hell is Mr Jones doing here?"

Rob looked at his brother and then at the 7-foot copper, "Good question, Grace; what are you doing here, Mr DS Jones?"

"Rob, that photograph the guy from the Special Branch showed us and asked if that was Rob Hat standing on the edge of carriage with a large case next to him waiting to be helped down was, in fact, you, Rob. When DI Reynolds and myself went back to Reading Police Station, Reynolds went straight up in the lift to question how DCI had insisted on knowing what the Special Branch was looking for. It seemed that the CIP had told DCI Gordon in confidence that the PM had lost track of his red parliamentary case when the two trains collided. They have, from all accounts, been looking for anyone that could have hidden this case in a bag or case when all the passengers were taken off the train. It turns out from the BBC News coverage that case on the edge where you were standing was the only possible way of taking that case off the train without being seen. There it is, Rob. Unofficially, this is the reason I followed your brother here," DS Jones said. Rob looked at his brother wanting to moan at him for bringing the police to his workplace.

"You say unofficially?" Rob asked.

"Come on, Rob. Unofficially, I have helped you on numerous occasions when I should have not seeing it put my job at risk to help and support you."

"Speak to him, Rob, to what's…" Rob stopped him by raising his hand.

"Okay, Mr Jones, you need to meet me at 9 am tomorrow at the coffee shop on your left just as you turn into Ladbroke Grove from the Bayswater Road, and I promise to show you something that I will need your advice on," he said looking at Grace who for a change was nodding a yes.

"About time, Rob, you need advice," Tony said.

DS Jones got up shaking hands with Tony and Rob along with ruffling Grace's hair when Rob could hear her whisper, "Thank you," to the giant of a man. He was heading out of their cabin and getting to the door, when he turned and said, "Did you know George Almedia is back in the UK?"

Rob looked at the DS and said, "No, should I?"

"Will speak later, Rob, I need to get back to Gems; you're honestly doing the right thing more so seeing Special Branch is now assisting the PM in getting back that bloody red case sitting in a garage a few steps from our parents," Tony said out of ear shot following the DS out to Premiers' car Park.

Chapter 38
Machame

With the General Election fast approaching, the PM was becoming extremely anxious knowing his whole party was promoting promises from the government's manifest to the UK's population that will not be delivered.

Simon Davis sat in his department above 10 Downing Street thinking he should make the most of the lifestyle he had grown accustomed to these last five years. With those two manifests out there, he was fully aware they could bring his world come tumbling down around his ears, that is, if they were to be given to the media. Yes, he could resign, but he intends to make certain that all avenues have been covered to get those two manifests back in his possession before considering that option. Regarding the 20 million that's been asked for, this would mean he would need to sell their family home in Knightsbridge that his wife's family had given them.

"Simon, your lunch is on the table. Are you okay, darling, you look as though you're in a world of your own?" his wife Judith said walking back into their kitchen.

Just then, his mobile goes off, and he opens the message. "Call in ASAP G."

"Judith, I need to shoot next door, be back in about ten minutes," the PM called to his wife and then dashed down the stairs and out the back door.

Walking into Graham's office where he was sat looking at his open screen. "I truly need to have some good news," the PM said pulling a seat up to his desk.

"Read this Simon," he said moving his seat over a little and making room so the PM could get a better view of the screen and the message his chancellor feels he should read.

"Graham,

I checked once again all the people that flew from Kilimanjaro International Airport into Zanzibar around the Easter holiday period. On my first check, there was no sign that Robert Hat flew into Zanzibar.

On my second check earlier today, it turns out on the Easter Saturday, Mr & Mrs Alan Hat flew to the Spice Island. It turns out that Rob Hat is Alan's nephew making it a strong possibility it was Rob Hat that was standing in the doorway of the train after the rail crash.

I must admit when checking the first time seeing a married couple was to fly to Zanzibar, so when viewing the list and seeing a Mr & Mrs, I never looked any further to the full names on the flight list.

I am currently in Mombasa waiting for my connecting flight to Zanzibar, then I shall be heading to the office of DHL Nyerere Road Zanzibar, and I have booked into the Serena Hotel opposite the DHL office. Hopefully, the DHL office will have their CCTV available for the Easter Saturday when your parcel was sent from. Then I will fly to Kilimanjaro to meet Alan Hat, who lives in Machame on the foothills of Mount Kilimanjaro.

On investigating Alan Hat, he runs a charity aidintoafrica.org in East Africa, and I have managed to gain a clear photograph of him from his website, which might prove helpful.

Regards, SB."

"Granted, Graham, you know most of what I am about to tell you. Yes, I know Alan Hat when every man and his dog were trying to figure out who it was that was helping a great many charities. It was our government that had betrayed them by stopping their yearly funding because of the austerity measures we had introduced.

"Young Rob Hat had got hold of the stolen cash from the National Bank, and with this cash, he helped a great many. However, it took the Met over a year but all to no avail to discover who the hell were RH, LJ, MM, WS and FT. This method of signing appeared on every donation that was made that was sent to Portcullis House in the Houses Parliament for my ministers to deliver."

"I remember, Simon, I had three parcels to deliver to homeless charities in the West London area that had contained in total 60k," his chancellor said.

"The name escapes me, but the Met had arrested the wrong person for having the bank's cash. This was when Rob had decided he couldn't let another person take the blame.

"Unbeknown to Rob Hat, his uncle had arranged to have all the charities his nephew had and helped to attend a meeting at the Bridge Hotel close to London Bridge. Alan Hat had invited the BBC and ITV and numerous members of the press; also, the Met got an invite. Would you believe he had the audacity to invite Pauline Edwards, our charity minister, who had kept me informed via her mobile? She felt it would be an ideal opportunity for me to attend to explain why we had to cut charity's funds seeing we were getting a great deal of bad press.

"This was when everyone was introduced to RH, LJ, MM, WS and FT, which to everyone's astonishment was 17-year-old Robert Hat."

The PM still looking at the screen then added, "If Alan Hat is involved with my missing case, then heaven help us. It would be like trying to get blood out of a stone for him to admit his involvement."

The PM said getting up, "Have to go, Graham, seeing my lunch is on the table. Keep me posted," and he was then out the back door.

Chapter 39
Monkey

Linda picked up Grace a little after 6 pm from Premier Supreme Car Hire, and they headed for a little shopping down Oxford Street. First, Linda parked up her Mini Cooper at her hair salon just at Oxford Street. After checking on her staff with Grace waiting at the reception, they eventually wandered back towards the hustle and bustle of one London's busiest streets.

Waiting for the pedestrian crossing light to go green, crossing Oxford Street and heading for Marks & Spencer's. "Strange thing about the world's busiest city London I have noticed, Grace, no bugger speaks to anyone makes it at times a lonely place to live," Linda was saying that Grace never heard seeing she was more concerned about the smartly dressed African lady walking alongside her.

Walking into M&S, Grace pulled Linda back by her arm back into the street with Grace looking towards Tottenham Court Road, then turning in looking in the direction of Marble Arch. "Hell, Linda, that was Anna Kajeme that walked beside me crossing the road," she said. Then added, "But I couldn't see her amongst the huge crowds."

"You might have just thought it was her," Linda said pulling her back into the store.

"The last time I saw her was at Dar-es-Salaam Airport when she was putting the children's pink bag with the 750 diamonds stuck on putting it through the scanner."

Linda looked at Grace with her mouth wide open in disbelief. "Bloody hell, so this is the bag she had when the police dragged her off your flight to Kilimanjaro that she had wedged under the seat in front of her?" she said smiling watching Grace going up the escalator backwards making sure she was not being followed.

"Yes, Linda, this was the famous children's bag with the sparkly stones stuck on that Rob had taken from the seat to give to my younger sisters only to find out they were worth a fortune," Grace said turning around just in time to get off the escalator.

When they walked into the store's coffee lounge waiting in the queue to be served, Grace was looking everywhere. "Can't see her," Grace said.

"Two cappuccinos, Miss, please," Linda asked ignoring Grace, who was obviously anxious.

Sitting at a table in the far corner with Grace stirring the life out of her coffee when she spots in the other corner, Anna Kajeme sat with two guys with their backs to her, and she gave Grace a nod. Grace stopped stirring and dropped her spoon on the table that bounced onto the floor. "Don't look now, Linda. To your right in the corner, Anna Kajeme is sitting with two guys with their backs to us, and she has just nodded to me."

"Okay, Grace, drink up and let's head to the escalator. We go out the door from where we came in, and then rush down to the left in Oxford Street and come back in the other door. We then rush across the store and exit through the other door. Hopefully, the pedestrian crossing light is on green, so we can get across the road, and we make a further dash to my salon, pick up my car, and then get you home."

Grace gulped down her coffee and was on her feet, "Let's go then." Once again, Grace was going down the escalator backwards, and within seconds, they were out the door and charging down Oxford Street to reach the other door. Customers trying to figure out what these two young ladies were dashing across the store to the next exit must have caused something of a panic seeing a great number of customers started to charge to the exit. With luck on their side, they were across the road, and no more than twenty seconds later, they were sitting in Linda's Mini Cooper.

"Anyone would think I was a heavy smoker," Linda said coughing and spluttering while putting the key in the ignition. When they pulled into Oxford Street and headed for Marble Arch, Grace was looking behind her to see if she could spot Anna Kajeme following them, which was pretty pointless seeing there was a stream of traffic headed in the same direction. "Relax, Grace," Linda said as they passed the Hilton.

"That's easy for you to say," Grace said still watching all the cars that were behind them.

Other than catching the lights at Westminster Bridge, they pulled into the King George Estate at the Elephant Castle and turned into Saints House within twenty minutes of leaving Linda's Salon. With no sign of Rob's bright red Morris Van, Linda parked her car in front of Grace's mum's garage.

"Come on, Grace, I will walk you to your door." Reluctantly, Grace opened the door with Linda already out waiting for her friend to get out so she could lock the car. Grace noticed a car, which she thought was a Honda, parked by the flat's entrance. With the car locked, they were just about to walk when from nowhere came a black BMW screeching to a halt broadside to the Mini Cooper and two guys, who seemed to be in their 40s, jumped out of the car and approached Grace. With the back door swinging open, the African lady casually stepped out giving the guys a nod, and within seconds, Grace was heavily pushed backwards to the garage providing a large sound as her back hit the metal garage shutter. "What the fuck do you want of Grace?" Linda said from the other side of her Mini.

"This does not concern you, blonde; get back in your toy car and mind your bleeding business," Anna Kajeme shouted at her.

With Grace up against the garage, she felt herself shaking, knowing that she was going to take a beating. She knew hurting her would send a message to Rob.

When she looked to her right, she heard the Honda starting up with its headlights on; it accelerated hitting the rear of the BMW and pushing it forward to about twenty feet.

Grace and Linda both looked what seemed to be in slow motion. They watched George Almedia releasing his seat belt and get out of the car and strolled around facing the two guys. "I don't think so, gents," he said walking towards them and just as he went past Anna Kajeme, he slapped her around the face that sounded like a firecracker going off. "There's nothing for you here," he said as she swayed towards the Mini from the power of his slap.

With the two guys now facing George with their fists clinched, he guessed showing them that they were ready to put up a fight. "Okay, I guess, guys, this lady," he said looking at her now rubbing her cheek, and if she had been a white lady, it would have been bright red. He then continued to say, "Is paying you to put the fear of Christ up such a young lady here; surely, this is not the norm for you guys?" He said whipping off his jacket and tossing it to Linda, who had not got back in here Mini. "Anna, you need to call your monkey's off Grace."

One of the guys put his hands up and walked aside with the other simply starred at George and said, "Who you calling a fucking monkey," and swung his right arm looking to hit George, who stepped back making the guy miss.

"Wrong move, son," he said kicking him in the crutch. Initially, he seemed to lift off the ground with the power of his kick and then watching him going to his knees and screaming in pain. George pulled him up by his hair and slung him towards Anna, and knocking her over with him finishing up on top of her. George walked over and rolled the guy off her and helped her to her feet. "Anna, for the last time, what you're looking for, you won't find anything here for you. Now take your two boys back to bed." The guy that walked away shot into the back of the black BMW.

Just then, they heard Rosie call out from her doorstep, "Do you need any help?"

Grace was walking round the Mini putting her arm round Linda's shoulder. "We are okay, Rosie," Grace said as the three of them watched the BMW leaving Saint's House with no backlights and with all the light's glasses on the ground.

"Thanks, George," Grace said with Linda tossing his jacket back and watching George Almedia get back into his motor and winding down his window.

He leaned over to be heard, "You're welcome; oh yes, tell Rob to call me."

Still holding each other, they watched him turn round, and with a simple wave, they saw his taillights vanish out of the estate.

Just then, Rob pulled into Saints House and parked up next to Linda's Mini. "Are you leaving, Linda?" Rob called out from his open window. "Trust you girls had a great evening?" Rob then added watching Linda reverse out of the garage, and then he pulled in to where she had just left. "I guess there's been an accident here seeing all this broken glass on the ground?" Rob said locking his van.

“Okay, Grace what have you been up to.” Grace looked at Linda in her Mini with her back to Rob, who was making sure his van was securely locked for the night.

She put her index finger to her lips and turned from the Mini and faced Rob. “Just a coffee and a browse around the shops,” she said and then said, “I will tell you more a little later; oh yes, you need to give George a call.”

Waving Linda off, they made their way to the lift that just might be working?

Chapter 40
The Right Thing

Rob heard the post coming through the letterbox and then heard his dad coughing down the hallway to collect the mail. "I have one for you here, Son," his dad called out going back into the kitchen. Rob came out of his bedroom dressed for work, "Tea, Son?"

"Please, where's my post?"

His dad smiled, and put a leaflet on the table, "It says homeowner."

"I was joking, Son, the best place for it is in the bin." Rob picked it up, and the moment he noticed the title was 'Manifest for 2015/2020,' he tucked it in his pocket whilst his dad was at the sink. Drinking down his tea, he rushed out of the flat and flew down the stairs two at a time.

Getting to the bottom, the lift opened at the same time with Grace coming out with two bowls of cornflakes, and sticking out of her top pocket was the self-same leaflet Rob had. With their cornflakes eaten and the Morris Van rolled back a little, they were in the garage taking the red case out of the dusty old sack. With the case now on the rickety table, they took out the two manifests and compared them to their leaflets that the postman had delivered.

"He's doing it, Rob, our PM is promoting the lies," Grace said now looking at what he intends to deliver over the next five years. Rob kept the two manifests and put the case back into the sack and chucked it into the corner.

"He's either really very brave or bloody stupid," Rob said closing the garage and locking it up and jumped into the van.

"Why are you taking those two manifests with you?"

Rob started the van and said, "A promise is a promise. DS Jones."

Just leaving the Elephant & Castle, Grace's mobile goes off. "It's a text from Linda."

"What's she saying?"

"Hi, Grace, in case you have not had your post yet. Our PM is a real arsehole seeing he's making promises that he will not stick to. It's time Rob handed what he has to the media. Linda," Grace read out.

Going over Westminster Bridge Rob's mobile buzzes on the dashboard, which he slides across. "Get that for me, Grace."

"It's from your uncle."

"And he's saying?"

"Rob just looked at the government's website. Do the right thing and hand them over to the Media. Love A & Y. PS When are you two coming back to

Tanzania again?" Grace read the text out once again, and they sat in silence until they turned right down the end of Ladbroke Grove and headed for the gates at Premier.

"Well, say something, Rob, what do you intend to do now?"

Rob never answered and drove in and parked up and headed to the office where Jenny came out with the keys to their arch also waving the same leaflet they had. "I have never voted for the Peoples Unite Party but having read the party's manifest I now know where my cross is going," she said handing Grace the arches keys.

"Don't believe all you read, Jenny. Our PM just might not deliver all the promises," Rob said showing his line manager that he also had the leaflet.

"Makes you wonder just how many people will be taken in by believing what we know is complete garbage landing on their mats today. I can't speak for you, Rob, but I am far from happy knowing that the population is being hoodwinked by Simon Davis, our PM for the Peoples Unite Party." Rob looked at Grace knowing that she wanted him to go to the media and his uncle said, from the offset, he should drop this information on the laps of the media.

Only fifteen minutes ago, Linda's jumped on the bandwagon. "Bloody say something, Rob, your silence is driving me mad."

Still, he says nothing. Once in the arch, they both entered their cabin where Rob puts the kettle on. Grace was putting on her wet gear that she left in their cabin last night before Linda had picked her up. "Tea is served, sit down on your arse and listen."

"Go on, then speak up!" Grace shouted at him.

"I will contact Paul Lawson, the editor of the Daily Mirror, and ask his advice. I am sure he would like such a story that would bring down Simon Davis."

Grace hobbled over to Rob with one wellington boot on. "Love you, Rob, you're going to be doing the right thing," she said hugging him.

"First, Grace, I need to meet up with DS Jones since I did promise to show him something," he said checking his watch. "I am getting late, hold the fort here for the next hour for me." And then Rob rushed off carrying the two manifests.

Chapter 41

Sorry, It's Only Black and White

Whilst Rob was rushing to meet DS Jones, Freddie Andrews from the Special Branch had unpacked his overnight bag for his short stay at Serena Hotel on the Nyerere Road, Zanzibar. From there, he crossed the road to DHL and showed the young guy behind the counter his ID and asked to speak to the manager.

"Hi, Arthur Chapman here," the DHL manager said shaking the hand of the guy from the Special Branch UK.

"Mr Chapman, you sound as though you are American," Freddie said with the manager nodding.

"You have good ear, Mr Andrew."

Freddie told him that he needs to see the DHL CCTV for the Saturday transactions of their shipments they dealt with. "This is for the Saturday after the Good Friday."

"Please come through to my office and let me see what I can find," Arthur Chapman said lifting the counter at the far end of the 'Goods-In' area to allow him on the other side of the counter. Freddie followed him down the hallway into his office.

"Can I ask what this is all about?" Freddie was thinking he would love to tell him, but he knew if it got out that the UK's PM was desperate to get his contents back from his missing red case, then the Tanzanian media would have a field day.

"All I can say is that the UK's government would be extremely grateful if DHL could assist them."

Arthur Chapman booted up his PC and beckoned the Special Branch agent to join him at his screen as it flashed the DHL Logo on the screen. He entered his password, and once in, he went straight into the CCTV programme. Once opened, he entered the consignment date and the number relevant to the package sent. "Here we go; these are the clients that brought their parcel into our office on the given day." Freddie was totally impressed with the DHL CCTV programme they had.

"How many consignments came into your office for sending on that Saturday?" he asked.

With a couple of clicks, "Sit back, my friend, there were 265 brought in. Here we go," and the CCTV started to run, and two hours later, there was no sign of Alan Hat. The only thing in the two hours was a scruffy little urchin bringing in a parcel and handed over four 10.000 Tanzanian shilling notes.

"Arthur, I need you to rewind to where that little lad handed over that large currency notes?" Freddie watched the Manager rewind the tape. "Hold it there please," the SB agent asked him.

"I give you this much it's not the norm that one of the street children would have 40.000-shilling notes."

"Arthur, that coverage was at 4:30 pm. Do you, by any chance, have an outside coverage of around that time?" The Manager changed to the location of the parking area and fast-forwarded to 4:25 pm then slowly he forwarded the tape.

"Here you go." They both could see the lad going to a small Toyota jeep where the lad was giving a lady the consignment note, and they guessed the change. Then they watched her hand the boy that could be a couple of Tanzania notes and she leaned out of the jeep and ruffled the boy's hair.

"Fast forward slowly for me, stop." They could see her talk to a passenger, but they could not see if her passenger was a male or female. "Are you able to print me a still of the lady ruffling the lad's hair?" Freddie asked.

The Manager took the tape back to what the Special Agent asked for. He paused the screen, "This okay?" Where the woman's face was very clear.

"Great, my friend." Arthur pressed print on his keyboard.

"Sorry, it's only black and white," the Manager said and, within seconds, handed Freddie the still photograph.

Back out in the 'Goods-In' counter. "As a thank you, would you like to join me at 8 pm this evening for dinner at the Serena Hotel?"

Sitting at the bar at the Serena Hotel, Freddie Andrews from the Special Branch was hoping to discover that Alan Hat had sent that parcel via DHL to Portcullis House in the House of Commons for the attention of Simon Davis, the PM. When, in fact, all he gained was a black and white photograph of a woman in the car park of DHL. His only hope was that this lady was Mrs Hat, Alan's wife.

Whilst Freddie Andrews was wondering if it was Mrs Hat at DHL, back in the UK, Rob was sitting outside the coffee bar in Ladbroke Grove with DS Jones, who was reading the two manifests. "Hell, Rob, you're like a bloody magnet when it comes to picking up things that could get you locked up," DS Jones said while starting to read them once again what the Peoples Unite Party will, in fact, deliver. Putting the two manifests down, he looked directly into the eyes of Rob and said, "Give them to the media and bring him down." Rob sat there in total silence listening to what his DS friend was saying.

"Okay, the election takes place on the 7 of May, so on the 5 of May, I will hand his bloody case and contents over to the media seeing you all can't be wrong."

The DS leaned across the table and said, "You make sure that the press doesn't know it came from you." Rob never said anything; he knew that he would leave it at a security box at Waterloo Station and send the key to the Daily Mirror. What Jones was saying made a great deal of sense since he was going to take the manifests to the Daily Mirror.

“Changing the subject, are you sure, Rob, you don’t know that George Almedia is back here in the UK?” Rob never answered; he just shook DS Jones’s hand and was about to leave. DS Jones still had hold of Rob’s hand and pulled him towards him and, looking down to him, he whispered in his ear, “Of course, even if you knew, you wouldn’t let on?” Just then, the copper’s mobile went off.

“Saved by the bell, speak soon,” Rob said and headed back to Premier on foot.

Chapter 42
Coffin

"Charlie, look at the gate monitor. It's Colin Thomas from the Sandhurst Funeral Parlour at the gate pressing the life out of the buzzer, and why the fuck has he brought a bloody Hurst is beyond me?" Glenda shouted from upstairs.

Charlie pulled the chain in the downstairs toilet and went to the monitor. "What's your problem, Thomas?" and under his breath was saying, "Can't even have shit in peace."

"Let me in, Charlie." With the gates swinging open slowly, Charlie went to the front door and pointed for him to drive around the back and smiled seeing his mother wasn't joking, there was a coffin in the back.

"Hope that box in the back of the Hurst is bloody empty?" Charlie said when Colin Thomas came into earshot as he was walking towards the front door.

"No, it's empty. I am on the way to Frimley Park Hospital to collect a client."

"Hope he's dead?" Charlie laughed at his own remark that he guessed the undertaker would have heard such stupid comments a great many times. Peter was going to reply to his silly remark when Glenda Baines pushed Charlie aside.

"You taking the piss bringing that Hurst and coffin in here?"

Colin went to sit on the sofa. "Hang on, don't make yourself comfortable, you're not stopping. The sooner you get off our premises with that Hurst, the better," Charlie said standing next to his mother.

"You might have a big problem coming your way?" Colin Thomas said looking to the floor feeling what he was about to tell them he just might find himself thrown in that coffin at the back of their home.

"Spit it out, you pervert!" Glenda Baines shouted at him.

"Paul Stevens, who's worked for me many years, is immigrating to Australia at the end of April. He came into my office an hour ago just as I was to leave for the hospital and demanded 5k." Glenda looked bewildered at her son who just shrugged his shoulders much as to say, 'How the bloody hell do I know what's that got to do with the Baines family.'

"It turns out that when your Trevor was in my office when we were setting our deal, he overheard part of our conversation. I honestly thought he had left the building when Trevor arrived," Colin said thinking the worst is yet to come their way.

"What the fuck did this Paul guy overhear?" Charlie screamed at him.

"All he said was that he knew Trevor Charles Baines was not in that coffin at Honour Oak Cemetery. Other than your mother, Charlie, and yourself, no one knows what's buried seeing the arrangement was to loan you the keys to my funeral parlour and, overnight, I allowed you to undertake whatever you wanted to do."

Charlie now started to march up and down their lounge and looked at his mother and said, "What shall we do?"

"Colin, you now need to tell me how your conversation finished up with this creep Paul?" Glenda asked seeing her son had stopped his marching and was waiting for what this child molester had to say.

Colin coughed and looked scared of both of them. He said, "You have 48 hours to come up with the cash, or he's going to the police seeing he knows your husband is still alive."

"Colin, can we trust him?" Charlie asked.

"This arrangement I had with your father was back in January, so from then until now, Paul's never said sod all, but now, he's got the all-clear to live in Australia. He's come out of the woodwork to gain him and his family nice few quid to help them down under."

Charlie looked at his mother, and she nodded. "Okay, I will be at the Sandhurst Funeral Parlour at around 6 pm tomorrow evening," Charlie said.

His mother added, "Now, you can piss off."

With the Hurst now heading to Frimley Park Hospital, Colin Thomas noticed the Honda parked up down the lane with a coloured guy sitting inside looking as though he was reading a newspaper.

George Almedia couldn't for the life of him figure out why a Hurst had just left the Baines House. Five minutes later, the Baines Audi came by with Charlie at the wheel with his mother brushing her hair.

George Almedia started his car and followed the top of the range Audi.

Chapter 43
Shiny Black Shoes

In Machame, Yvonne was in their bathroom washing her hair, and Alan Hat was on his PC when he heard a car pull up outside. Going to the window, he could see a smartly dressed guy with his blonde hair tied back in a ponytail paying what must have been a taxi. The guy straightened his tie and, doing up his jacket, walked towards their bungalow carrying a holdall.

With a knock on the door, Bernie charged up to the front door getting excited to who it might be. "Bernie, get back. There's no food for you," Alan said stepping over the pig and opened the door.

"First time I have been greeted by a pig," the stranger said with Alan Hat pulling Bernie aside and pushing him towards the kitchen.

"Can I help you?" Alan asked with the guy going to his jacket and pulled out his business card and handed it to him. Alan looked at his card and said, "What brings the Special Branch UK to my door in Tanzania?" Of course, he had half expected a visit but not from such a high-profile authority. "You better come in."

With them both sitting in Alan's office. "What is this visit all about?" Alan asked with Bernie coming into his office and plonking himself on the floor while staring at the visitor's highly polished black shoes.

"I am currently working directly with the UK's government," he said pulling a photograph out of his inside pocket from his jacket. "Is that your nephew, Robert Hat, standing on the edge of the opened train door?"

Alan took the photograph and looked at it and, without any doubt, it was his nephew. "It's very blurred, and I believe Rob is much shorter," he said handing it back to the SB Agent. "Sorry, I can't see that being Robert Hat," he said looking at his card. "Sorry Mr Andrews, I can't be of any help." Whilst this was going on in his office, his wife was listening in the hallway to everything that was being said.

"Did young Robert visit you here in Machame over the Easter holidays?"

Alan looked at Freddie, "What's he done wrong then? Yes, he was here until the Tuesday after the Good Monday, and Grace, his young lady, was here to visit their godchild who hopefully is still sleeping. Yes, they also looked after our place whilst Yvonne, my wife, and I spent the holiday on Zanzibar."

With this, Freddie from the Special Branch pulled out a further photograph from his jacket. "Is this Mrs Hat ruffling the kid's hair?" he asked handing him the photograph. Just then, Yvonne Hat came in holding baby Grace who was pointing to Bernie, who was cleaning the shoes of their visitor.

“Sorry, Freddie, my wife is far more attractive and, dare I say, a little older.” Freddie sat there knowing he got it totally wrong. “Show my wife the photograph that you think might be of Robert Hat.” Yvonne handed baby Grace to her husband and took the photograph to the window where her glasses were.

“Sorry, it’s not very clear, and I am sure Rob is far smaller,” Yvonne said taking baby Grace back off her husband.

“Do you fancy a drink, Mr Andrews?” Alan asked.

“No, I am fine, thank you, but I would like if you could get me a taxi seeing I have a flight from Kilimanjaro back to the UK in two hours,” he said looking at his watch.

Alan got up and took his keys off his desk. “I need to be in Arusha so I could drop you off on my way,” Alan said giving his wife a kiss on the cheek and noticed the SB guy putting the photographs in his holdall. He whispered in his wife’s ear, “That was close.”

“Thank you! That would be kind of you, and thank you both for your time,” Freddie Andrews said following Alan Hat out of their bungalow with Bernie following his wet shiny black shoes.

Chapter 44
That's Got to Be Lucky

George Almedia's rented Honda, with its damaged front lights that happened after his run-in with Anna Kajeme and her two heavies at Saints House in South East London, was due in later today for repair at 'Rent A Car.' Keeping two cars back from the Baines's Audi, they seemed to be heading south of the Thames.

One hour later, now three cars at the back of the Audi turned right into Manor Road. Then, they turned right where the sign said Honour Oak Cemetery. Now knowing that parking is not allowed between 8 am until 6 pm in Manor Road, George drove down a further 200 yards and parked his motor in the small shopping parade. Jogging back, he entered into the wooded area and figured where he entered, he could be directly in the line of the Baines's grave.

Through the bushes, he could see Charlie Baines and his mother in their Audi. It seemed to where he was crouching, they were having an argument. Five minutes later, which seemed like an hour, they left the Audi and were walking directly towards him. The only difference this time was that Glenda Baines was not carrying any flowers. When they reached the grave, Glenda knelt down looking all around and making sure there was no one close to their proximity. He could see Glenda beckoning her son, who was a few steps behind her. Charlie holding a similar holdall he had when he left the grave the last time he was in the wooded area, walked into the bushes and was no more than 50 feet away from where he was crouching. George looked down at his shoes and brushed off some dog's shit with some leaves. When he looked up, Charlie Baines was nowhere to be seen.

With his knees starting to throb from the crouching, he sat his arse onto the damp ground. Staring ahead to the last place, he saw Charlie before he vanished. It was a good ten minutes when the ground seemed to lift up, he couldn't be certain, but he thought he saw a flash of light when he saw him appear once again with his holdall looking that it could burst open.

He watched Charlie walk out into the open and was standing talking to his mother. George Almedia took a white handkerchief from his pocket and tied it to a bush he was sitting behind as a future marker when at some stage, he comes back.

Watching the pair walk from the grave and getting back into their Audi, George waited until they left the cemetery. He got up and ventured back to Manor Road looking in both directions and making certain there were no traffic or pedestrians. With all clear, he left the wooded area and strolled back to the small shopping parade.

Brushing himself down before he got back into the Audi. When brushing his arse, he made certain that there were no leaves on his trousers. Bringing his right hand back, he said out loud, "That's got to be lucky." Looking at his hand seeing further dog's shit on his fingers.

Chapter 45
Asante Sana

With Alan Hat dropping off Freddie Andrews from the Special Branch at Kilimanjaro International Airport for his flight back to the UK. He had flown over from the UK to discover if it was his wife Yvonne that had sent the package via DHL on Zanzibar to Portcullis House for the PM Simon Davis.

From the airport, he headed for Arusha for his meeting with the owner, Tony Mullins from Southern Ireland, who had started Kibo Safaris back in 2000.

Tony must have heard Alan Hat pull up outside his office in his old jeep. "Karibu, Alan," he said watching Alan get out of his jeep, and he followed Tony back inside his office. "Would you like a cup *chai*?" Tony asked.

"Asante," Alan said pulling out copies of the invoices from his pocket he had earlier sent. Whilst double-checking them, Tony was making the *chai*.

"Are you on your own?" Alan called out.

"I have all my motors out working, and my wife Irene is busy shopping; hence, I am making the *chai*," Tony said coming back into his office with two *chais*. Sitting behind his desk and pulling out his top draw and sliding an envelope over to him, "It's all there; it's in dollars, $1000."

"Asante," Alan said starting to drink his *chai*. Tony then went to his safe and brought out a further envelope and handed it to Alan.

"Last month, I took 25 clients up Mount Kilimanjaro; hence enclosed is $2500 for your 'Climbing for A Brighter Future' project that you turn into food for the orphans and street children." He then said, "Kibo Safaris are pleased to be involved in such a worthy project." Alan looked at the envelope where written on the outside said 'For Aid into Africa.'

"Asante Sana," Alan said.

"Alan, I have a job for you this Saturday."

Alan got out his diary and flipped the pages, "Saturday, I am clear by 4:30 pm."

"Perfect. At 6 pm, can you pick up once again Peter Goodman from the Tato Hotel who is flying back to the UK?" Alan scribbled it down in his diary.

"Where is he flying into?" he asked.

"Sorry, I don't have that info," Tony said locking his safe.

On his way back to Machame, he decided to pull over and text his nephew.

"Hi Rob,

I had Special Branch here two hours ago; no problem will explain more by email later. The main reason for this text is to tell you I am picking up Peter Goodman (TCB), who is leaving Tanzania this Saturday at 6 pm from the Tato Hotel, not sure where he is flying into. Will text you Saturday to give you all the details.

Rob, the last thing you want is for Trevor Charles Baines to get to the so-called Baines's grave before you have the opportunity to find out if what you believe is true.

Hopefully, George Almedia just might hold the KEY to a solution?

Tell Grace that baby Grace is doing well.

Love from all in Machame."

Chapter 46
Kenya Flight 253

With a two-hour delay at Kilimanjaro International Airport for Freddie Andrews flight to the UK, he was unable to come to terms that Alan Hat was not involved in sending that parcel to the PM for the Peoples Unite Party. He also had to accept it was not Yvonne Hat that was able to get a little street child to go into DHL to send that parcel.

What if that was Robert Hat standing on the edge of that train waiting to be helped off. Then with the large case by his side, that was big enough to hide the red parliamentary case; yes, it looks a possibility. If it was him, he would have realised that the government would investigate the whereabouts of this case that held confidential papers.

Yes, if he was guilty, then to a degree, he made a good decision to throw any investigators off their track by sending those items from Zanzibar.

Taking his takeaway coffee from Costas, knowing he still had a considerable wait, he went to the comfortable lounge when he decided to take a look at the Aid into Africa's website run by Alan Hat. He did have a brief look earlier to see if there were any photos of Yvonne, his wife, on his site, but all to no avail.

Booting up his laptop, going into Google and entering the web address, he reads Aid into Africa started back in 1996 and approached companies in the UK to part with any obsolete educational materials along with medical equipment.

"That looks impressive," he said in a whisper seeing the lounge was full, and his flight was not the only flight to have long delays.

He sees AIA delivered 350 tonnes of obsolete aid in the UK that would not be obsolete in the third-world. He reads on, the aid he delivered went to Thika, Nairobi, Kwale, Mombasa, and Diani in Kenya. In 2000, he commenced delivering aid to Dar-es-Salaam, Songea, Moshi, Arusha, Kilimanjaro, and then over to Zanzibar in Tanzania.

From 1996 to 2003, 20x40-foot containers were used, and it highlighted that AIA never ever asked for any cash, just materials that would benefit the children, schools and hospitals in East Africa.

Freddie Andrews had to smile where it said that Alan Hat was the nearest you could get to Oliver Twist seeing it kept asking for more.

The list of companies that supported these projects into East Africa was highlighted on a full page of his website. What amazed him was Staedtler, the Pencil and Pen Company, that had donated some seven million pencils and a million pens when AIA commenced their projects back in 1996. Reading on the next line was a company that would have saved a great many lives in the third-world. Intersurgical, based in Berkshire, had donated over a million respiratory kits. Looking further down this list of donors, he saw the Open University had given 100,000 books for higher education.

"Bloody hell," he said out loud this time where it was highlighted that AIA had letters of support from Buckingham Palace and Hillary Rodham Clinton when her husband was America's President.

Reading further on, he spotted that two pallets of respiratory equipment were shipped over to Iraq when the war was raging that went into hospitals

The next page was AIA's future project, 'Climbing for A Brighter Future.' Yes, Aid into Africa's goal is open, a Food Bank in Arusha to feed the orphans and street children. His method seems he will be gaining tour companies that sell the trek up Mount Kilimanjaro for each client that wanted to reach the Roof of Africa would pay the tour company and extra $100 that would be given to Aid into Africa who would turn into food for the less fortunate children.

Of course, Freddie Andrews knew he would not face any problems in the UK seeing there are already so many food banks in the UK simply because of all the austerity measures that the Peoples Unite Party had introduced.

Having read extracts from the Aid into Africa website got him thinking that would Alan Hat risk everything he's accomplished by getting involved in a red parliamentary case that's gone missing?

He scribbled a note in his diary. To ask Alan Hat at some stage if he had accomplished his goal in Tanzania.

Going back into Costas for a further coffee, he sat in the coffee bar to read the Tanzania Times. Then over the tannoy, "Kenya Flight 253 to the UK, please would you make your way make go to gate 10," the African lady said in perfect English.

Waiting in Gate 10, he knew he had to inform the Chancellor that it was not Rob Hat's uncle that had sent that parcel to the PM.

Grabbing the straws, he thought he had nothing to lose by calling the CIP (Corps of Intelligence Police) and gain their assistance from their force to get involved without telling them all the reasons as to why Special Branch needed them, not that he knew himself what was in the PM's red leather case.

Much to his surprise, he got straight through to Colonel Jameson, the top man in the CIP. Getting in the tail end of the queue to have his passport checked, people in the queue could clearly hear him say: "Yes, Colonel, you heard me correctly. I need a 24x7 on him until I tell your office otherwise." He then ended his call.

Chapter 47
Backburner

In Reading Police Station, DCI Gordon Taylor was in DI Judy Reynold's office with DS Jones and DS Richardson listening to him rollicking DI Reynolds. "Reynolds, I don't pay you inspector to deliver stolen credit cards to Bracknell Police Station," the DCI shouted in Judy Reynold's face, who appeared to be close to tears in the way she was being spoken to more so with her two DS's in her office.

It was the telephone ringing on the desk of DS Jones that brought the DCI's shouting at their DI to a halt. "Yes, Colonel, our DCI Taylor is with us downstairs. I will pass your call over to him who's with our DI, CIP governor," Jones said transferring the call.

"Good evening, Sir, how can I help you?" DCI Taylor said.

DS Jones leaning towards DS Philip Richardson and whispering: "Yes Sir, no Sir, three bags full, Sir. What an arsehole we have as a boss?" With Philip turning with his back to their DCI, trying not laugh.

"Yes, Sir, if you wish," the DCI said putting the telephone under his chin while trying to tighten his tie as though Colonel Jameson could see him. He then started to write something down on a sheet of A4 paper he had pulled out of Judy Reynolds's printer. "So, Sir, I take it that my contact will be this Freddie Andrews from the Special Branch, and I am to use the contact details you have given me," he said with their DCI having the most stupid smile on his face. "Of course, Sir, I will use my DI Reynolds and DS Jones whom I believe know him." DI Reynolds sat at her desk with her boss's back to her giving him the middle finger that made both her sergeants smile. "Of course, Sir, you can trust me to handle this, and I must say Sir, thank you for having faith in me to gain what you are seeking." He was going to crawl further, but the line went dead, "Damn it, the line was cut off."

"Richardson, tea for me," their DCI asked.

Judy Reynolds sat there thinking that her boss is such an ignorant bastard and said, "PLEASE Philip, would you be so good as to get Jones and myself a tea and, of course, yourself."

The DCI took the hint with Reynolds emphasising the word PLEASE. "Two sugars for me, Sergeant, thank you," he said going to the door, "Nature is calling."

Using DS Jones's desk, Philip put the tea cups down. "Okay, listen up, as you know that was the boss at CIP who's put me in charge of what I am about to tell you. Firstly, I am pulling you, Reynolds and Jones, off the Trevor Charles Baines case. As for you, Richardson, I am leaving you to keep tabs on Glenda and Charlie Baines." their DCI said.

"And us?" DI Reynolds asked.

"I want you both to keep a 24x7 on Rob Hat. You have both met Freddie Andrews of the Special Branch. From all accounts, Simon Davis, our PM, seems to have lost his red leather suitcase case, and Freddie Andrew feels there is a possibility Rob Hat might know the whereabouts of it."

"The SB Freddie Andrews had shown both of us the photograph of the young guy standing at the door of the train after the rail crash where the PM had left his red case. We both weren't sure that it was Rob Hat, but it now seems the Special Branch might believe otherwise." DI Reynolds said looking at Jones, who was looking uncomfortable seeing he had earlier advised Rob to hand those two manifests over to the media. With the DCI handing the A4 sheet of paper containing where he scribbled down the contact details of the CIP Colonel Jameson and Freddie Andrews, he said, "Everything you unearth, you are to contact me seeing I am your superior and I will speak to the CIP with the information you gain." He then took his tea and left DI Reynolds's office.

"Looks like, Jones, you might have been right seeing the Trevor Charles Baines case as just found its way to the backburner?" DI Judy Reynolds said and then added, "Our boss is what's known as an arse licker." Both her sergeants nodding in their agreement.

DS Philip Richardson took his jacket from the back of a chair and said, "I am off home and, yes, first thing in the morning, you will find me in Sandhurst."

"I'll walk with you to the garage. See you in the morning, big guy," Judy said with DS Richardson opening her office and waited for her to follow him.

Jones, now alone, took out his mobile and decided to text young Rob Hat. He wrote, "You now have DI Reynolds and me on your back. See you at Saints House at 8 pm in your van."

The only saviour for Jones, as he saw it, was there had been no mention of the two manifests. All the CIP and the Special Branch were seeking was the parliamentary red leather case, not its contents.

Chapter 48
Please Don't Hurt Me

On the dot at 6 pm, Charlie Baines drove his Audi round the back of the Sandhurst Funeral Parlour and parked up beside the company's Hurst. Colin Thomas came out of the back door to greet him, "Paul Stevens is waiting in my office trying to wear out my carpet; he's a bag of nerves knowing your coming." Charlie never said anything; he just followed the pervert in through the back door noticing the room on the left where a young couple was paying their respects to whoever it was in the coffin. Walking further down the hallway into the parlour's main entrance, Colin Thomas opened the door on the far end of the reception area. It was just then the young couple appeared.

"Thank you, Mr Thomas, my mother looks very peaceful," the young lady said holding what could be her husband's hand.

"As promised Mr & Mrs Eddery, I will be with you at 10 am tomorrow with your mother along with the two cars that you have requested," Colin Thomas said seeing the young couple leaving the funeral parlour.

Charlie Baines looked at Colin Thomas and said, "Very sad." Then, he followed Colin into his office. Both of them could see Paul Stevens crouching in the corner looking petrified seeing Charlie Baines walking in and taking a seat at the desk and looking directly at Paul Stevens in the corner. "Please don't hurt me," the elderly guy said getting brave and stood up but remained in the corner.

"Okay, Paul, now you need to tell me what you know that's worth 5k?" Paul stood there wiping that could be his sweaty hands down his trousers.

"Mr Baines, all I know is that your father is not in that coffin that was buried at Honour Oak Cemetery," he said taking two steps towards Charlie Baines, who stood up and walked towards him.

"Don't hit me."

"So, who and what do you know is in that coffin?" Charlie yelled at him.

"Mr Baines, I honestly don't know or even care what's been buried," he spluttered out and then said, "All I want is a little something for my silence for my family to get us started in Australia and you will never hear from me again." Charlie sat back down again and waved him over to sit in his boss's chair opposite him.

"Sit down, Paul, and here's the deal if and when your mouth opens, then Mrs Stevens will be looking for the services, such as Sandhurst Funeral Parlour have to offer. Now, do you fully understand that the Baines's arms can reach as far as Australia?"

Paul Stevens sat there shaking, "My lips are sealed."

Charlie Baines went to his pocket and pulled out an A4 jiffy bag and tossed it over to him, "Don't you dare count it. There are one hundred 50-pound notes enclosed."

"Colin, our business is now completed," Charlie said getting up and leaving his office. He went back down the long corridor and out through the back door.

Paul Stevens sat there, this time wiping the sweat from his brow with the cuff of his jacket. "Paul, you don't fuck with Baines family seeing you will lose if you ever cross them," Colin said, "Knowing you can't beat them."

Chapter 49
Saucy Git

Rob was in the library in Edgware Road and decided that he would set up a Hotmail account. He went for hoodwink@ hotmail.com; he then went to his Help account that he set a few years ago and found the email addresses of Paul Lawson, the editor of the Daily Mirror and his brother, Ben Lawson, of the Daily Mail. He then started to compose the email that he would send early in May.

After being satisfied, he tucked his message away into drafts and checked his watch and then headed back to Premier to pick up Grace seeing he had arranged an appointment to meet up with George Almedia at 6 pm in Costas at Waterloo Station.

Rob parked up at Waterloo Station, hoping to avoid a penalty for parking on a yellow line. "Rob, you need to remember you're meeting with DS Jones at Saints House at 8 pm, so we don't need to hang around too long in Costas," Grace said walking into the station's concourse.

"We have plenty of time. First, I need to go into the Safe Security Company, opposite platform 11, and get myself a security box for these two manifests." Rob had tucked under his arm in an A3 jiffy bag.

Grace waited outside the Safe Security Company whilst he was signing up for his box. With Rob walking out, "What name did you register under?" Grace asked looking to her right, seeing George Almedia walking into Costas.

"Paul Lawson," Rob said holding Grace's hand and using his other hand to put the key to number five box in her pocket. "Please don't you lose it."

"Saucy git, George has just gone into Costas."

Grace was dreading this meeting with George simply because this could mean that Rob would be joining him to prove that Trevor Charles Baines's stolen fortune could be in his casket six feet under the ground.

George was sitting by the window, and he must have seen them coming from the Safe Security Company as the young male waiter was putting three drinks on the table. "Grace, you get more attractive each time I see you. Heaven only knows what you see in Rob?" George said getting up to greet his two trusted friends.

"There you go, two cappuccinos for my friends and English tea for myself," George said sitting back down.

"Thank you, young man," he said giving the young waiter a £5 tip.

"What were you two doing over at the security office?" he asked stirring his black tea with Grace starting to slurp her hot cappuccino.

"I have taken everyone's advice, including your good self. Yes, as of the 5 of May, two days before the general election, the Daily Mirror along with Daily Mail will discover that what's inside security box number five will be proof without any question of doubt that Simon Davis, our PM, is prepared to hoodwink the UK's entire population to gain the keys again to 10 Downing Street."

"Rob, you are doing the right thing. You should feel proud that a young guy is capable of bringing down the Peoples Unite Party before they were possibly going to cause misery to millions," George said helping Grace wipe down the table. Listening to Rob and George, she stirred the life out of her coffee feeling relieved that this nightmare of the leather red case and two manifests will soon be coming to an end. "Now for me being a Tanzanian and always ready for a fast Tanzanian shilling, I would have blackmailed the bastard."

Rob looked at George after that comment. "Don't think I hadn't thought about it," he said that got him a dig in the ribs from Grace.

She then said, "I hope you two are joking." With George shaking his head much as to say no, he was serious.

"Okay, you two, I have seen Charlie Baines twice now going into the woods just behind his father's grave and come back with a holdall stuffed out that could contain cash. On the second time, I was no more than fifty feet away from him tucked behind a bush, and the sod disappeared before my very eyes. A few minutes later, just like magic, he appeared again. Granted, the bush didn't give me a clear and, with the sun going down, did not help, but there he was again with a holdall going back to the grave to join his mother, Glenda."

Just then, Rob's mobile went off informing him he's got a text. "It's from my uncle."

"Is there a problem, Rob?" George asked.

Rob opened his text, "Here goes," and reads it out.

"Hi, Rob,

Peter Goodman is flying out of Kilimanjaro on flight Kenya Airways flight 256 to Heathrow Terminal four, and due in at 7 am on Sunday the 3 of May.

If you intend to do you what you said earlier, you need to find a way to keep him from Honour Oak Cemetery.

Love from all in Machame.
Alan."

"Rob, what your uncle is saying makes a great deal of sense. We don't need Baines to be at his own grave before we accomplish what we aim to prove. You need to send me that photograph you have of Trevor Charles Baines whilst he was at the gate of Majame for his climb up Mount Kilimanjaro. I will greet him Sunday and get him out of reach," George said feeling the keys he had in his pocket that Rob's uncle had given him a while back.

Then Grace, who seemed concerned, said: "No blood, George."

With him smiling, he said, “You know me too well?” He then added, “It’s okay, Grace, I have a safe place for him.”

George Almedia’s mobile went off, making Grace jump. “It’s also from your uncle, Rob. He’s copied me on your message, and he’s added…”

“What, George?” Rob asked.

“Read it yourself,” George handed it to Rob, who read.

“George, when you were over in the UK for the christening of baby Grace, I loaned you the keys to our home in Bracknell Berkshire for you to stay should you so wished. As to be expected, you never did return them. Hopefully, you still have the keys, and of course, you have brought them with you.

94 Deansgate has a secure cellar that just might be useful. Wink, wink.

Alan.”

“I know the police are keeping tabs on Charlie and Glenda Baines, so you will be assured they won’t be meeting him at Heathrow,” George said taking the set of keys from his pocket and putting them on the table that brought a smile to Rob’s face and then went on to ask, “When are we going to the Honour Oak Cemetery and hopefully get our one million pounds reward?” He said going to the counter and ordered a further three drinks.

Whilst he was at the counter, Grace said, “This is getting bloody dangerous.”

This time George brought the drinks to their table, “George, can we get the 7 of May out of the way, and hopefully you can see that Baines finishing up in the strong arms of the law but not before the 7.”

“Okay, Rob, I will pick you up from Saints House when you are ready?”

“George, we need to shift. I have a meeting with your friend, the 7-foot copper, at 8 pm at Saints House. It seems I might have a problem?” Rob said gulping down his drink. Grace was looking first at Rob and then at the African and back again to Rob thinking these past few years that frequently our lives faced problems after problems.

“Call me if you need a helping hand?” George said, once again wiping up the overspill of coffee from Grace’s fast stirring.

Chapter 50
No Followers

6:30 pm at the Baines family home, Lamberts, the estate agent, was putting up the for-sale placard. Inside, Glenda was looking out from their window in their lounge. "I hate Frank Taylor for doing this to us, making me sell our home to pay what your father owed the git," she said turning to see her son reading from his mobile.

"Mum, just like you, I hate the fucking Frazers, but let's face it, my father put us in this situation that we have no control of," he said getting up and handing his mobile to his mother, who was still staring at the for-sale sign.

"Read the text," he said sitting back down again. Glenda noticed the text was open to read.

"Charlie, coming into Heathrow with my last £20 and a few Tanzanian shillings, I hope to change before leaving Kilimanjaro. I will be making my way to Wokingham Station so pick me up around 10 am Sunday. No followers needed."

Glenda, now sitting opposite her son, looking angry that this is the first she had heard from her husband since he pissed off to Tanzania. "Okay, Charlie, early Sunday, I will take the Audi and visit your Nan, and hopefully, the old Bill in the grey Ford Focus parked up will follow me. Then you should take my Mercedes and pick up your father."

"I'm going downstairs to the cinema. Mother, I am truly pissed off in the way we are both being treated," he said picking up his pack of Marlboro and lighter along with a bottle of whiskey plus a glass, then buggered off into the basement.

Glenda sat there and turned on the TV, and the moment the X Factor came on, she turned over to watch the lottery draw. She would have checked the numbers but seeing she hadn't bought a lottery ticket for a number of years, there was very little point. So, she started to flick through the channels without bothering to look what was on.

She knew Charlie was right. The 30 years being married to Trevor has been bloody hell. She knew from the offset her husband was a gangster, and she had lost count of the times she had come forward to provide an alibi for him. The only time he had said he loved her was on their wedding day and when she gave birth to Charlie.

Although Trevor had never hurt her, she was fully aware they didn't come more violent than him, more so in the early years of their marriage. It was not until he reached middle age that he stepped back and ordered others to do his dirty work. She never asked him, but she was absolutely certain he was responsible for a number of murders.

Whilst he was in East Africa, she had kept him up to date with everything that's been going on, but he never responded. Now Charlie had received a text with no mention of his wife that had stood by him for far too many years. Even tonight he was giving out his orders treating them like his servants.

For the life of her, she had no idea what the future had in store for her son and herself. Snapping herself out from feeling sorry for herself, she looked to see what channel she was at. "Shit 999," she knew she could telephone that number and put an end to her misery.

Chapter 51
York

They were ten minutes late for their 8 pm meeting with DS Jones when they drove into Saints House and parked up in front of the garage. Rob noticed the Sergeant getting out of his motor at the far end of the garages and started to stroll towards where Rob had parked, and they were now standing at the back of his old Morris Van.

"Rob, could we talk inside the garage?"

"Sure," he said and jumped back in his van and let off the handbrake to let his motor roll back enough so Grace could lift the garage shutter up.

With the garage closed, the three of them were inside the garage, and Grace put the overhead fluorescent light on. With them now leaning on the rickety table, "So the text you sent me says that DI Judy Reynolds and you are on my case, meaning what?"

DS Jones pulled out a photograph from his jacket with Rob standing on the edge of the train door waiting to be helped off and put it on the table. "This is the first time I have seen this, and, yes, Rob, that is you with Rosie's old case by your side."

The 7-foot copper smiled and said, "Yes, Grace, I know, and Rob knows, but the Special Branch are not sure and have ordered the CIP to make certain if that photo is in fact of Rob Hat. So now our DCI have given DI Reynolds and me the task of keeping tabs on you."

Grace picked up the photograph for a closer look. "I can see why they doubt; Rob's got his hand on his head looking away from the camera. I guess for me to be sure it was Rob that ancient case that belongs to Rosie was the giveaway by his side."

"Yes, you two are lucky since there is no mention of the contents inside the case. All Special Branch want is the red leather parliamentary case back with the PM," the DS said putting the photograph back in his jacket.

"As I said, when we met for coffee, you are doing the right thing in giving the media those two manifests. Would love to be a fly on the wall when the PM reads the papers," the DS said then asked: "When are you giving the press those two documents?"

"On the 5 of May, Paul Lawson, the editor of the Daily Mirror, and his brother Ben, the editor for the Daily Mail, should be picking them up on Wednesday from box number five at the Safe Security Company at Waterloo

Station," Rob said looking at the sack in the corner that had the red case inside and nodded to Grace.

"The way to get the Special Branch and the Met off your back is for the parliamentary case to turn up. Remember, Rob, for obvious reasons, it's not common knowledge that Simon Davis and his Chancellor Graham Johnson are only concerned with its contents, the two manifests," DS Jones said.

Grace seeing Rob looking at the sack and nodding to her she went to the sack and plonked the sack on the table and said to DS Jones, "You want it? Be our guest."

The Sergeant pulled out the red case from the sack. DS Jones, now seeing the red case on the table, put his hands up. "Wow, I can't be seen with it," the DS said and took a step back from the table. "Clean it off of all fingerprints. Make sure it's found, then you won't have DI Reynolds and me being found in your shadows, giving you two the freedom to move."

The Sergeant mobile went off, sounding much louder in the garage. "Lift the shutter, Grace." DS Jones went outside, and they could hear him saying: "No, it's very quiet here; yes, Rob's van is here. Okay, I will stop here until midnight. Goodnight."

Back inside the garage, he said: "I am back here again Sunday until 2 pm, then my boss Reynolds will relieve me waiting to see who you meet and where you go." He then took a sheet from his notebook and wrote down something and gave it to Rob.

"So, what's with this address?" Rob asked handing it to Grace who never even looked what was written and tucked it into her pocket.

"Our PM Simon Davis's elderly parents live at that address you have, and thanks to your taxes, the Met at our station are providing the PM with two cars and two motorcyclists to escort him to visit his parents. They will be leaving 10 Downing Street at 9 am Sunday," DS Jones said.

"So, you want us to leave the red case on Downing Street?" Rob said knowing it would be impossible and started to laugh.

"Now be serious, Rob. I figure if you leave now with that case, you can be back here by 4 am Sunday," he said.

Grace took that piece of paper out of her pocket and looked at the address written. "Hell, they live in York."

"Have a safe journey; the M1 should be relatively quiet by the time you reach it," the DS said leaving the garage and walked towards his car.

Part 3

Chapter 52
He's Safe

George Almedia's Saturday evening was in Camberley rushing from shop to shop to buy what was needed, and by 11 pm, he was at 94 Deansgate that laid back from the main road with a high hedge on three sides, making the house very secluded. By the time he had everything in place, it was 1 am when he eventually got back to the Castle Palace Hotel. He put a 5 am early call in.

At 5:45, with him being the only person in the restaurant having a coffee and three slices of toast, he noticed that he had a text. He opened the message and read.

"Good morning, George, it's 4:30, and I'm back from York. Anyway, I'm about to get my head down for a few hours' sleep. Simon Davis's parents are in for a bit of a shock when they take their milk in only to find a red parliamentary red case tucked in their porch. DS Jones, your friend, informed me that the PM will be travelling at 9 am from 10 Downing Street to visit his parents.

Hope your day goes to plan.

R & G."

George thought he should reply even knowing having Rob's mobile going off would more than likely wake him. "Sod it, I'm awake so you can join me," he said in a whisper and wrote: "Brilliant choice to offload it, G."

"Good morning, Rob," he said in a further whisper and pressed send.

Dunking his toast in his coffee, he had to smile and wishing he could see the PM's face when he discovers those manifests were not in his red case.

Passing by the reception of the Castle Palace Hotel to hand his key over to the night porter, coming through the door was a face he knew only too well coming in. "Glad you could make," George said.

Whilst his friend's wife was checking in, "Can't stop, I am off to Heathrow to meet a guy that will be surprised that he's being met."

With his friend putting his index finger to his lips, George understood what it meant. "It's okay, my friend, my lips are sealed," George said heading out of the hotel to get his car from the hotel's car park.

7:30 standing in arrivals at terminal four with the Kenya 256 flight from Kilimanjaro landed at 7:25, so he decided to wait for Trevor Charles Baines to appear from the customs hall holding a large card that read Mr Peter Goodman.

At 7:45, a great surge of people came through, but this Goodman character stood out so clearly from the photo that Rob had given him. His shaven head with a few wisps of grey hair and bushy moustache with a rucksack on his back wheeling a large red case with two walking sticks strapped to the side and, he was glaring at George Almedia standing there displaying his name. "Who the fuck would you be, mate?" Trevor said walking up to him and standing there. Taking his rucksack off, he looked totally confused.

"We need to talk," George said pointing to Costas. With George wheeling his case, they walked over to the coffee bar.

"Black coffee for me," he said.

With their drinks on the table. "Charlie Baines called me last night to warn you that his mother and Charlie have been arrested for holding back the knowledge of the whereabouts of his cash father's stolen cash, and to make things worse, it seems Charlie is being charged for setting light to the Frazer's night club in Wokingham."

Baines took out his mobile. "Wrong choice, Mr Goodman, seeing they are still in custody at Reading Police Station." Baines sat there stroking his moustache and then rubbing his shaven head that he knew had to shave at some stage.

Trevor was totally aware that he had pissed off his wife Glenda a great many times, and they had drifted apart. Now her being questioned about his cash, would she break and spill her guts? That could see him spending a great many years locked up. Yes, he knew he could not afford to be seen. Now he wished he had remained in Tanzania but the fear of all that cash buried felt he should be home. He was more than happy that his son Charlie had set light to Frank Frazer's night club; he only wished he had waited for his arrival then he would have fucking blown the place up with Frank and his twins in it.

"So, who the fuck are you then?" Baines asked.

"It should be me asking you that question. Why would Charlie Baines wanting to protect a Peter Goodman from showing his face back in Berkshire?" Trevor Charles Baines never responded.

"Peter, I honestly don't give a shit to who you are. Charlie Baines said I would be well rewarded if I could put you in a safe house until their problems are sorted," George Almedia said drinking his coffee and feeling confident that he had successfully pulled the wool over Trevor's eyes.

"Keep an eye on my bags whilst I go for a piss?" Trevor asked and strolled towards the toilets at the far end of the arrival hall. Seeing he had left his mobile on the table and never one to miss the opportunity of keeping Baines away from making calls, George removed his sim card but never fully fastened the back of his mobile hoping that might make Trevor think it had fallen out.

In George's Honda driving out of the car park. "I take it, Peter, that your one of the late Baines's team that the police would like to speak to hence his son's concerns about getting you safely tucked away from the law?" George asked putting his parking ticket into the machine.

“Something like that, but shut the fuck up, and you’re paid to get me safe seeing that’s what Charlie is paying you for.”

George was more than happy to see Trevor Charles Baines had nodded off with an extremely loud snore as they drove down the M4. Taking the 329 towards Wokingham, but headed left towards Bracknell.

“Time to wake up, Mr Goodman,” George said stopping outside 94 Deansgate. “You’re in Berkshire,” George said taking his bags out of the boot and walking to the front door with Trevor trying to figure out where he was but still followed him into the house.

They were both standing in the hallway when George opened the cellar door and said, “This is a copper’s house, and the family is away.”

“You’re fucking kidding me,” Trevor said thinking this is not a good idea.

“Mr Goodman, it doesn’t come any safer than under the roof of a copper. Between the hours of 10 and 12, when a Mrs Sampson comes in to feed the fishes and the hamster that you might hear her at night having her work out on the wheel. You will be safe here,” he said pointing to the stairs.

Eventually, Trevor decided this unknown character could be right and carried his rucksack, and George heaved his red case down the half a dozen stairs down into the cellar. “There’s an air vent so you won’t suffocate,” George said. Trevor was looking around seeing a chemical toilet, camp bed, bedding, a small stove, box of tin food, and even two cartons of long-life milk along with tea bags and a bag of sugar.

“When Charlie calls me, hopefully, in a day or two with the all clear, I will pick you up. In the meantime, make the most of a bad thing. There are even a few magazines at the bottom of the box,” George said going to shake his hand, but Baines ignored the gesture and turned away and sat on his camp bed.

George left him and walked up the stairs and, without making any noise, pulled the two bolts across the door and walked into the kitchen and took a chair and wedged it under the door handle.

In his Honda, he took out his mobile and sent Rob a text.

“Hi, Rob. He’s safe.”

Chapter 53
Daily Mirror

Sunday morning, Rob was down on the fourth floor with Grace, who was taking care of her younger sisters, Jane and Janet, whilst her mother, Jean Long, was at church. "Grace, did you ever set up your laptop I bought you?" Rob asked.

"Thanks to Linda, she's set me up with Talk-Talk that's also Mum's phone provider," Grace said going to her room where Rob could hear her moving boxes. "Here you go, one hardly used laptop," she said placing it on their coffee table in their lounge.

Rob booted up her laptop, "And your password is?"

Grace started to blush, "Okay, all I could think of was lovehat1."

Rob smiled and entered lovehat1. "Here we go, we are in. Oh, yes, love you too Grace1." He entered the new account Hoodwink@hotmail.com account and opened the message he had done and put it into drafts at the library in Edgware Road. "Have a read of this, Grace, and let me know what you think." Going to his address book, he entered Paul Lawson and Ben Law's email addresses to the email he was looking to send.

Having read it twice, Grace said, "Rob, I agree the press should know that the case turned up in York at the PM's parent's home."

"Subject: With the following information, the 2017 Election will not take place.

Good morning Paul & Ben of the Daily Mirror and the Daily Mail

Your tabloids covered the rail crash that happened from Vauxhall station, where a train going to Waterloo had a head-on collision from the train coming out of Waterloo Station.

As you reported, our PM and his chancellor were on this train. What your papers never knew was that the PM had left his red parliamentary case on the train containing confidential papers.

Whilst the media was not informed about the loss of this case; however, the Special Branch was ordered by our government to find the whereabouts of the red case. They then used the CIP from the Met to join the hunt.

Note their task was to recover the red parliamentary case with no mention of its contents.

As of today, the 3 of May, in the early hours, the red parliamentary case was delivered to the PM's parent's home in York. Of course, minus the confidential papers that will no doubt finish the career of Simon Davis, the leader of the Peoples Unite Party.

By the end of play today, at security box number five, a key will be left at the reception of the Daily Mirror. Yes, if you want to know more, take the key and go to the Security Company opposite platform 11 at Waterloo Station.

The box is registered in the name of Paul Lawson."

"It's good, Rob, send it."

"Okay, Grace, put your coat on, and we need to deliver the key to the Daily Mirror."

Driving over Blackfriars Bridge heading for Fleet Street. "Rob, please make sure that your face is not seen at the Daily Mirror."

Chapter 54
£500,000

Slamming the door behind him, he shouted out to his mother, knowing that with his Audi outside, she was back from his grandmother's. He failed to notice a black Mercedes parked at the side of the so-called mansion. "I waited at Wokingham Station until noon but there was no show." Walking into the lounge, he was taken aback seeing old man, Frank Frazer, sitting in his wheelchair with his oxygen cylinder by his side and his mask over his face that he took off and spluttered.

"Girlfriend let you down then?" Glenda sat there, hoping her son doesn't answer his question.

"I told you, Frank, we were expecting a potential buyer for our property that Charlie was going to meet—Mr & Mrs Jenkins at Wokingham Station," Glenda said looking directly at her son, who was still standing in the doorway and nodding.

"Three hours I waited, I called Jenkins' mobile number four times, and each time, it went straight into voicemail."

"Okay, Charlie. If you like, I believe you where others might not. Now, what I am here for is, I want two million pounds. Now seeing I am not a vicious person, so I want you to sign over the deeds to this spectacular home to me."

Glenda was about to protest when Charlie said, "Okay, we agree but you need to give us a further few weeks seeing we might sell very soon, and your two million pounds will be forthcoming."

"Two weeks, Glenda, and my solicitor will be here to do the deal," he said taking a draw from his oxygen and then taking his mobile out. He was tapping in some numbers. "George, I am ready to go."

Two minutes later, his driver helped him out of the Baines's home and took him away. "Good riddance to bad rubbish," Glenda said sitting in their lounge while taking out her mobile from her handbag.

"Your father is not picking up; Christ knows where the git is," Glenda said whilst Charlie was on his mobile talking to Kenya Airways, checking that a Peter Goodman was on their flight 256 from Kilimanjaro to Heathrow.

"That was a fucking waste of time since I can't prove over the telephone that I am Peter Goodman's son, they would not confirm or deny if he was on that flight."

Just then, their monitor at their front gate came to life in their lounge. "Who the hell is that at the gate?" Glenda asked. They both could see a very tall smartly dressed lady that could be an African.

Charlie tapped the answer button that would stop the buzzing and asked, "Can I help you, miss?"

"I need to speak to Peter Goodman."

"Open the gate, Charlie!" Glenda screamed out as she was walking into the kitchen.

Her chauffeur-driven Mercedes pulled up to their front door, and this elegant lady got herself out. "Wait here for me," she said to her driver while walking to the front door, where Charlie Baines was waiting to greet her.

"I need to speak to your father, Peter Goodman."

Charlie looked at her appearing to be confused; it was then his mother called out, "Let her in, Charlie!"

Now all three of them were in their lounge sitting in silence. "My name is Anna Kajeme. I had spent some time with Peter Goodman before he climbed Mount Kilimanjaro. When Peter was due to return to the Tato Hotel in Machame on the foothills of Kilimanjaro, the tour operator for Kibo Safaris sent their driver to the hotel to pick me up to enable me to greet Peter at the Machame Gate to be there on his arrival."

Glenda looked at this very attractive young lady. "I am sorry, Anna, you have truly lost me as to why you are here." Then once again, the room went silent with the three of them looking at each with neither of them knowing what to say.

It was Charlie that broke the silence, "Can I offer you a drink, Anna?"

"Vodka and coke would be fine." With that, Charlie went to the drinks' cabinet with his back to his visitor, and his mother poured herself a large scotch and downed it in one gulp. He didn't need to have a big IQ to know where this arrival of Anna Kajeme was going. Doing a further scotch for himself and a Vodka and Coke for Anna, he poured his mother a large brandy that he knew she would appreciate more so with this African lady arriving and asking to speak to Peter Goodman, who did not exist.

It was Anna that started to add wood to the fire knowing that shortly the fire was going to erupt into a giant blaze and said, "I never actually got to greet Peter; it was the Kibo Safari driver that blew the whistle on him. Don't ask how he knew that Peter Goodman was, in fact, Trevor Charles Baines, one of the UK's most notorious criminals." Charlie looked at his mother and watched her gulp down her brandy.

"My husband passed away a while back and is buried here in the UK," Glenda said looking at her empty glass and handing it to her son, who went back to the drinks cabinet and returned with a further large brandy.

"Mrs Baines, this was my problem seeing when I checked out the name Trevor Charles Baines; yes, he was buried at Honour Oak Cemetery in South East London." She then pulled out a couple of photographs that showed Peter Goodman with his right arm around her having dinner that could have been at the Tato Hotel and then handed the photos to Glenda. "At first, I began to think perhaps the Tato driver might have been mistaken but when I looked at those two photographs again, I could plainly see the Tattoo on his right hand TCB. Yes, I have to agree with his shaven head and large moustache, it is a good disguise from his photo on the website that was shown on the BBC news coverage at his funeral."

It was Charlie who said, "If what you are saying is true, what do you need from us?" She sat there as cool as a cucumber and finished her drink, handing Charlie her empty glass.

"Thank you," Anna knew the fire was smouldering, but her next thing was to start the blaze and said, "Thanks to good old Google, I see that Trevor Charles Baines has a great deal of stolen cash that the banks are offering a million pounds reward for its safe return. Mrs Baines and you, Charlie, I am not a greedy person; it's now Sunday, and we should all be at church, so I think it's best that we conduct our business shall we say 6 pm Monday?"

"What do you want for our silence?" Glenda said looking at her son, who nodded in agreement with what she was asking.

"As I said, I am not greedy. Shall we say £500,000?" Anna said, and got up to go and then added, "Thank you for your hospitality."

With Glenda and Charlie standing by their panoramic lounge window, they watched Anna Kajeme leaving their home. Then they saw the gates closing behind the Mercedes. "Charlie, to say today's been a bad day would be an understatement."

Chapter 55
Darling, Can We Have a Bet?

Sunday, just before lunch, the PM arrived at his parent's home in York. With all the kisses and hugs over at their front door, they walked through to their lounge to be greeted by his red parliamentary case sitting on their dining room table.

"Your father went to the front door to pick up the Sunday papers that the paper lad leaves in the front porch with the milk," his mother said and then asked, "Cup of tea, darling?" Without waiting for him to answer, she waddled off to the kitchen. "Henry, put that paper down and talk to your son, who's taken the time to drive all his way from London," his mother, Dorothy, called out from the kitchen where her son could hear filling the kettle up.

"What's with your case arriving here, Son?" his father asked putting the Sunday Times down the side of his old rocking chair.

"Dad, you need to trust me; it's a long story that you don't really want to know," Simon Davis said with his father going back to his paper. One thing Simon was grateful for his father was not in the least interested in politics, which made their conversation limited. Simon sat there staring at his red case, really scared to open it to see if those two manifests were still inside.

"Cup of tea, Son?" his mother said while sitting at their dining room table.

"Mum, you said you were going to the doctors to sort out your memory loss. Yes, I would love a tea; thank you," he said fearing his mother could be at the early stages of Alzheimer's.

His mother got up and slowly walked to the kitchen and he heard her say, "Oh, I have already filled the kettle, silly me."

A full fifteen minutes later, his mother returned from the kitchen. "Henry, where did you put the cups?" Henry put the paper back down and went out into the kitchen. "When did you put them up in the second cupboard?" she asked his dad, who was going back to his rocking chair and going back to his paper.

"Here you go, darling," she said putting his tea on the table beside his red case.

"Any chance of a tea for me, Dot?" his dad asked looking at his son, who was shaking his head.

"She's getting worse, Son." Simon got up and went into the kitchen.

"Let me help you, Mum." With Simon coming back into their dining room and handed his dad his tea and then said, "Dad, I will get a doctor in to see her, and if need be, I will get her into Harley Street to get her sorted." His dad never made any comments; he just starred over the top of his paper and nodded.

Drinking his tea at long last, he opened his briefcase, and it was no surprise his two manifests were not inside. Simon took his mobile out from his jacket since he needed to text Graham Johnson, his chancellor.

"Good afternoon, Graham.

You may not know, but I have visited my parents in York only to be greeted by my red case that turned up on their porch. That's the good news, so you MUST call off the Special Branch. I guess you have already guessed what the bad news is? Yes, you have it in one; there's no sign of those two manifests.

Speak Monday,
S."

"Come on, you two. I am taking you for dinner at the Marriot Hotel, where we should get a great view of the York Racing Course." His mum rushed to get her coat with his father looking far from being happy having to put his paper down.

"Darling, can we have a bet?" his mother said looking excited. "Henry, where is my purse?"

Chapter 56

No Good You Protesting

Later Sunday, Grace and Rob were looking over the balcony where they could both see DI Judy Reynolds sitting in her old Mini at the far end of the garages. "I assume that is DI Reynolds, but in all honestly, I recognise her Mini," Rob said, and as he said it, the Mini pulled out of Saints House and sped away.

"Let's hope, Rob, that the CIP and the Special Branch now know that the red case has been found, and they have called off keeping a watch on us?" They were just about to go inside Grace's flat when they watched a BMW pull in to Saints House and parked up where the Mini had just left. "Bloody hell! Rob, that's your uncle and aunt getting out of the BMW. Oh, Yvonne's getting baby Grace out of the car!" she shouted out. Rob was just about to say, that's fantastic to Grace, but she was gone, and he could hear her charging down the four flights of stairs.

By the time Rob got downstairs, he could see Grace was all over her godchild. Grace put her down, and she came walking towards Rob with her arms open, much as to say, 'It's your turn to make a fuss of me.' After a brief cuddle and a kiss, he gave his godchild back to Grace. Yvonne gave him a kiss on his cheek and the three of them walked towards the flat with the females on their way into Saints House. Alan and Rob were left standing by the car. With the boot lid up, Rob took the highchair from the boot.

"What a pleasant surprise having you here," Rob said and closed the boot of the BMW.

"I was hoping our friend George would not have told you we were in the UK since your aunt wanted to give you both a surprise," Alan said taking a holdall from the back seat.

"George has been in contact with me, and the moment he told me that you two were going treasure hunting in the so-called Trevor Charles Baines grave, Yvonne booked a flight for the three of us. Yes, before you ask, we are booked into the Castle Palace Hotel and as we arrived early this morning, George was on his way out to meet Peter Goodman at Heathrow. By email, we both agreed you should not be involved in designating a grave seeing if you are wrong, and there is a body, you will lose all the credibility you have in London overnight; hence, you should not be at Honour Oak Cemetery."

Rob was about to say something. "No good you protesting you're not getting involved. Yes, you're in charge, and only you will say when we do this, George and I are working for you, and that's final."

"Now, let's go and see my brother and sister-in-law," Alan said while taking the highchair from Rob and walking towards Saints House.

Rob looked at his uncle, "You want the good news or the bad news?"

"Okay, let's start with the good news."

Rob smiled and said, "Thank you for your support and caring for me." Alan couldn't think what the bad news could be as he pressed the call button for the lift. "Oh yes, the bad news is the lift is not working," Rob said heading for the first flight leaving his uncle to handle the highchair and holdall for the five flights.

"Nothing changes at Saints House then," he said struggling with the highchair that was refusing to stay folded.

Chapter 57
Do You Trust Me?

Grace eagerly offering to look after baby Grace whilst Alan and Yvonne took his brother and his wife, Julie Hat, out for dinner. "Rob, it's okay if you want to join them, I and this little darling will be just fine," Grace said bouncing baby Grace on her lap. "It's strange how sick babies always smell the same," Grace said taking a wet-wipe off Yvonne and cleaning her T-shirt.

"Sorry, Grace. I should have mentioned your godchild has been eating chocolate on our way over here and you bouncing her made a mess of your T-shirt," Yvonne said with the Hat family seeing the funny side of Grace helping her to bring her chocolate up.

9 pm with baby Grace out for the count in Grace's arms, Rob, who had decided not to join them anyway, had recorded a film he wanted to watch. "What are we watching now then?" Grace asked.

"Man on Fire." Grace put her godchild down on the sofa and went to the kitchen.

"Tea, darling?"

"Yes, please dear," Rob could hear her giggling.

"What's so funny out there, Grace?"

Stopping herself from her giggles, she said, "We sound like an old married couple."

"One day we will be," Rob said knowing Grace Long one day, for sure, would be Mrs G Hat.

"Who the hell is that at the door? He or she better had not woken my little darling!" she said and then heard Rob say at the door.

"You better come in."

"Who is it, Rob?"

"DS Jones, duck too late."

"Tea, Sergeant?"

DS Jones came into their lounge while holding his head. "Please, Grace. No sugar, I am on a diet," he called out.

With the tea now in their lounge, "Are you hoping being on a diet you might lose inches in your height?" Rob asked DS Jones, who was still rubbing his head.

"That's not funny," DS Jones said looking at Grace, who was trying not to laugh.

"This is a great film; I think it's based on a true story?" Jones said.

"Mr Jones, what brings you here? I am sure it's not to watch Denzel Washington meet his death." Grace asked picking up baby Grace, who was woken up with all the talking going on.

"No, but this is still a good film, Man on Fire," he said when Rob froze the screen.

"Anyway, it appears that you two had done a good job in delivering that red case in York. Of course, you will be pleased to know that Special Branch and the Met have no longer any interest in you," DS Jones said.

Rob chirped in and said, "It was all thanks to your advice." Rob told him, but since Jones had come round to see him, he decided not to mention that he kind of guessed as much seeing DI Reynolds had earlier pulled out of Saints House.

DS Jones knew his uncle must be over from Tanzania since Grace with her godchild was a kind of a great clue and said, "Just how long is your uncle here for?" Rob just shrugged his shoulders much as to say he had no idea.

"Rob, I wonder what the press will do once they are aware that the Peoples Unite Parties leader, Simon Davis, was capable of hoodwinking the entire population to gain the keys again to 10 Downing Street."

Rob looked at the frozen screen desperately wanted to press play. "Well, come Monday, they have the opportunity to find out the real PM and the lengths he would go to be our PM once again."

"Do you trust me, John?"

The DS smiled and not waiting for what he was about to say, he said, "In all the time I have known you, you have never used my Christian name."

"Listen, no promises, but there's something going down that could possibly see you getting a promotion." The DS sat there rubbing his head while trying to figure out what Rob was on about.

"In answer to your question, do I trust you well over the time I have helped you and given you heads up to help you that if my DCI knew I would be sweeping roads now?"

Rob looked at Grace, who would have guessed what he was going to ask. "Okay, on and around the 7 of May, I might need you to watch my back as a DS."

DS Jones never pushed Rob to tell him more, but yes, he knew he trusted the young lad and always would do since it was Rob that kept his mentally ill son in education back in 2013 from the stolen cash from the National Bank he had found on a train at Waterloo Station.

"Okay, press play. I might as well spend my evening with you more so seeing you're about to watch a fantastic film."

"Sergeant, do you want some bad news?" Grace asked.

"Spit it out, Grace," Rob looked over to Grace, thinking what the bad news is.

"Mr Jones, your head is bleeding," Grace said handing him a baby wipe.

Chapter 58
Ten Thousand Tanzanian Shillings

Trevor Charles Baines, in all his years, had only been camping once, and that was a disaster. Yes, he spent two weeks listening to the pissing down of rain hitting the canvas, now a bad memory of his. Granted, he was not camping, and he was never going to hear the rain some 12 feet underground. His camp bed, he was dreading stretching out on it, even sitting on the end of it tossed him onto the concrete floor

Looking at his chemical toilet, he was hoping his bowels will hold out until the large African guy releases him from his jail.

With a couple of dozen bottles of wine to choose from would be good, but no corkscrew amongst the box of materials that was left for him. Checking his watch, he realised that since it was fast approaching midnight, so there was very little chance, he would be out today.

He took out his mobile and was thinking he could risk it and call his son. Then he noticed the back of his mobile had not been closed and, to make things worse, there was no sim card. Other than using his mobile when he texts his son from Tanzania to meet him at Wokingham Station, he had not used his mobile. He knew he was going to call his son from Heathrow, but the African advised him not to.

Now sitting in the middle of his camp bed, he started to wonder if the coloured guy, whom his son had sent, had taken the sim out of his mobile whilst he went for a piss.

He lights up his stove for the third time since he has been in hiding for a further coffee.

Here, he was a very rich guy but locked in this shit-hole with only a few quid that should get him to Wokingham and ten thousand Tanzanian Shillings that he never managed to change at the airport. "I fucking hate this!" he shouted out knowing he should stop talking out loud since it could be seen as him going bloody mad. "Fuck it," he took a bottle of red wine and smashed the neck of the bottle on the first step of his hell hole. Using the toilet roll has a strainer, he placed a couple of sheets over a mug and poured himself a mug full.

Turning off his stove, he settled down on his camp bed and decided to get himself pissed until Monday when he's hopefully let out.

Chapter 59
Thomas Cook Holiday Voucher

At 9 am Monday, at Daily Mirror in the office of Paul Lawson— the Editor of the Daily Mirror—was calling down the front desk. “Peter, who left this small jiffy bag marked for my attention?” he asked looking at the key with the number five on his desk that the fob said ‘Security Company Waterloo Station.’

“Sorry, boss, I had my back to the desk. When I turned, I just got a glimpse of an old lady that looked more like a bag lady leaving the building.”

Paul was now thinking this lady could have been paid a couple of pounds to deliver. “It’s okay, Peter. No problem.”

Logging in to his PC, he noticed he had half a dozen messages, but the one that grabbed his attention was also addressed to his brother, the editor of the Daily Mail. “Strange,” he said and opened the email.

“Subject: With the following information, the 2017 Election will not take place.

Good morning, Paul & Ben of the Daily Mirror and the Daily Mail.

Your tabloids covered the rail crash that happened from Vauxhall station, where a train going to Waterloo had a head-on collision from the train coming out of Waterloo Station.

As you reported, our PM and his chancellor were on this train. What your papers never knew was the PM had left his red parliamentary case on the train containing confidential papers.

Whilst the media was not informed about the loss of this case; however, the Special Branch was ordered by our government to find the whereabouts of the red case. They then used the CIP from the Met to join the hunt.

Note their task was to recover the red parliamentary case with no mention of its contents.

As of today, the 3 of May, in the early hours, the parliamentary red case was delivered to the PM’s parent’s home in York. Of course, minus the confidential papers that will no doubt finish the career of Simon Davis, the leader of the Peoples Unite Party.

By the end of play today, a security box number five key will be left at the reception of the Daily Mirror. Yes, if you want to know more, take the key and go to the Security Company opposite platform 11 at Waterloo Station.

The box is registered in the name of Paul Lawson.”

Leaving his office, he saw Shirley Evans just about to sit at her desk. "In here, Shirley, and a coffee."

"Hell, Paul. I am only ten minutes late." Paul ignored her and returned to his office to read the email again before she arrived.

A few minutes later, with two coffees, she closed the door with her backside. "Sit down, and read this." Whilst she was reading the message, his brother Ben entered his office holding a printed copy of the email. He put it on Paul's desk noticing Shirley was reading the self-same message.

After reading the mail, she was looking at the two brothers. "Looks like we just might have a scoop here if this is not some nut case," she said whilst Ben was dangling his car keys in front of his brother.

"Shirley, whilst we are at Waterloo Station, you need to go to the front desk and get Peter to show you the CCTV, and let's see if we can identify who handed this jiffy in with this key enclosed," he said showing his brother the security key.

It was an hour later, when the brothers returned carrying an A3 jiffy bag while Shirley was sitting at the editors' desk. Ben took the two manifests out of the jiffy bag and placed them on his brother's desk. "Shirley, whilst you're at my desk, you need to find the government's website and search for the Peoples Unite Parties manifest that they are promoting with for their election."

Two minutes later, "Got it." The two brothers now stood behind her starting to read the government's promises to the population.

"Ben, you need to check these promises against those two manifests we have here on my desk." It took Ben a few minutes to check after he had moved Shirley from Paul's desk.

"Oh, fuck! Our Simon Davis is a crook seeing he's promising with no intentions to deliver," Ben said looking up from the desk in disbelief that a PM would go so low to gain the keys to the black door.

Shirley was now looking at those two manifests. "Hell, boss, he's even been stupid enough to sign both of them. It's even put it in writing in pen; this is what we promise the population. Then on the other manifest, he clearly says this is what we deliver."

Paul Lawson started to walk up and down his office. "How the fuck he manages to pass this past his ministers is beyond me," he said and sat down at the far end of his office.

"Shirley, you said earlier we could have a scoop here providing it was not some nut case sending that key. Nut case, no seeing our PM is the nutcase losing these two legal documents. Cheers, we have one fucking scoop here," the Editor said.

Then, Ben said, "I will drink to that," while going to his brother's desk and pulling out a bottle of scotch.

With three small whiskeys put in plastic cups from his water providing machine. "Shirley, how did you get on with Peter on the CCTV he's got for the front desk?"

Shirley started to smile. "I have saved the best bit to last that will make you smile or even laugh."

"Spit it out!"

Shirley finished her drink in one swallow. "Yes, it did seem like a bag lady that brought in that jiffy, but Peter never looked at the CCTV we have outside the building. Let me show you two gents." After a few clicks. "Now this will make your day," she said getting up and letting the brothers look at the screen. "Now, press play."

"That's our dear friend, Rob Hat, handing her something that could be a £5 note," Paul Lawson said going over to Shirley putting his arm around her giving her a kiss on the cheek.

"You're wasted here, Shirley. You should be working for the Met," Ben said.

"No more kisses, Ben," Shirley said putting her hands to her cheeks.

"Okay, let's now be serious, yes we have a scoop, but I see no reasons why we should involve young Hat," Paul said with his brother nodding in agreement.

"I think we should give him something to thank him for choosing the Daily Mirror and the Daily Mail for this scoop we have here."

Ben then said, "I agree with you, Paul, it would be so wrong of our papers to highlighting it was young Hat being known for the guy for bringing down the Peoples Unite Party."

"Okay, you arrange it. Shirley, let's give him a £2,000 Thomas Cook holiday voucher," Paul said pouring out a further three whiskeys.

Chapter 60
Is Daddy Okay, Mummy?

Simon Davis, our PM, arrived back at 10 Downing in the early hours of Monday morning on the 4 of May. Not wishing to wake his wife, he decided to spend a few hours' sleep on their couch in their extremely large dining room.

With his two manifests still out there, sleep was never going to happen. Even though his mother was ill, he should be giving her his full attention, but it was those manifests that were his priority. He knew he was selfish neglecting his mother in preference to worrying about what the outcome would be if his papers finished up with the media.

Of course, he never knew that at this juncture, the wheels were in motion to see him tossed out of 10 Downing.

At 7 am, "You should have disturbed me instead of sleeping on the couch in your suit," his wife said bringing him a coffee and two digestive biscuits that she placed on their 12-foot dining room table.

"Tough day in York. I really should have stopped home since I have a great many problems here," Simon Davis said with no mention of his mother, who was adamant in placing a bet on at the Yorkshire Race Course. He then took the 50p out of his jacket pocket that his mother wanted him to put on Red Rum and spun it in the air, knowing if it's heads, he loses that his wife trod on to stop it from spinning on the wooden floor. "What's it say, Judith?" he asked. Taking her foot off the coin, she looked down.

"Heads," she said picking it up and placing it on the table by his coffee.

"How is your mother, Simon?" Judith his wife asked.

"Sorry love, what did you ask?"

"Your mother, how is she?" she asked again watching her husband leaving the dining room and she could hear him walking up the stairs.

A few minutes later, their youngest 6-year-old son came into the lounge. "Is Daddy okay, Mummy? He passed me in the hall and went straight into the bathroom, and I think I heard him crying."

Judith looked at Gerald and said, "I think he's worried about your granny?" But she knew she was not telling him the truth.

Since that rail crash, he's never been the husband that she loved and admired. She felt they were drifting apart these last few weeks. Perhaps she should see that her husband visits his doctor. She was hoping he would acknowledge that he's struggling on a daily basis not only as a PM, but she felt their relationship with herself and their children were going in the wrong direction.

Looking at the cold cup of coffee and the two digestive biscuits, the tears started to roll down her cheek as she picked them up. Walking back upstairs, pleased that their older children were away in university since they would have picked up their father's strange moods that hang over him.

Back in the kitchen, her husband was on his mobile in their bedroom, and she just caught the last of his conversation. "I feel my days are now possibly numbered." She was just about to leave the kitchen and enter the bedroom that the door was wide open. She asked him who he was talking to on his mobile when he came out in a fresh suit doing his tie up. "Can't stop, Judith. I am already late for a meeting," the PM said totally ignoring his son sitting on the landing.

Chapter 61
The Door Was Slammed Behind Her

At the so-called mansion in Sandhurst. "Well bloody lie, Charlie. I am dammed if I am going to give that African bitch a single penny with her screwing my husband, she can fuck off." Glenda Baines shouted at her son with her cheeks appearing to burn. She then calmed a little and added, "Hopefully, we sell or we sign our home to the Frazer's, and then we shall vanish but, in the meantime, bloody lie to the black cow."

Charlie thought his mother should have said this earlier since it was fast approaching 6 pm, which not giving him a great deal of time to come up with something to fob her off with. "Mum, it's 5 pm; how the hell do I buy this time we need?"

"Give her some legal crap that's delaying us to gain your father's funds?" Glenda said and left the room, and slammed the door behind her.

Charlie had earlier cancelled his bank account from Barclays to the Spanish Santander. Using his cancelled bank account, he wrote a cheque for £500,000 and signed it C Baines. He sat in their lounge watching the monitor come to life and listening to their tall oak grandfather's clock tick away the seconds that chime every quarter.

As the clock chimes went off at 6 pm, the monitor came to life seeing the African lady's chauffeur-driven car at the gate. Charlie opened the gate and, watching her car drive up to their front door, Charlie dashed round and opened the front door and walked back into the lounge with Anna Kajeme, who followed him dressed in her full black leather suit. "Good evening, Mr Baines. I assume your mother is unavailable?" Charlie never answered; he just nodded. "Mr Baines, I believe my wages are now due?"

"Of course, Anna," and handed her the cheque from his trousers pocket. "Note I have not addressed it to anyone; I never knew how to spell your name; hence, I will let you fill it in."

She looked at the cheque and said, "I would have rather you provided me with cash." Anna Kajeme said staring at Charlie.

"Problem, Anna. All the legal matters regarding my father's estate have not been completed and will not be until mid-June at its earliest," Charlie said with his fingers of his left hand crossed in his left leg of his trousers.

"So, you're saying this fucking cheque is worthless until mid-June when your so-called dead father's estate is completed?" she asked.

Charlie looked at her and said, "Anna, hopefully by then, I will be able to pay you in cash, which you seem to prefer?"

Charlie had a while ago had bought a Pay as You Go mobile. "Let me have your number; call me on this number 07775 690445." She entered on her mobile and then dialled it to which Charlie answered then ended the call. "So now we can keep in touch," Charlie said feeling he was starting to sweat with all these lies he was telling.

Yes, if there's one thing to say about Charlie Baines, he might have the same genes of his father, and yes, he was always going to follow in his father's footsteps but telling lies, he would not follow in his father's footsteps.

"Charlie Baines, you need to listen and listen well. On the 6 of May, I fly into Thika in Nairobi to attend a family funeral, and I shall be back by the 15 of May. If, for whatever reasons, my £500,000 is not available, I will be going to the police and claim the reward the banks are offering. Is that clear? I will prove that Trevor Charles Baines is still alive and fucking kicking," Anna Kajeme said and left his lounge and, for the second time in two hours, Charlie jumped when the door was slammed behind her.

Chapter 62

Will It Be Okay in Here?

Back in her chauffeur-driven car. Charlie noticed from their conservatory that Anna Kajeme got into the front with the driver, making him think that her driver was more than just a chauffeur.

"Sid, get me out of this mansion. This Baines character must think I am bloody stupid," Anna said lighting two Marlboro at the same time and handed one over to Sid.

"Cheers," he said waiting for the gates to swing open.

"Sid, whilst I am in Thika, I want you to keep an eye on the Baines family. I wish I knew where Trevor was. Whilst I can tell the police and prove to them that Trevor Charles Baines is alive, but that will not get me any reward from the banks since I don't fucking know where his millions are stashed away. That arsehole of a son, Charlie, is trying to convince me that his father's money is with their solicitors and waiting for his father's estate to be settled. All the time I spent with this so-called Peter Goodman at no time did he pay by card, it was always cash; it was as though he was a walking safe," she said filling the car with smoke.

"What you want me to do other than keeping an eye on them? If you want babe, I can beat it out of him," Sid asked.

"It's a good idea perhaps at a later stage, but in the meantime, as I said, just keep an eye on Charlie Baines and his mother. I don't bloody trust him; he's given me a cheque that's not worth Jack shit."

Sid just nodded and put his hand between her legs. "Not here," she said pushing his hand away.

"When it comes to being fucked to me, it's two a penny, but when it comes to me being what's owed to me, I always turn up with sod all," Anna said not wanting to lose out again.

"You got me now, and I am one lucky bastard when it comes to money, and of course, I have not heard you complain when it comes to sex," Sid was saying rubbing his crutch.

"Don't kid yourself, Sid; you're good but not that good."

She sat there smoking the life out of her cigarette thinking of the time she had planned the perfect diamond robbery from Johnson Diamond in Mwanza in Northern Tanzania. Sitting on the half-full plane from Dar-es-Salaam to Kilimanjaro with 750 Diamonds glued to a children's pink bag that were worth millions—then being dragged off the jet by the law leaving her fortune tucked under the seat in front of her. Only to discover much later, an 18-year-old Rob Hat had helped himself to her diamonds. "Shit money always has a habit of running away from me," she said making Sid wonder what the hell she was going on about.

He said, "Penny for your thoughts?"

"Nothing, just drive."

"When I get back, and my money is not forthcoming, I will want you to burn the Baines home down."

"No problem, anything for you. Where to now?"

Anna sat there, lowered her window and tossed her cigarette out. "Saint's House, let's hope his bloody black bodyguard is not with Rob Hat." Sid looked at her knowing the last time with Harry, his brother, at Saints House, the guy had beaten the shit out of him, and she got a good slapping.

Sid then put his hand back on her leg stroking the inside of her right leg. "Leather really turns me on, babe," he said pulling into the Premier Inn in Sandhurst and then said, "Will it be okay in here?"

Anna checked her watch; it was a little after 7 pm. "If they have got a room, you can have an hour to enjoy my body seeing I don't want to be too late getting into London."

Chapter 63
Take Me to the Hospital

Rob and Grace had arrived home Monday at 9 pm after day's hard graft at Premier with Grace shooting upstairs seeing she was already late for dinner.

George and Alan Hat were in the Castle Palace Hotel, both drinking a diet coke before they were to meet Rob at Saints House at 9:30 pm. "Looking forward to reading the press Tuesday morning, that's assuming they have picked up those manifests from Waterloo Station," Alan said finishing his drink.

"It seems with the help of our friend DS Jones who had told him to leave those two documents at the parents' home of the PM in York because Sunday Simon Davis was due to travel to meet his mother and father," George said. "What a great choice to leave it," he was saying when his mobile went off.

"Are you two leaving the hotel?" George had to smile with Rob being bossy.

"Leaving now boss," and then George ended the call.

"I guess that's our boss, George?" Alan said watching George gulp down his coke followed by a large burp.

With both of them arriving at Saints House seeing Rob sitting on the side of his bright red Morris Van. George parked his Honda at the far end of the garages out of sight behind a 15cwt Ford Transit. They were just about to walk to Rob when a Mercedes pulled into Saints House and stopped immediately across the Morris Van blocking his van if he wanted to escape. George and Alan tucked behind the van to see what was occurring.

Anna got out and waited for Sid to join her before heading to Rob, who was still sitting on the side of the motor with its door open. "My, my all alone? So, where is Mr Big Black man?" Anna asked with Sid taking a step closer to Rob. Rob sat there and simply shrugged his shoulders and glanced to his left while waiting for his uncle and George to appear.

Sid walked straight to Anna's enemy and dragged him from his van, pushing him into the Garage shutter and was about to throw a punch. "Not yet, Sid," Anna said that stopped him just in time before him getting Hat to suffer a blow. "Rob, over a year ago, after you got your reward, I said you owe me and once again last month when you drove me to Moshi Town in Tanzania with my friend Peter Goodman when I said once again you fucking owe me. Well, here I am, I have come to collect my share of the reward that Lloyds paid you. Last time I came here to warn your very attractive lady friend with a beating to convince you that I will stop at nothing to gain what's owed to me. It was your so-called guard that saw the three of us off," Anna said. She and Sid did not notice anyone creeping down the side of the garages; they were George and Alan Hat.

Within seconds, George was now standing directly behind Anna, and Sid was still holding Rob up against the garage with his back to Anna waiting to be told to hit Rob. "Anna Kajeme, won't you ever learn there's nothing here for you?" She turned in shock to face the African and put her hands up like one does to surrender, but in her case, it was the wrong choice to surrender seeing George grabbed both her arms and swung her around twice and flung her over the Mercedes and heard her scream out in pain.

"Young man, you would be wise to release my nephew alone." Sid was not going to argue after seeing what happened to Anna and stepped aside. George stepped forward and pushed Alan aside.

"Alan, don't be nice and polite to the likes of this piece of shit. The only thing he will understand is this…" George lifted him by his neck and, other than Anna Kajeme seeing Sid's feet doing two to the dozen off the ground, it was then that George lowered him to the ground and head-butted him so hard with his head hitting the metal garage shutter. It was so hard that it made Alan and Rob jump.

Grabbing hold of him, he dragged him to the black shiny Mercedes and smashed his face down on the bonnet where they heard his nose crack, and they could see his blood running down the bonnet into the road.

Walking round to the other side of the car, Anna was sitting up on the ground trying to stop the bleeding from her head that was running down her skin tight black leather suit.

He pulled her to her feet and looked directly into her eyes and started rubbing the blood all over her face. "Anna, now listen. You are really out of your depth here. If I ever see you again trying to hurt my good friend, I promise all your beautiful looks will turn to you being one ugly bitch—that's a promise." He opened the door to the Mercedes and threw her in, hitting her head on the steering wheel, which they could hear Anna scream out in pain again.

Going to the front of the motor on the near side and opening the door whilst the guy was still face down on the bonnet. Stepping back to the bonnet, he said, "The only thing you have gained this evening is you don't have to fucking drive." With the passenger door open, he lifted Sid off the bonnet by his hair and pulled him off and dragged him to the open door. Lifting him high enough, he threw him into the motor with his bloodied face landing on Anna's lap. He then slammed the door.

Anna started the motor and started to make a three-point turn. Before driving out, as hurt as she was, she looked at Rob's uncle and started to think George and Rob's uncle were here to find out where Trevor Charles Baines's stolen cash was.

"Take me to a hospital," Sid said with his head back while hoping to stop the bleeding from his broken nose.

"George, I know now never to upset you," Alan said watching the black Mercedes drive away from Saints House.

"Granted, I have a short fuse, but I would never hurt the people I love and respect," George said while giving Rob a wink, who was laughing.

Chapter 64
She's a Wise Old Lady

George took a rag out of the side of Rob's van and wiped his hands from the blood he had gained from the ruckus. "So, that's how you scare the shit out of them?" Alan Hat asked.

"Given half the chance, they would do likewise to gain what they wanted," George said throwing the bloodied rag back into the van.

Just then, Rosie came along on her mobility scooter. "Bloody hell, big guy. I have only ever seen what you did to those two on films on television. You okay, lover boy?" she asked looking at Rob.

"Fine, thank you, my favourite girl. Any chance we could use your sitting room seeing we need somewhere for a private talk," Rob asked.

"What are we going to talk about then?" she asked.

"Private, Rosie," Rob said going over to her giving her a kiss on the lips. "What about you being the tea lady?" Rosie turned her scooter around and headed back to her flat.

"What's up, Miss Rosie? Have we upset you?" George called out after her.

"The kettle won't boil itself."

Rosie put three teacups along with a plate of assorted biscuits, custard creams, digestive and bourbon on the table. Leaving her nice and tidy sitting room, Rosie turned to her guests. "That's my husband, Billy," she said pointing to the mantelpiece at the casket, which took centre stage with photographs on every side. "If you gents need advice, I will only be on the other side of the door."

With Alan and George looking at each other smiling, it was Rob who said, "Hopefully, not with your ear to it?"

"I guess we are all now waiting to see the outcome of what happens next with our PM," Rob said dunking his custard cream in his tea that decided it would break into two with a splash.

"I am proud of you, Rob, for doing the right thing with those two manifests. Without any doubt, the media was the right place for them. I actually had a bet of 10,000 Tanzanian Shillings with your aunt that you would do the right thing seeing the UK's population need to know what their potential PM would do once in power again."

"Yes, I am in agreement. Although if I am honest, English politics does not concern or interest me in Tanzania, yes—as I have said to Grace—I would have blackmailed the git."

"Okay, Rob, when do we see what's in that coffin, and hopefully, we don't find it's just a body?" Alan Hat said.

"You now know, Rob, you're not getting your hands dirty on this project. Rob, there's a small shopping parade a little further down Manor Road where you can park up, and Alan or I will keep you informed to what we find," George was saying with Alan nodding.

"Rob, what we want to find out is when are we going to tackle this?"

"Okay, my A-Team. The election is planned for the 7 of May, which is not likely to take place now. Anyway, either way, we do it at this Wednesday evening," Rob said with George and Alan both putting their thumbs up at the same time.

"Listen, I want to run this scenario by both of you. We all must agree that DS Jones has helped me. Now, he also helped you, George, at Waterloo Station when we took those diamonds out of the Security Company, and I know you invited him to Mwanza for a holiday with his wife and two children.

"Be assured he knows nothing about us searching for Trevor Charles Baines's stolen cash. I was about to tell him the other evening, but the film Man on Fire stopped me."

"That's a great film, Rob, I have watched it."

"Rosie, take your ear from the door," Rob said with George and Alan doing their best not to laugh.

"Of course, the Met has been trying to work out where his stolen hoard of cash is for a great many years. My intentions are that DS Jones figures out where that cash is that should give him a promotion in the Met. I would have him parked up, hopefully, in a police car in Manor Road on the pavement with his blue light flashing by the wooded area giving you two the cover to go about what you have to do without any risk."

It was George that spoke first, "If he agrees, I think it would work."

Alan then said, "I am in the agreement seeing no one would be able to pass him into the wooded area with the law there."

"Mind you, DS Jones will be pissed with me since I have lost count in how many times he's asked did I know that George Almedia is back in the UK," Rob said hearing the front doorbell going off.

They all could hear Rosie shuffling up her hallway and opening her door, "Hello, darling, I guess you're looking for lover boy. You better come in, darling, he's in my sitting room with Billy and his uncle along with the big African in a private meeting."

Rosie shuffled back to her kitchen, pottering about, singing, and leaving Grace to come into where Rob was with George and Alan. "You have not finished all your biscuits," she said taking a digestive. Then asked, "Where and who is Billy?"

It was George that pointed to the casket. "Shit," she said now knowing what her late husband's name was. "Rob, I and many others were looking over the balcony where George beat the life out of those two. It's a wonder why no bugger called the police to see what was going on."

"Rob, this came to you around 2 pm by a courier company. Your mother held on to it, and when she saw we were back, she thought you might be with me. Tonight, she gave me this letter when I got home for my dinner while leaving you downstairs waiting for your uncle and George to arrive," Grace said. Rob opened the A4 white envelope and pulled out a handwritten letter.

"Read it out, Rob," Grace asked sounding very curious why a special delivery by a courier company.

"Hello, Rob.

You, of all people, should have known that we have CCTV outside the Daily Mirror offices. Please don't be alarmed; we at the Mirror and the Daily Mail will at NO time mention that it was you that provided our tabloids with one of the biggest scoops we have had for a while. Thank you!"

Rob tipped out on Rosie's table a voucher that said 'Thomas Cook Voucher.' He handed it to Grace, who flipped it open. "Wow, Rob, we have a £2000 holiday voucher."

"Grace, if you're in agreement, I would like to give it to Rosie?" Grace never answered; she just gave him a hug.

"Rosie," Rob called out. She was still singing the 'Hills Are Alive with The Sound of Music.'

"I knew, at some stage, you were going to be asking my advice; what do you want to know, lover boy?"

"Why we never asked you to our meeting was because we were not sure we would be able to do what we wanted to. Give it to her, Grace." Before she could open the voucher, Rob said, "And don't ask me to take you to the airport; you're a bloody pain in the arse when you have to travel."

"My God, Rob, it's a large voucher. Can Pauline, my friend, join me when we decide where to go?"

"Of course, darling," George butted in.

"Miss Rosie, when you choose where you would like to go and it cost more than £2000, you're to inform Rob and I will make up whatever the extra is," George said going around the table to give her a hug.

"Listen, Rosie, I believe that £2000 will cover two flights to Kilimanjaro, and you both can stop with Yvonne and me in our bungalow on the foothills of Mount Kilimanjaro," Alan said, also getting up to kiss her on the cheek.

"Whilst you're in Kilimanjaro, you should fly to Zanzibar and spend a little time on the Spice Island, and, of course, I will pay everything for such a charming lady," George said with him giving her a kiss followed with a further hug.

"Thank you so much. You're all so kind. Can you let yourself out? I must go and wake Pauline up and give her the good news," Rosie said leaving them, and they could hear her shuffling at speed down her hallway, perhaps to get her keys.

They were all about to leave when Rosie put her head inside her sitting room and said, "Rob, George and your uncle are right seeing handing Simon Davis documents to the press was the right thing to do for all of us, well-done lover boy," and she was out of her front door. Within seconds, they could hear her knocking the life out of Pauline Shaw's door knocker.

With George and Alan both laughing, it was Rob who said, "Let's all hope that's all what she heard."

Grace gave Rob a dig in his side and said, "Whatever she might have heard, it won't go any further than her flat."

"Rob, she's a wise old lady," Alan said putting his jacket on with George doing likewise and taking his car keys out of his jacket.

Leaving Rosie's flat and walking towards the entrance to the block. "Grace, contact my brother and sister-in-law and tell them that on Wednesday evening, we are all going on a jolly night out at Honour Oak Cemetery."

Grace was hoping that he was joking and said, "That's not bloody funny."

Rob smiled at her, "I agree it's not funny, but that's where we are all going."

Chapter 65
Good Luck, I Will See Myself Out

Midnight at 11 Downing Street with the Chancellor mobile ringing on his bedside table. "Graham, you going to get that?" Dawn, his wife, said turning over and putting her pillow over her head. In the dark, Graham Johnson was picking up his phone, and the moment he saw the callers ID, he jumped out of bed and walked into his wife's walk-in-wardrobe.

"Freddie, it's midnight; what's so urgent?" There he stood amongst his wife's clothes while listening to why he called. "Are you at the gate of Downing? Stay there, be with you in a few minutes," and then ended the call.

Back in their bedroom, he had to put the light on and was looking for a pair of jeans at the bottom of his wardrobe. Leaving his pyjamas' top on, he slipped on a pair of trainers and took his bodywarmer that was hanging behind the door. "Graham, what the bloody hell is going on?" Dawn said from under her pillow that the Chancellor could hardly understand what she was saying.

"Explain later, go back to sleep," Graham said turning off the light.

"If only," his wife grunted coming up for air.

He did the short walk to the gate where he could see Freddie Andrews pacing up and down the pavement. "Graham, I rushed out and forgot my clearance pass for all areas within government," Freddie said.

"Arnold, let him in. I will vouch for him he's from the Special Branch," Graham ordered and walked into the small security hut at the gates and signed him in and jumped in his Audi for the short journey to 11 Downing Street's back entrance and parked up.

Graham noticed from the back; the PM had his office light on. "Follow me, Freddie," he said as they walked through the side gate of number 11 and then walked through the side gate of number 10.

"There's no rest for us in government," Graham said as they both walked in the back door of number 10.

"You both might have a long rest if what I have been informed is true," Freddie Andrews said whilst Graham knocked on the door of the PM's office and getting no response, he knocked again a bit louder. There was still no answer. Graham opened the door to see Simon Davis dead to the world in his suit on his sofa. With a gentle cough from Graham, it managed to wake up the PM.

"Hell, Graham, what's going on?" Graham sat on the corner of the sofa as the PM swung his legs off it.

“Simon, you need to listen to what Freddie Andrews has to say,” Graham said watching Freddie sit on the side of the PM’s desk.

“Mr Davis, you set Special Branch the task to see if young Rob Hat had taken your red parliamentary case from the train after the rail crash. We then checked to find out if it was Hat’s uncle had sent you a few contents of your case from Zanzibar. Sorry PM none of this we could prove.” Freddie looked at the PM and Graham to see their reaction. “Now, with no involvement from our office, your case turned up at your parent’s home in York, and it was your chancellor who called us off the case, excuse the pun.” Simon appeared to look uncomfortable fidgeting on the sofa.

“Mr Chancellor and you, Mr Prime Minister, have not been totally honest with me. It was not the red case you wanted it could have been the remaining contents you needed to find that you could have feared these contents could go public.” There was no response to what the officer for the Special had said.

“Mr Davis, it’s none of my business what you are looking for, but I have come to warn you both that Fleet Street is buzzing. My contact told me only an hour ago that the buzz in Fleet Street concerns two high profile members of the Peoples Unite Party were heavily involved. Out of fear for his position, he refused to say what this involvement was.”

“Mr Andrews, I truly thank you for keeping my chancellor and my office informed,” the PM said and got up from the sofa. He straightened his attire and walked over to shake the hand of Freddie Andrews.

“Good luck, I will see myself out,” Freddie Andrews said knowing something in the very near future was likely to have a foul smell that was going to hit the fan.

Chapter 66
Get Me Out of Here

Whilst Simon Davis, the Prime Minister, along with Graham Johnson, the chancellor, was coming to terms that their days of living at 10 and 11 Downing Street could be short-lived.

Back in Bracknell, Trevor Charles Baines was getting to understand just what stir crazy was like. He looked at his watch seeing it was 2 am knowing he had been in this cellar now for around 36 hours. He looked on the shelf and counted six bottles of empty wine bottles without their necks. Normally that amount of alcohol he would have been pissed with his head going round like a merry-go-round, but that was not the case. Although he wished he was stoned living in a cellar with no more 12 foot by 8 foot.

There was no sound of cars, even a person's voice would help him from going fucking insane. Strange as it might be seen, he was beginning to enjoy the sound of the broken glass under his feet from the necks of the wine bottles.

He was even toying with the idea of talking to himself, but there was going to be negative; he would find it hard to think of what to say.

Knowing he should not be heard, however, if a person had been passing by earlier, they would have heard him scream out: "I am a fucking very rich, assumed dead and a professional criminal. So, get me out of here!"

Of course, Trevor Charles Baines never knew that he was going to be in this cellar for longer than he was led to believe. He also never knew he would not be seeing his son or his wife for a while. As for him seeing his stolen fortune, he would have a far better chance of him picking six lucky numbers for this coming Saturday's Lottery.

Chapter 67
A Heart of Gold

Seeing the workload for them at Premier was heavy with so many cars to clean plus a 10 am wedding booked for the two Rolls, they arranged to leave Saints House at 7 am after Alan and George had left Rosie's flat for their hotel, the Castle Palace.

Of course, Grace and Rob knew it was also to pick up the Daily Mirror and the Daily Mail to see what's been printed about the PM's attempt to hoodwink the UK's population.

With his mother and father still sleeping, he decided to text DS Jones and wrote:

"Good morning, John.

We hope to be at Premier by 8 am; we do need to speak to you ASAP.

At the gate, enter the code of 1904 and then PLEASE forget that number, come in and park up in our car park.

Rob."

With Grace sitting on the wall opposite their garage with two bowls of cornflakes beside her, she was waiting for Rob to appear out of Saints House. "What you turned over a new leaf then?" she asked jumping off the wall seeing Rob jogging out of Saints House to join her at the wall to have his breakfast.

"Meaning what?" Grace never responded seeing she knew that he knew he was by and large always late.

Driving out of the Kings Estate round the Elephant & Castle and headed to Westminster Bridge, Rob's mobile went off. "Grace, get that for me."

She took his mobile off the dashboard. "It's a text from DS Jones."

"What's he saying, love?"

"I will see you then. The BBC1 News, news flash Peoples Unite Party to be scrutinised by Scotland Yard, more to follow. DS."

"See you when and where Rob?"

"I did text him earlier asking to meet us at Premier. We need to make certain that DS Jones can help us on Wednesday." Grace was also hoping that he will look after their backs while George and Alan go digging for what might be a body.

"Rob, I enjoyed last night seeing Rosie so excited about going to your uncle and aunt's bungalow in Machame. I say this about our friend George Almedia yes, he's a hard man and you wouldn't want to upset him but the guy's got a heart of gold. Did you see how quick he was to cover Rosie and Pauline's cost for their trip over to the Spice Island?" Rob just nodded because he knew first hand just how tough and generous his friend was.

"Grace, deep down he's a real softy. Look at all the lovely gifts he brought from Tanzania for baby Grace's christening." It was now Grace's turn to do the nodding.

Chapter 69
Now for the Icing on the Cake

At 8:10, they were at the gate of Premier Supreme Car Hire. Rob pressed in the code 1904 and entered where they could see DS Jones waiting outside their arch. Jenny, their line manager, came out from her office with the keys to the arch. Rob was thinking he was in for a rollicking for giving out the company's gate code. "Morning, Jenny. You're in really early seeing you're normally here at 9 am," Rob said.

"Just as well seeing I pulled up to the gate the same time as Sergeant Jones who's been here before. He said he needed to speak with you. So, I let him in and, as you can see, he's waiting by your arch for you," Jenny said with Rob thinking that was lucky because he knew he is not allowed to give out the code for the gate.

"Thanks for coming in early, Rob. As you have to get the two Rolls ready by 10 am plus I believe you have a further twenty cars to clean from the night shift drivers who will be back at 5 pm," Jenny said handing Grace the arch keys and headed back to her office with Grace going over to the arch with the keys whilst Rob went into the driver's arch to pick all the car keys from the Drivers Key Peg where Premier drivers leave them. At other times they leave them with Jenny but seeing she came out with only the keys to the arch.

"Good morning, John. I'll do you a tea in a minute. Grace, if I pull the two Rolls out, can you please start to clean them for me?"

"Wow, this is now the second time you used my Christian name," DS Jones said smiling and knowing it didn't come naturally to young Rob.

Grace went into their cabin and put the kettle whilst waiting for Rob to get the motors out for her to make a start. A few minutes later, Rob made the tea and took a cup out in the arch for Grace who would have to turn the hose off to drink it. "Rob, please put it on the side for me."

DS Jones and Rob were sitting in the cabin facing each other. "I have yet to get the papers, hopefully, I will shoot out later and pick them up," Rob was saying stirring his tea and then handed the teaspoon to the Sergeant.

"As I said in my text, there was a news flash on the BBC News where they said the Peoples Unite Party are facing being scrutinised for their actions by Scotland Yard, more to follow later," DS Jones said tossing the teaspoon in the sink. "Okay, young man, what so important in getting me here?"

"I guess you would have heard this when you were a kid? Are you sitting comfortably if so, I will begin?"

"Yes, Rob, even though this wooden bench is hard on the arse."

"I was going to ask you the other evening, but Denzel Washington stopped me. What I am about to tell you, you should gain a benefit from within the Met," Rob said looking at DS Jones who was looking confused to where this meeting was going.

DS Jones said, "Okay, get it off your chest, no doubt you're going to be asking for my assistance?"

"You were at the funeral of Trevor Charles Baines?"

"So, what's new then?"

"I was in Tanzania at my uncle's place in Machame after that funeral for Baines. The purpose of our visit was for Grace to see baby Grace.

"I helped my uncle out who had a job for Kibo Safari Company but he and my aunty, Yvonne, were due to go to Zanzibar, so I took it on for him. The job was to pick up a Peter Goodman from the Tato Hotel in Machame and take him to the Machame Gate where he would start his climb to the Roof of Africa. We had to meet up with a further tour operator at the gate who also had climbers. Before I left the gate, I was asked to take a photo of the entire group." Rob took his mobile out and went to photos and found the photo he was looking for and handed his mobile to DS Jones for him to see.

"Nice Rob, what the hell is special about this photograph," he asked.

"Look at the guy second from the end on your left as you're viewing it."

He was looking closer, "Yes, a very attractive young lady at the end."

"Are you blind, John? Look at the guy's right arm around her shoulder, now look at his hand." It took DS Jones a further 30 seconds for the penny to drop.

He looked up from the photograph, "Fucking hell, TCB!" and picked up his tea and downed it in one gulp forgetting his tea was very hot and started to kind of choke and spat some back into his cup.

"For a great many years, the Met has been trying to find out where Baines stolen millions are hidden. Well of late, the case has gone into the long grass seeing we have been hitting brick walls at every turn."

"Now don't you go shouting at me, but George Almedia has been here trying to see what's in the Baines's coffin," Rob said seeing DS Jones was not a happy bunny, knowing Rob had not said he knew he was here when he had asked him.

"I am not shouting at you, Rob. So, you believe Baines's money is in the arsehole's coffin?"

"George followed Charlie Baines, his son, with his mother, Glenda Baines, a couple of times to Honour Oak Cemetery. On each of these occasions, Charlie had gone into the wooded area behind Baines's grave and came back each time with a holdall looking stretch out to its maximum."

DS Jones came around the table and put his arm around Rob's shoulder. "You are a clever sod; you should have been a copper."

"My uncle is over here to help with this job, and they both have insisted I should not be seen designating a grave seeing if I am wrong and there is a body then my uncle and George feel what credibility I have will be lost overnight for raiding a grave."

"Right, John, we are hoping to gain the million-pound reward that the banks are offering for the safe return of their stolen cash."

"Fair enough, and I agree with them that you should not be seen robbing a grave, but my question is why are you telling me this and what the hell do you want from me?"

"I take it, John, you have a blue light that you can place on the top of your car?" DS Jones was getting more curious by the minute.

"I do and, in all my years in the force, I have never had to use it," he said moving his cup aside and leaning over the table looking directly into Rob's eyes, "Okay and what's coming next?"

"I take it your office has been a little concerned seeing George back in the UK?" DS Jones never answered; he just nodded. "If I am right that his coffin is filled with cash, then George Almedia will be claiming the reward. Now you have been checking to what George was up to, and you have been following him."

DS Jones put his hand to stop him. "As it so happens both DI Reynolds and I have been told to keep an eye out to see what he's doing in the UK."

Rob thought this couldn't be better. "Okay, John, 7 pm Wednesday night you follow George and my uncle to Manor Road, that runs alongside Honour Oak Cemetery, where they will park up and enter into the wooded area. You park behind George's Honda with your blue light on top of your car flashing, this alone will stop anyone going into the wooded area."

"That makes sense," he said knowing his blue light to be the perfect deterrent.

"Okay, so George hopefully finds Trevor Charles Baines buried treasure and will in due course get the reward. You will gain promotion for being a shrewd police officer," Rob said and felt that DS Jones would go along with this scenario.

DS Jones got up and put the kettle on again. Whilst waiting for it to boil he asked, "What about Trevor Charles Baines, we must get him and put the git away?"

Rob picked up the cups and put a teabag in each cup. "Four sugars, John?" he asked him.

"I told you earlier, I am on a diet. Mind you, that last cup what I drank of it tasted good with sugar in it."

With their teas now on the table. "Now for the icing on the cake," Rob said.

"I love cake, go on then tell me."

"We have Baines. He's hiding in my uncle's cellar in Bracknell and the guy's going nowhere fast. On the Wednesday night, after we prove where his cash is, you can pick him up but, for obvious reasons, not at my uncle's house. George will tell you more later how this will work."

John drinking his tea and put his cup down. "How the hell did you get one of the UK's most wanted and assumed dead criminal into a cellar in Bracknell?"

"Leave it, for now, John. I am sure George and my uncle will tell you in due course," Rob said putting on his wet gear and just then noticed Grace had left her wet gear hanging behind the door with her wellington boots under the bench where DS Jones was sitting that he took out to the arch.

"Rob, you need to tell them I will be at Saint's House on Wednesday at 6:30 pm to follow them."

Chapter 70
Gone with the Wind

Of course, DS Jones knew there was a BBC1 news flash saying the Peoples Unite Party were being scrutinised, and, in turn, he had informed Rob. If Rob had turned his TV on, he would have also known and, if he had stayed at home until 8 am, he would have also seen a police car arrive at 10 Downing Street from Scotland Yard. An hour later after its arrival, the PM and the Chancellor were seen leaving Downing Street and following the police car.

It was in the early hours of Tuesday when Freddie Andrews from the Special had marked their card that the press was buzzing in Fleet Street. Having left Simon Davis and Graham Johnson to ponder over what faces them should his two manifests go live.

"Simon, I bloody warned you! Having those two manifests together in your case was dangerous more so seeing you highlight that what we go to the Nation with is a lie. Now you have had all your ministers in the UK selling those lies and even many tabloids have commended the Parties Road we are travelling to stay in Downing." Simon Davis was marching up and down his office listening to him in his crumpled-up suit from his hours sleeping on his sofa.

"Hell, Graham, we would have very little chance of winning the next election tomorrow if we had publicised what our intentions were." Graham sat there in his pyjama top while shaking his head in disbelieve to what his friend the PM was saying.

"Graham, when we put this course of action together, you were in full agreement with it."

Still shaking his head, "Yes true, but I never knew you would be so stupid to carry those two manifests around with you. To seal it, you bloody signed them!"

Just then, there was a knock on his office door. "What is it?" the PM shouted out.

With the door opening, "Excuse me, Sir, but we have a DCI Miss Sandra Willis wanting to speak with you, and your chancellor. Is he available?" the nervous security officer said.

"You need to show her to the library for me."

"Shall do, Sir," he said leaving the PM's office a damn sight quicker than he entered.

Graham left his office and went out the back door to get changed while dreading this DCI's visit was not related to those manifests that's brought Scotland Yard to number 10 Downing.

The PM dashed up the stairs to brush up and get out of his crumpled-up suit. Whilst in their bedroom getting changed, Judith, his wife, came out of their on-suite. “Simon, you working all night won’t see you making old bones,” the PM’s wife said taking her hairdryer out from a draw on her dressing table.

“Sorry, dear, can’t stop. I have an officer from Scotland Yard down in the library,” he said putting on his suit jacket and kissed his wife on the cheek and left their bedroom.

On his way down the stairs, he heard his youngest son calling out, “Daddy, there’s a police car outside our house.” The PM decided not to answer but carried on down the stairs and went straight into their library. He noticed Graham was already in there making small talk with the very young attractive DCI dressed in torn jeans and white tea shirt with the logo on the front that read, ‘I Love New York.’

The DCI Sandra Willis handed them both her card that neither of them looked at but put them in their jackets. “Please don’t think me being rude, but you seem extremely young to have such a high rank in the Metropolitan Police at Scotland Yard,” the PM said looking at his chancellor who was now sitting down on their very large red chesterfield sofa at the far end of the library with the two matching armchairs opposite.

“Yes, Sir, I agree young, but I am extremely good at what I do,” the DCI said walking towards the armchairs. She sat down beckoning the PM to join them in what could be the reading area of the PM’s very large library.

With all three of them seated, the PM was looking very uncomfortable and his chancellor was wondering when this young inspector was going to say why she was here. “Prime Minister, it’s come to the attention of the CIP that the media are wanting to go live with a piece that is detrimental to the Peoples Unit Party, and you only have to thank Colonel Jameson that he’s gained you a 24-hour delay on whatever this story is looking to go into print with. The Colonel is requesting that you and your chancellor attend a meeting at Scotland Yard to give you the opportunity to defend any accusations against the Peoples Unite Party,” DCI Willis was saying while getting up and starting to browse through the vast array of books.

“Graham, can you arrange that your driver takes us to Scotland Yard, and it would be ideal if we follow the DCI?” the PM said. The Chancellor was immediately on his mobile making the necessary arrangements.

“Ten minutes, Prime Minister.”

“Can I offer you tea, Inspector, whilst we wait?” The Inspector never answered the PM; she just nodded reading the book, ‘Gone with the Wind.’ Graham thought that was an appropriate choice of books to browse through.

Simon Davis left the library and, with the door open, they could hear him asking what could have been a maid. “Tea for three in the library.”

The DCI turned away from the book and said to the Chancellor, “Please or thank you cost nothing,” and then returned to the book.

The three of them leaving 10 Downing Street with a smartly dressed guy standing by the police car. “Everything okay, Governor?” her DS said opening the car door for her.

Once in the car, she said, “Yes, it went well. He won’t ever be getting my vote.”

Chapter 71
Yako Sod Wajanja

Leaving Premier at 6 pm. "I don't understand Rob why the Mirror or the Mail had not made any mention of those two manifests," Grace said looking through the two papers again, then glancing at Rob with a puzzled look on her face.

"Something must have happened since DS Jones said there was a BBC1 news flash regarding the Peoples Unite Party being scrutinised. My question is who the hell is doing the scrutinising? Perhaps there might be more this evening on the news?" Rob said while thinking the general election is going to be taking place tomorrow. This made him wonder how they can stop this election at such short notice.

If Grace and Rob were worried but not half as worried as Glenda and Charlie Baines seeing Trevor Charles Baines who was due in at Heathrow early Sunday morning and was then making his way to Wokingham Station where Charlie was meant to meet him.

It was now Tuesday evening, and to say Charlie and Glenda were worried would be an understatement. "Charlie, you knocking back the whiskey won't get you any closer to finding out where the fuck your father is," Glenda said leaving the lounge and once again slamming the door. Then, she immediately came back again into the lounge. "Charlie, what doesn't make sense is if he was due to come into Heathrow, why then travel to meet you at Wokingham Station?" Charlie listened to his mother, and yes, she was making sense in what she was saying.

Charlie took out his mobile and read his message again from his father. "Mother, he was definitely coming into Heathrow. Perhaps he's confused? Or perhaps he's being scared of being recognised and decided not to take a direct route to Wokingham. Other than that, I don't have a bloody clue as to why." It still didn't make any sense to Glenda, who left their lounge again. Instead of slamming the door, she left it wide open and went into the kitchen.

Of course, the Baines were not aware that George Almedia, who they never knew at this stage, had taken the sim card out of Trevor's mobile whilst he had been taking a leak on Sunday morning at Heathrow.

Putting the Baines sim card in his own mobile, he had to smile noticing all his contacts were saved to the card and not to his phone. To him, it made sense to call Charlie Baines just in case they decide to go to the police and come clean that Trevor was still alive. He or his wife might have feared his father had been kidnapped, which he had been, or worse killed. "Hold that thought, George, that's not a bad idea, killed?" he said in a whisper.

He called Charlie Baines, which Charlie answered on its first ring. "Where the fuck is you?" George never responded. "Hello, Dad, where do you want me to pick you up from?" Charlie shouted down his mobile so much, so George had to take his phone away from his ear.

"Trevor is honestly very safe and, in a perfect world, he will be with you later this week," George said now knowing what he had to make certain Charlie or his mother never went to the police or never showed their faces on Wednesday night at Honour Oak Cemetery.

"I don't know who the fuck you are and what you want," Charlie said, still shouting down the phone.

"Mr Baines, on Wednesday night around 10 pm, I will be at your house in Sandhurst, and you will know who I am, and I promise to tell you what I want," George said and then ended the call.

George Almedia, the big African normally dressed so smartly in his designer clothes and Saville Row suits, sat back on his bed in his underpants' and T-shirt and said out loud:

"Yako sod wajanja." (you're a clever sod)

Chapter 72
Her Double Bed

Grace and Rob got back to Saints House at 6:50 pm and ran up the four flights, and dashed along the landing to Grace's flat. "Why are we rushing, Rob?" she asked trying to get her breath back.

"Channel 4 News at 7 pm."

Grace started to giggle putting the key in the lock. "I thought we were rushing so you could get me into bed," she said with Rob seeing the lounge was empty and switched on the TV.

"If your mum agrees, then we will go to bed but not until after the news," Rob said that go him a dead leg.

"Here we go Grace," seeing the news programme had just started.

"Good evening. Earlier this morning, a police car was parked up at 10 Downing with a very attractive young detective in torn jeans and a white T with the logo that could be reading 'I Love New York,' showing the policeman on duty outside number 10 what could be her warrant card.

"It was five minutes later the door opened, and she was invited in," the Newscaster said.

"DS Jones, of course, never knew this or decided not to tell us," Rob said with Grace standing in the doorway with her eyes glued to the TV.

"What's going on, Grace?" her mother asked coming out of the bathroom, and Grace could hear her young sisters playing in the bath.

"It's okay, Mum. Just a news programme we wanted to watch."

"At 9 am, a BMW arrived at 10 Downing Street with the young Detective coming out and followed by the PM and Chancellor. The police car pulled away with the BMW following with the PM and Chancellor in the back."

"Breaking news at 6 pm this evening that all media were informed that the 2017 general election will be delayed until further notice. There has not been any further information as to why the Metropolitan Police were at 10 Downing Street."

"Other news…"

"Mother, did you know the general election has been delayed until further notice?" Grace shouted out to her mother, who was back in the bathroom laughing with Jane and Janet.

"No, darling. That will save me having to vote on Wednesday."

"Yes, it is Mum."

"Janet, don't put that towel in the water," her mother shouted back from the bathroom.

"I guess the PM and Chancellor were being brought in to possibly Scotland Yard to answer questions regarding what the Mirror and Mail were going to go live with their scoops," Rob said and then added: "Shall I ask your mother if we can use her double bed."

Grace walked away from the doorway and, once again, he got a clip round the ear this time. "Don't you dare," she said giving Rob daggers because he had started to laugh.

Jean had managed to dry off her daughters, and they were now busy in their bedroom playing games and fighting along with arguing between games.

"Rob, would you like to stop for dinner?" Rob looked at Grace, who had become the Churchill's nodding dog.

"Depends on what it is, Jean," that got Rob a further dig from Grace.

"Just joking, Jean, you know me; I am not a fussy eater," he said putting his arm around Grace and kissing her on the cheek.

"Don't think you're going to be invited to stay the night, yes I heard you from the bathroom about using my double bed. As you said, Rob, I am just joking, but I am serious when I say you can't use my bed," Jean Long said laughing as she went out into the kitchen.

"I always said you have a big mouth; you must learn to whisper," Grace said with both of them joining her mother in the kitchen and were now laughing themselves.

Chapter 73
Truth or Tell Her Porkies

"Charlie, your dinner is on the table," Glenda called out from the kitchen. "It's your favourite sausage and mash."

Glenda and Charlie were now sitting on stools at their breakfast bar. "Who was that you were talking with on your mobile?" Glenda asked. Charlie shoved half a sausage in his mouth giving him time to think should he tell her the truth or tell her porkies.

"I don't know who it was, but he was using my old man's mobile, and he was telling me your husband Trevor is safe and could be back with us in a few days," Charlie said taking a beer out of the fridge. "You want one?" His mother just shook her head.

"Charlie, what I want is your bloody father back. It seems the silly bugger has gone and got himself kidnapped," she said taking a swig from her son's can of lager.

"Did they say what he wanted?" she said going to get hold of his can of lager that Charlie had put out of her reach on the quick.

"No, the guy said that around 10 pm tomorrow, we will know who he is and what he wants," her son said. Glenda sat there trying to figure how this person knew that Trevor was still alive. Surely, he couldn't have recognised him seeing she had a problem to recognise him from his passport for Peter Goodman.

"Charlie, I told him he should have had that TCB tattoo removed from the back of his right hand. It seems some bastard seen it and looked at the possibility of gaining a few quid," Glenda said stretching across her son and grabbed his can of lager.

"We will know more on Wednesday night, but I am not going into my father's safe until I am given proof of life," Charlie said going to the fridge and taking out a further two cans of Lagers.

Part 4

Chapter 74
Shame on You

Whilst the nation is now fully aware that the 2017 general election has now been delayed. However, only a few knew why and they consisted of Colonel Jameson, who ran the CIP at Scotland Yard. Then we have the Lawson brothers, who are the editors for the Daily Mirror and the Daily Mail. These two tabloids who are currently waiting to be given the clearance from the CIP's after Colonel Jameson is 100% certain that the PM and the Chancellor were trying to HOODWINK the entire population to gain the keys to number 10 Downing Street once again.

It was at 9:30 on the 4 of May 2015, on the eve of the would-be general election, the DCI Sandra Willis's driver drove into the underground car park for Scotland Yard. A few yards back, the BMW carrying Simon Davis and Graham Johnson's driver parked next to the police car.

Leaving the DCI's sergeant and the Chancellor's driver by their motors, they walked to the far corner of the garage where the lift was situated. With none of them talking, the DCI pressed for the tenth floor.

Once out of the lift, they followed DCI as they walked along the very large corridor passing a great many offices with their brass plaques letting people know who was behind their doors. Getting to the far corner was the door they needed to enter that had two brass plaques: the top one said Director CIP and below it said Colonel T Jameson.

DCI Sandra Willis knocked on the door when an elderly lady dressed in a very smart grey suit opened the door. "Good morning, Mrs Jacobs. I have brought the PM and his chancellor to speak with the Colonel," the DCI informed the Colonel's private secretary.

"Please come in, Sandra. My boss was expecting you but not sure when," she said and then added: "Good morning, gentlemen. Can I get you, gentlemen, tea or coffee?"

Simon looked at Graham, who was shaking his head. "No, we are fine, thank you."

"The Colonel is currently in a meeting with his officers that should be concluded very shortly," she said looking at her watch and at the large wall clock on the wall behind her large desk that had five or more telephones on it along with her PC and laptop that were both open. Picking up her telephone, she made a call. "Sir, your two guests are in my office," then she hung up. The PM took a seat in her large office with an enormous glass coffee table with an array of magazines. Graham Johnson took a seat next to the PM after picking up a motoring magazine.

It was around ten minutes later, some ten police officers walked out of the Colonel's office, all dressed in their smart uniforms. Other than the last officer, they totally ignored the PM and the Chancellor when he looked over at Sandra Willis. "Good morning, Detective. I see you have had a good nick here," he said looking at the PM and the Chancellor. "Hi, Mr Prime Minister, you be okay in there? He's in a good mood for a change," the officer said pointing to the Colonel's door. "Bye, Mrs Jacobs, I was told for you to send in the PM and the Chancellor," he said giving Sandra Willis a sly wink and left the Colonel's private secretary's office.

Mrs Jacobs came from behind her desk and beckoned the PM and Chancellor along with the DCI to follow her; she then knocked on the Colonel's office door and entered. The PM was half expecting his office was going to be lush, but it was quite the opposite. Just a basic desk with two chairs facing his desk already in place for the PM and Chancellor. There was a flip chart at the far end with a dozen or so chairs facing it. In the far corner, there was a water cooler. There was not a piece of carpet to be seen, just a wooden floor that could do with being varnished. The PM noticed all this whilst the Colonel was on the telephone, who eventually waved them in. "If you're trying to piss me off, you're doing a bloody good job," Colonel Jameson said and then slammed his telephone down on his desk that bounced off his desk and hit the floor clattering. Then, it started to spin round on the wooden floor. His private secretary went to pick it up. "Leave it, Martha. Besides, I don't wish to be disturbed, and I most definitely do not wish to take any calls," he said seeing he had not put a chair out for others. "Sandra, pull up one of the chairs by the flip chart and sit on the left of me," he said sounding much calmer.

Colonel Jameson was defiantly old school with his spotted bowtie and tweed waistcoat; he must have been all of 60 totally bald.

"Good morning, Prime Minister and, of course, you Chancellor, please excuse my outburst earlier," he said looking at his telephone on the floor that the DCI picked up and placed it on his desk before settling her chair some five feet from his desk.

"Let's me conduct this meeting. You may or may not know that Freddie Andrews from the Special Branch requested my assistance in locating your red parliamentary case, hence, I used DI Judy Reynolds and her DS Jones from the Reading Police Station to look into your problem. The reason I used them was simply that they both knew Rob Hat who, Freddie informed me, you suspected him of having your case, but your suspicion was unfounded, so you, Simon Davis, and you, Graham Johnson, had barked up the wrong tree."

So far, the PM and Chancellor had not said a single word until now when the PM said, "Regarding your office assisting me to gain my parliamentary red leather case back, I must say thank you."

The Chancellor noticed the small microphone on his desk by his PC. “Colonel, is this meeting being recorded?” Jameson sat there and then pulled out his tape recorder and placed it on his desk.

“Yes, of course. Why is that a problem?”

The Chancellor never replied, and it was the PM that said: “Colonel, I expected our meeting to be recorded.” He said looking at his friend Graham who was looking uncomfortable for asking that question that finished up embarrassing himself.

“The word ‘expected’ you use makes me concern seeing I expected you would have brought a government solicitor along to this meeting?”

The PM leaned forward putting his two hands on the Colonel’s desk and looked straight into the eyes of the man that managed the CIP and told him, “I honestly could not see a valid reason why I should need a solicitor for this meeting.”

Mr Jameson then replied, “Really, Prime Minister?”

“I believe, Mr Davis, that whoever had your red case and its contents, Freddie Andrews from the SB informed you that they wanted a very large reward and that they would use this reward to help put right the wrongs the Peoples Unite Party were planning. A further option he or they offered for you to get your case back was for you, the PM, to resign?” Both the PM and the Chancellor were shaking their heads. “Freddie Andrews also told you that failing any of those options, they or he would hand certain papers to the media,” the Colonel said leaning across his desk and, like the PM, looked directly into the eyes of Simon Davis.

“I can confirm to both of you that the contents of your case were handed to the Daily Mirror and the Daily Mail that they obtained via a Security Box at Waterloo Station. Because of the nature of those contents, Paul Lawson, the chief editor, needed to be certain your documents were kosher before going to print. To this end, I sent DCI Sandra Willis to investigate Monday afternoon.

“Officer Willis, would you kindly highlight to these two gentlemen from the Peoples Unite Party what your investigation uncovered whilst you interviewed Paul Lawson, the editor,” the Colonel said opening a draw on his desk but never closed it.

The DCI stood up while straightening her ‘I love New York’ T-Shirt and taking her notebook, which she was struggling to get out of her back pocket since her torn jeans were ridiculously tight. “Mr Prime Minister, the Colonel more or less has covered it.” Reading from her notebook, “When I asked the Editor, do you know who had left the documents at Waterloo Station? He said he had no idea. I then asked him, have you been asked that your paper needs to pay a fee for the information or did your brother Ben Lawson’s paper, the Daily Mail, had to pay for the confidential documents. He went on to say not a penny was paid but then said normally something of this nature we would have expected to pay for the privilege to have a scoop of this nature printed in our tabloids,” the DCI said. Looking at the Colonel, who was nodding his head in agreement with what she was saying. Then she turned her attention towards the PM who looked beaten.

"Then Mr Lawson said seeing what they had was a rarity on his desk, we would have been expected to pay. We had to make certain the papers we had were genuine; hence, he called in the CIP to check it out before going live. So, he then admitted losing a day in going live or risk facing a liable case if this was a hoax," the DCI said and giving up in trying to get her notebook back in her back pocket.

With the Colonel's draw on his desk still open, he lifted out an A3 jiffy bag and slid it across his desk towards the PM. "Mr Davis and you, Mr Johnson, the CIP is giving you the opportunity to prove that the contents in that A3 jiffy bag are a forgery or that you both knew nothing about the contents enclosed," the Colonel said sitting back his chair. The PM never answered and peeped inside the jiffy bag while shaking his head in disbelief that his legacy will be that the UK Prime Minister, Simon Davis, attempted to HOODWINK the UK's population.

"Gentlemen, I take it your silence speaks volumes?"

The Colonel picked up his telephone and called his receptionist, "Martha, please would you call Paul Lawson, the chief editor of the Daily Mirror, and inform him that Mirror and the Mail have their scoop, but I would appreciate it if they would send me a draft this afternoon."

The PM and his chancellor walked over to where the flip chart was and were out of reach to the ears of the Colonel and the DCI. "Simon, we are fucked simply because you wanted to see yourself as a statesman at any cost with no consideration to the people of the UK who you were willing to betray. Sorry to say this, Simon, but shame on you." Simon never responded to his friend, but he knew he was right.

Back at the Colonel's desk, "Excuse me, Colonel, can I ask what is in that large Jiffy bag?" the DCI asked.

"Thank you for your help regarding this matter. As for your question, when you read the Daily Mirror or the Daily Mail, you will know everything you need to know tomorrow," Mr Jameson said and walked over to where the PM was talking to his chancellor. The PM looked as though he was not far from crying.

"Gentlemen, perhaps now might not be the right time? But you need to be aware that in the not too far distant future, the chances are DCI Sandra Willis will be bringing you both in for questioning for attempting to deceive the people that would have voted you into government as their PM," the Colonel said walking back to his desk. Mrs Jacobs came inside his office and just nodded much as to say she did what was asked of her.

"Martha, would you be as kind as to see Simon Davis and Graham Johnson back to their car in our garage, and please pick me up a cup of coffee on your way back from our restaurant." Martha simply nodded her head once again.

With the PM hanging his head with the Chancellor walking a few steps behind him, they followed Mrs Jacobs down the long corridor to the lift.

Chapter 75
Treasure House

Tuesday afternoon George Almedia and Alan Hat were in the cemetery at Honour Oak, gaining their bearings to where Trevor Charles Baines grave was to where they should park in Manor Road. Plus, George agreed with Alan that he had not seen the location. "Why bring flowers then?" Alan asked.

"Bloody hell, mate, it is a graveyard," George was saying while, at the same time, taking the gravel path to the right with headstones on either side with many neglected that stood out from the few that were cared for. At the end of the path in the far corner on the right, George saw the small white painted wicker fencing that went around the three plots. The centre plot had flowers that were starting to wilt. There a black marble headstone that read:

Trevor Charles Baines 1950–2015. Rest in Peace, my Darling. Your Loving Wife.

"Over here, Alan," George said.

Alan went over and stepped over the small wicker fence and read what the headstone said. "I would find it extremely difficult to get sad when there's no body beneath." Alan then turned his attentions to the plots, one on either side of the Baines grave that had small white wooden crosses in the ground that clearly said 'reserved.'

With no one they could see visiting their loved ones in the very large cemetery, they walked into the wooded area. "What you looking for, George?" Alan asked seeing George was walking further into the shrubs.

"Found it, Alan," he said waving a handkerchief he had tied to a bush earlier. Alan walked over and stood beside George, who was once again tying his handkerchief back around the bush. "Alan, around twenty feet from here, Charlie Baines disappeared. One minute I could see him through the bushes, much to my regret, I looked down and saw I had trod in some dog's shit and I was wiping it off with some dried leaves and when I looked up, Charlie boy had vanished. I waited when all of a sudden, as though by magic, he appeared holding a holdall that looked full and walked back to his mother, who was, I guess, attending her husband's grave when, in fact, her husband is tucked away in your cellar in Berkshire who is very much alive, well he was when I left him Sunday."

"Okay, George, somewhere between your handkerchief and the grave, there is an entrance that will get us under the ground to the coffin."

George looked at his friend and said, "It does sound impossible, but I know what I saw."

"Alan, you need to make your way out in a straight line into Manor Road and wait for me. I will get my car from the car park and come and pick you up, so we will both know where we stop when we come back Wednesday evening."

Ten minutes later, Alan jumped into his Honda. "Now we know, George, where to park up," Alan said pointing to the block of flats opposite that said Treasure House on the side of the block.

"That's the perfect omen," George said with them both laughing.

On their drive back to the Castle Palace Hotel, "Your nephew will be pleased when he would, I guess by now, know that the general election has been delayed. Makes me wonder that those two manifests might have come to life."

Alan turned around and, on the back seat, he could see the bunch of flowers George had at Honour Oak. George noticed him looking in the back seat. "Yes, those flowers are for Yvonne, your wife."

"If you say so, George," Alan said knowing the big African could say things off the cuff.

"Alan, before we head back to Castle Palace Hotel, I am going to see if someone is okay."

Alan didn't need three guesses to know where they will be heading.

Chapter 76
Only the Lonely

With so much going on, the general election being delayed along with the PM and Chancellor following a police car, which could be heading to Scotland Yard. Then we have George Almedia and Rob Hat's uncle Alan hoping they can find a secret entrance into the Baines's Grave to hopefully gain a million-pound reward.

There is one person Trevor Charles Baines that does not have the foggiest idea that all this was going on and that some people were trying to get their hands on the cash he had grafted for and, in some cases, killed for.

Other than talking to himself since Sunday, as far as he knew, he could be the last man person alive in the UK.

He was treading on the glass from the broken necks of the wine bottles he had drunk, and he still loved the sound it made under his foot. Looking in the small wine rack on the far wall, he starts to count just how many bottles he had left to drink.

"Please would someone come for me, even a copper? I wouldn't mind just anybody," he called out, then he pulled over the empty carton that some of his food was in and tipped it over and put his pack cards on it. Then started to try again for what must have been his 60th time to get out with Clock Patience.

Then started to sing in a whisper, "Only the lonely knows the way I feel tonight."

Other than his son, he knew no one gave a shit about the stinking rich Trevor Charles Baines. All the others wanted was his fortune that was out of reach and out of sight.

Outside Alan's house in Bracknell, "Granted, it's your house, but please not a word," George said and opened the door and saw the chair he had put under the doorknob at the cellar door was still in place.

"Mr Goodman, I am sorry I have not brought the key with me for the cellar," George shouted out knowing full well he would be there. It took Trevor a few seconds to understand he had heard a voice that, to him, sounded a relief having been living in silence only his own voice to listen to.

"Get me out of here," he said with Alan hearing all the glass cracking as Baines came up the few steps to get close to the cellar door.

"Mr Goodman, Charlie Baines was let back home this morning. Glenda, the wife, was still having pressure applied since the law believes her husband could still be alive and well."

“I don’t give a shit if Trevor’s alive or dead now, you just get me out of here, and I will get lost,” the so-called Peter Goodman said behind the locked door.

“Charlie also told me an hour ago that his mother is likely to do a deal with the DI Officer Judy Reynolds,” George was telling him that Alan had to step into his own lounge for fear of laughing with George pulling the wool over Baines’s eyes. If he never knew the lies George was spurting out, he would himself have believed him.

“Wednesday evening, Charlie, your son, will be giving me a flight ticket for you to go back to Kilimanjaro. The moment I have it, I will be straight back and get you to possibly Heathrow.” There was only silence from behind the door, but the African could hear him breathing.

“Whoever you are that Charlie is paying you to protect me, you don’t want to fuck with me,” he said banging the cellar door.

“See you tomorrow. Besides, I have to get you out since the copper, who owns this place, has decided to come home early Thursday.”

They were back in his Honda, “So, now I am a copper with broken bottles in my cellar,” Alan said that George never replied to. He just drove with a huge smile on his face flashing his white teeth that stood out against his dark brown skin.

Before heading back to the Castle Palace Hotel, they stopped in Bracknell Town Centre and popped into Thomas Cook, where George bought a one-way flight ticket for a Peter Goodman to Kilimanjaro International Airport.

Chapter 77
Bombshell

"If we hadn't had been asked by Jenny to give her motor a clean, we might have got home for the 6 pm news," Rob said falling arse over tip getting his wellingtons off.

"Less haste, more speed," Grace said, already ready to go home, sitting on the bench doing her best not to laugh.

Thirty minutes later, they had only got as far as Marble Arch. Grace had wound down her window; she was stretching the top half of her body out to see what the newspaper stand was displaying to entice people to pick up the free Evening Standard. Rob noticed her antics and grabbed hold of one of her legs in case she fell out. She was back in their van with hair looking a total mess since they had got up a little speed driving down Park Lane. "I couldn't read all the heading on the paper stand but what I managed to read was, 'Breaking news Peoples Unite Party top officials could be responsible for the delay of the General Election,'" Grace said trying to straighten her hair with her fingers.

Rob slid his mobile across the dashboard. "Grace, text your mother and ask her to record the 6 pm BBC1 News for us."

At 6:45 pm, they drove into Saints House and parked in front of Grace's mum's garage. Locking up his side of the van, he was off and called out, "Lock your door," and was in their block and dashed up the four flights of stairs. Just getting to the fourth floor, he heard the lift open and watched Grace stepping out. "As I said earlier, darling, less haste, more speed. Even if you had beaten me to the fourth floor, you couldn't have got in," Grace said tossing him her door keys.

Walking down the landing with Grace in front, Rob was breathing heavily behind her. Grace heard him say, "That's not funny."

With them standing in their lounge, Grace noticed a note on their coffee. "What's it saying?" Rob asked.

"She's saying what?"

"Off out to visit a friend with your younger sisters in town. I have recorded the BBC News for you. Dare I ask why? Mum. Ps, your dinner is in the oven."

With Grace putting the kettle on, Rob put the TV on and went to recordings and opened up the recorded BBC1 News and then paused it and went out into the kitchen and put the milk and sugar in their cups.

Back in the lounge, "Press play, Rob."

"Good evening, George Harvey here. Welcome to the BBC1 extended News.

Early this morning on the eve of the General Election, the entire nation was totally confused without any explanation that the election was put on hold until further notice.

Earlier, the PM and the Chancellor were seen by the BBC following a police car that we believe to be heading for Scotland Yard. When we asked the Yard, they were non-committal that if those in charge of the Peoples Unite Party were brought into Scotland Yard." With the Newscaster looking directly into the camera, "We can now shortly go over to Downing Street where Prime Minister, Simon Davis, and his chancellor, Graham Johnson, will hopefully explain why at the last minute have they decided to delay the General Election?"

"I am guessing the PM wished he had not gone to the Southampton airport to promote the Peoples Unite Party for this election," Rob was saying getting up from the sofa and sat on the floor only a few feet from the television. Grace, not to be outdone, kicked over the soft pouffe next to Rob and sat next to him. "You're my hero," she said ruffling his hair.

"You won't say that if it comes to life that I was involved with the election being delayed."

Then George Harvey in the BBC1 studio said, "Here we go to Downing Street."

"Thank you, George," the onsite broadcaster said. "We are still waiting for the PM and his chancellor to come out from number 10," the BBC reporter said with the BBC camera focusing on the two portable podiums both in place fitted with their microphones. The camera then fanned around capturing the ITV and Sky cameras along with at least thirty reporters from the many tabloids eager to understand why this delay in the election.

Now with the camera firmly focused on the black door waiting for it to open. It was 6:45 pm when they both strolled out of number 10. Graham Johnson went to his left and stood behind his podium. There he stood looking somewhat nervous seeing the interest from the media. Looking to his right, where everyone could see Simon Davis giving the nod to his chancellor indicating that he should commence.

"Good evening, thank you. My task is to inform you that the General Election will not be going ahead tomorrow. There is a reason for this delay that my Prime Minister will endeavour to give you all.

"Please believe me, I do this with a heavy heart from the immediate effect because of reasons outside of my control. I will be resigning from the Peoples Unite Party."

"Why are you resigning, Chancellor?" the reporter from one of the National's called out that was totally ignored by the Chancellor.

"At this juncture, I feel I should let the PM answer any questions from you the people from the media." Graham Johnson said looking that he would have rather been anywhere else but here in Downing Street.

With the cameras and those from the press now all focussing their attentions to their left to hear not only why the delay but why the devastating bombshell that the Chancellor had just dropped. With the microphones all switched on, you could hear the journalist talking amongst themselves in dismay and all looking eager to know why the Chancellor was quitting parliament as of this evening.

"Thank you for turning up in numbers wanting to understand the reason why the General Election has been delayed," the Prime Minister said just as his chancellor, Graham Johnson, was fidgeting behind his podium while knowing this would be the last time that he steps out of 10 or 11 Downing Street to address the nation.

"Like my chancellor, my friend, said I want you all to believe that today, I do this with a heavy heart. The Peoples Unite Party is the only party that could put the great back in Britain. I have to put my hands up to overstepping my position as your Prime Minister. No doubt come tomorrow that would have been election day, you will all read how I attempted to deceive the population into enabling me, your PM, to remain in charge of the great Peoples Unite Party. Using my chancellor's words, I am informing the nation that I resign with immediate effect from my leadership of the Peoples Unite Party."

With the cameras still focused on the PM, many could be seen and heard trying to ask questions as both the PM and Chancellor were ushered away by their security people.

There was one journalist that had pushed his way to the front just before the door to number ten was opened for them to both to enter and shouted out: "You say deceive; how dare you attempt to HOODWINK the people that would have voted for you?"

The PM turned around before entering number ten and could be seen mouthing the words, "I am sorry."

"Well, George, I will hand back to you in the studio with this story we have heard that will no doubt will roll and roll for a good time yet."

Back in the BBC Studios, "I guess we all need to wait and read the full details of this astonishing news in Wednesday's press to discover the truth."

The recording then finishes on Grace's mother's recorder.

"At least, Rob, we know what the Daily Mirror and the Daily Mail story will be when they are going to publish," Grace said taking their empty cups out into the kitchen.

"That's true, but my fear is I hope my name is not going to be mentioned. It is one thing being known for helping the less fortunate, but to be known for bringing the government down, I couldn't handle."

Chapter 78
You Should Be So Lucky

In real-time Tuesday evening, Linda and Tony were watching the BBC1 News. "Bloody hell! Tony, your brother just brought down the government and yes, rightly so," Linda said and started to laugh at the thought that Rob had the balls to pull this off.

"Simon Davis, our PM, who thought he was a great statesman was, in fact, a bloody great liar," Tony said. Taking out his mobile, he texted his brother. "Congratulation, you deserve a treat. Pick you up at 8 pm, Tony."

George and Rob's uncle were heading back to the Castle Palace Hotel after convincing Trevor Charles Baines that he would be out of his cellar on Wednesday night. "Put the news on, George. Let's listen to what's happening in this crazy world we all have to live in." Granted, they only got the tail end of the Radio 1 News, but they both heard enough to know that Rob Hat had pulled off something that could possibly change politics and put the government on the spot to make them change all the crap they come out with.

George gave Alan his mobile, "Text your nephew."

Alan wrote, "You're one in a million. Well done, G & A. PS meet us at the Castle Palace Hotel at 8:30 pm; dinner is on us."

At Reading Police Station, their DCI Gordon Taylor ordered DI Judy Reynolds and DS Jones to his office along with DS Richardson if he's not watching the movements of Charlie Baines and his mother, Glenda.

Up in the DCI's ivory tower, she knocks on his office door, and on her third knock, Reynolds gave up and walked straight in only to see DCI Taylor at his window using his binoculars to see what was going on in Reading. Knowing her boss was more than likely searching to see any nudity in the tower block some fifty yards to his right.

"Did I say come in?" DI Reynolds was bloody angry and did an about-turn and was just about to leave his office. "Don't be childish, Reynolds. Take a seat and where's the huge DS?" he asked putting his binoculars on his desk.

"He's been keeping tabs on George Almedia since we need to know why he's back in the UK."

"What I say within these four walls stays within them?" he said looking angry. Judy Reynolds never answered; she just nodded. "I gather, Reynolds, you have seen the news?" She just nodded again.

"First, I had Freddie Andrews from the Special Branch giving me balls shit about my team finding the PM's parliamentary red leather briefcase. Then I get

Colonel Jameson from the CIP putting me in charge to find this fucking case," DCI Taylor was now shouting in the face of his DI.

"What's your point, governor?" she asked knowing he was the biggest arse licker in the Met.

"My bloody point is, it was not the case they wanted, it was its fucking contents," he said banging his right hand down hard on his desk. Taking a deep breath, then he shouted again. "Then the Corps of Intelligence Police (CIP) fucking use Scotland Yard to bring in the PM and his chancellor when that should have been this office to handle this," he said taking a bottle whisky from his desk and pours himself a very large measure.

"Those contents look like bringing down the PM and Chancellor and, like everyone else, we will have to wait and see what the hell was in his red leather case on Wednesday morning,"

DI Judy Reynolds said getting up and walked out of his office even though she heard her boss saying, "I have not yet dismissed you."

Back at Saints House, Grace tipped her dinner from the oven in the waste bin. Now, all dressed up and waited for Rob to come back to her flat all showered and smarten up for their dinner at the Castle Palace Hotel.

With Rob back down from his flat dressed in his suit that Linda had bought him back in 2013 for his court appearance at the Crown Court. Unfortunately, it was for his involvement with the stolen cash from the National Bank close to Reading, where a younger Rob Hat had helped thousands with this stolen cash that he had found on a train.

"Before you ask, darling, I have called Linda, and yes, they will be at the Castle Palace Hotel around 8:30 pm." Rob smiled knowing it was only 8 pm.

"Does that mean I am on a promise?"

Grace then pushed him towards the door and said, "You should be so lucky."

Chapter 79
Getting Your Arse Kicked

As per the norm, Grace and Rob arrived last at the Castle Palace Hotel. The waiter took them to the far corner of their restaurant out of earshot of the full clientele for the evening. Grace was seen darting to the far corner of their table where baby Grace was sitting in a high chair getting agitated since she had a plastic spoon, but no food was coming her way. "I am sitting here," Grace said sitting up close to the high chair.

"I did tell you, Yvonne, that you should have asked for two high chairs," Rob's uncle was saying with George Almedia and DS Jones along with Tony laughing but little did they know Grace would have tried to squeeze into one to be equal to her godchild.

"You're looking a smart lad tonight, Rob," DS Jones said and then added, "If my memory serves me right, you were wearing that suit at the Crown Court."

Rob looked down, and he could see his trousers were a little on the short side. "John, I was not aware you were coming this evening," Rob said trying to pull his trousers down a shade before sitting next to Grace.

"I invited him seeing we need to make sure we are all singing from the same song sheet for tomorrow evening," George was saying pouring out the Hock Wine for everyone minus one, of course.

"I hear congratulations are in order, Rob?" Yvonne said giving baby Grace her two-handed pink plastic mug that looked as though it contained milk that immediately was thrown to the floor.

"Here you go, darling," Grace said, who had picked up her mug.

Just then, three waiters wheeled over a trolley and placed two large pieces of Chateau-Brands on their table with three large bowls of roast potatoes plus two plates of mixed vegetables along with two jugs of gravy. "Hope you enjoy," the waiter said ruffling baby Grace's hair and walked away whilst the other two waiters were cutting the fillet beef up and serving the potatoes and vegetables.

Baby Grace might only be a baby, but if looks could kill, those waiters would all be dead since she was given bugger all to eat. The looks to kill were soon changed to all smiles when the young waitress put a plate of fish fingers and chips in front of her. "Enjoy, you little sweetie," she said with baby Grace putting both her hands on her head fearing having her hair ruffled again.

"DI Judy Reynolds told me an hour ago that our DCI is on the war-path seeing our own CIP and Special Branch had not been telling his office the truth. We were ordered to find the PM's parliamentary red case when all along it was the contents that were needed. Then the CIP using Scotland Yard when he felt it should have been his office in Reading, yes it would be an understatement to say he's effing fuming," DS John Jones said giving Rob a playful dig on his left arm.

"Grace, that's the third glass of wine you have had. Surely you remember the last time we were here, I had to help you to the toilet," Linda said.

"I can hold my drink these days. Besides, we still have a further two bottles of wine on the table to drink; it would be an awful waste to leave them."

Rob looked at Linda and said, "Leave her, Linda. If she brings up in my van, she can clean it out when we get home."

"Tony, would you and Linda like to join Grace and me tomorrow evening when we park up in the small shopping parade in Manor Road whilst George and my uncle go digging at the Honour Oak Cemetery?" Rob said looking at DS Jones and then George along with his uncle, waiting for them to object.

"Hell, Rob, this project is not one of your so-called Beano outings," George said waiting for his uncle to agree.

"Stop me if I am wrong, it was agreed that I am in charge of this grave robbery, but you oldies won't let me dig?"

"True," Alan Hat said looking at George Almedia, who just shrugged his shoulders knowing that was what was agreed.

"That's settled then, Linda and Tony, if they wish, can be at Saints House at 6:30 pm Wednesday when we will leave. George and my uncle will follow us to Manor Road. Then DS John Jones will follow and then park behind them whilst George and my uncle go digging. With DS Jones' blue light flashing on his unmarked police car, we can make certain that they are not disturbed," Rob said demonstrating that he's the boss.

"Listen, boss, if we come up with a body, you four better leave at a great speed since you're going to be getting your arse kicked, Rob," George Almedia said knowing there was no guarantee that they were going to come up smelling of Roses.

"There's no body, just money," Rob said with his fingers crossed under the table.

Chapter 80
I Hate You

With the grave diggers sleeping and hopefully dreaming of gaining a large reward from the banks, it was not the same for Grace since she was in Rob's Morris Minor Van having to clean up her dinner and wine that she had decided she no longer needed. "This is not funny, Mr Boss man," she was saying trying to clean the vomit off her window.

"You would have been wise to have opened the window first?" Rob said hoping she's learnt a lesson of drinking close on a bottle of wine to herself.

Rob and Grace never knew that half an hour to midnight at the rear of Downing Street, there were two removal vans, one for number ten and the other for number eleven.

"Daddy, why do we have to leave in the middle of the night? I am so tired," Simon Davis's younger son wanted to know why he can't go to bed.

"That's your young son asking you a question that you're unable to answer, heaven only knows just how many questions are coming your way in the coming months?" His wife said multitasking with packing and taping up a great many boxes to get ready for their moonlight flip. Simon Davis just sat there drinking whiskey as though they were cups of tea.

He knew his friend, Graham Johnson, would be having his ears chewed off by his wife. He also knew he should be feeling guilty about encouraging Graham to join him in attempting to deceive the population. As soon as he thought about what he had done to his loyal friend, he immediately dismissed feeling guilty.

Simon Davis was only worried about him and, for the life of him, he couldn't find a way to get out of the deep hole he had dug for himself.

It was Judith, his wife, who jolted him out of feeling sorry for himself when she threw the tape gun at him that landed at his feet and shouted at him that set his young son crying who stomped out of their lounge and they both could hear him running down the stairs screaming, "I hate you, you're the worse daddy in the world!" he said plonking his backside on the bottom step where he could hear his mummy getting angry with his bad daddy.

"Simon, we have two older children in University and, you know damn well, because of your stupidity, they are going to get ridiculed," Judith said throwing her youngest cuddly toys in a dustbin bag.

Simon Davis knew his wife was right in what she was saying but felt he should say something, "We can take them out of Cambridge and put them into University up north."

Judith just couldn't believe what her husband was saying. "Change their names to Smith or Jones, and you might bloody stand a chance." Then added, "As you know damn well, I hate bad language, but because of what you were planning to accomplish, you deserve being sworn at, pack that fucking whiskey in this box," and slung a flat pack box at him, "You're going to need it."

He still sat there and kicked the tape gun back to his wife and tossed the carton to the far end of their lounge. "It's high time you heard a few truths. Twenty-five years, I have stuck by you and listen to all the lies coming out of your mouth to the people that voted for you. These past years whilst you have been in power, you always believed that bullshit could baffle brains."

Simon got up and slurred his words, "Thattts noot tttrue."

Judith started to cry and said, "We are over. Our children and I deserve better than you; I want a divorce."

Chapter 81
Face the Music

It was much the same at 11 Downing Street, the only difference being it was Graham Johnson who was rushing around their apartment and throwing everything he came across into boxes. Outside their bedroom, he had already twenty boxes stacked up against the wall waiting for the removal team to be told to start loading.

Knowing he was going to have Dawn, his wife, to give him a rollicking, so he took a deep breath and entered the bedroom to see his wife in her nightdress sitting up in bed. “So, your so-called best friend, Simon, says jump and all you can bloody say is how high you want me to jump?” Dawn said taking a magazine off her bedside table and started to flick through the pages. Graham decided it was best not to reply and started to walk into his wife’s walk-in-wardrobe. “Don’t you dare touch my clothes. Besides, I am not coming with you to hide away in shame,” she shouted at him that brought him immediately back into the bedroom.

“Graham, your mess is your mess; it doesn’t involve me in any shape or form, so from now on, you are on your own.” Graham knew that coming Wednesday morning Downing Street would be packed solid with the media wanting answers.

“I can’t turn the clock back, Dawn. I never thought in a million years that my political career would finish up going down the drain because of Simon’s stupidity.”

Dawn put her magazine back on her bedside cabinet and said, “Let’s assume that you and your so-called Statesman Simon Davis had hoodwinked the Nation then if you had won the election, you would need to live the next five years lying to the people that voted for the Peoples Unite Party.” She said picking up her magazine again.

“We can’t stop here so, please get up so we can leave here before daybreak, plus I need you to help me to pack up everything,” Graham was saying, in fact, kind of begging her without going on his knees.

“Be the man I have always believed in and stand up and be a man, and if need be to ask for forgiveness that will prove you’re not the bloody coward that you are currently demonstrating that you are.”

Graham sat on the bed and took her magazine from her and threw it on the floor; he knew she was right. “Okay, I am going out to tell the removal team that we will not be leaving until lunchtime Wednesday,” Graham said knowing he would have to pop into number ten and tell Simon that he would stay and face the music.

Getting off the bed and walking out of the bedroom when he got to the door, “I love you, Graham,” Dawn called out, leaning out of the bed and gathering up her magazine.

Chapter 82
Could Be for His Own Safety

With big Ben just striking midnight, DCI Sandra Willis looked at the wall clock in her office at Scotland Yard and checking the time and felt stupid in doing so as though she was questioning that big Ben could be wrong.

"Well done, Governor, that was good arrest tonight," DS James Gardner said.

"Not before time people will sleep easy in Berkshire now Frank Frazer and his twins are locked up and, hopefully, they won't breathe fresh air for a very long while," the DCI said putting her coat on and picking up her car keys and headed for the underground car park. In her car, she thought she better check on her invalid mother, who must be desperate to get into bed. Taking out her mobile that had been in her car since they had left to arrest the Frazers at their nightclub in Wokingham. "Shit," she said noticing she had a text from Colonel Jameson, head of CIP. Before reading it, she called her mother who, to her surprise, answered on the first ring. "Sorry, Mum, for being so late. On my way home now."

"It's okay, darling. My neighbour got me into bed at 10 pm, drive safely on your way home," Mrs Willis said, then ended the call.

Checking the time that Colonel had texted her, "Bloody, 9 pm," and then opened the text.

"Do not wait for the press and the media to go live with our PM's problems. Make certain that you have Simon Davis at Scotland Yard for questioning. Trust me, it could be for his own safety. It seems his chancellor is getting away with it since there's no mention of his name within either of the attachments. I have not read what the Daily Mail addition is saying that's going live. I did call the Editor of the Mail, Ben Lawson, and he assured me that Graham Johnson's name was not mentioned.

Please read the two attachments. They are the draft copies to what the Daily Mirror has gone to print with for Wednesday's addition, and I dare say the Daily Mail's addition would be much of the same. C Jameson."

Having taken ten minutes to read the first attachment, she was thinking the Peoples Unite Party is going to want to lynch the PM, not to mention what the public might do to him. She then downloaded the second attachment, where she could see the two manifests duly signed by the PM. She read the first manifest that was saying, 'this is what the party will promote to the entire nation.' The other was clearly saying, 'this is what the Peoples Unite Party will only deliver.'

"What a bloody idiot!" she whispered getting out of her old Toyota.

Back up into her office, she managed to get DI Holmes and two of his DS to be ready to leave Scotland Yard by 2 am for Downing Street to take the PM into custody.

Knowing her mother would be worried and not wanting to explain why she might not be home until, hopefully, 9 am. Sandra texted her mother.

"Darling, something's come up. Don't worry, see you in the morning. S xxxx."

Sandra, not wishing to take the lift, charged down the four flights of stairs into the large control room. "Pipa, if you don't hear from me, would you please go to my place and get my mother out of bed for me in the morning?" the DCI said handing her a spare front door key.

"No problem, Sandra. I finish up here around 8 am. I will even have breakfast with her. She's a real darling, you must find it extremely difficult looking after your mother and holding down your high-profile position at the Met," Pipa said getting back to the telephone that had been ringing for two minutes.

"Hi, caller. Scotland Yard here, how can I help you?" the controller said as she waved bye to her friend DCI Sandra Willis.

Chapter 83
I Am So Sorry

1 am Wednesday at 10 Downing Street, Judith was carrying her young son who had cried himself to sleep. With him still sleeping, she strapped him in the rear of her Audi. The removal van was the lead vehicle with the PM's wife following close behind to their home in Kent. Simon Davis had made his way from the rear of the building and was standing outside number 10 as the removal van passed by followed by his wife's Audi, he waved out, but Judith looked the other way.

The PM went back into his office after getting changed into a pair of jeans, roll neck jumper and body warmer along with a cap that he was holding. Graham had told him half an hour ago that he was going to be staying but decided to wait in his office whilst his friend was seeing his wife and son off, hoping he could get Simon to change his mind.

"Graham, you do whatever you like, but as I said earlier, I can't face all the flack that's coming my way," he said pointing to the two suitcases by his desk.

Graham looked at him in disbelief that he thought he would not be recognised and said, "Are you for real, you fucking can't hide?"

"I am booked on a flight from Heathrow to Paris."

"You will not get airside before you are picked up."

Simon smiled and said, "When, in fact, I am going to stay with my parents in York to give me time to think," he said picking up his car keys off his desk.

"What about Judith and your young son? What is she saying about the stupid actions you are taking?"

Simon started to breathe heavily through his nose to hold back his tears. "I have lost everything, and that includes my wife. There is nothing for me here," Simon was saying going to pick up his two suitcases.

Graham put his hand on one of them, pushing it to the floor and then said, "What's been done, we were so wrong, and we are going to have to pay the price, and we will always be remembered for trying to deceive the people of the UK."

Simon nodded in agreement but could not think of anything to say other than, "Bye, Graham."

He got as far as his office door when Graham called out, "In your case, you'll also be remembered as a coward."

Simon stopped and thought of what his friend had just said. He dropped the case in his right hand to the floor and opened the door and walked out.

Graham sat at Simon's desk shaking his head when he heard the PM's Mercedes starting up.

Even at this unearthly hour, there were a few of the PM's staff mingling in the hallway, all looking confused about what was going on. Graham came out of the PM's office and started to head towards the back door and stopped and turned to face them and told them, "I am so sorry."

Chapter 84
Two Glasses of Champagne

Glenda Baines couldn't give a shit about the cancelled election, and as for the PM and his chancellor possibly having to go to Scotland Yard went straight over her head even if they finished locking the pair up, she wouldn't lose any sleep.

At 1 am Wednesday morning, she was doing her best to wear out her bedroom carpet as she paced from one end of her bedroom to the other end where their TV was. At each turn, flicking through the channels on her TV and not watching any of them. She had no idea where husband Trevor was, he was flying from Kilimanjaro International Airport into Heathrow. He had texted Charlie and told him to pick him up at Wokingham Railway Station. So, he's been back in the UK since early Sunday morning, and she was still none the wiser to where he is.

A further concern eating away at Glenda was Frank Frazer and his twins leaning on her and her son wanting the money her husband owed them from a large robbery from banks in Scotland. They have even forced her to put their home up for sale, or she would have to sign their large luxurious home over to the Frazer's.

"Where are you, Trevor? You're never here when I need you," she said out loud, making a further turn in her bedroom and flicking to channels and got to 503 BBC, the 24-hour news programme. She was just about to change to channel 504 when she heard the name Frank Frazer, so she immediately decided to pause the TV and set herself on the edge of the bed and pressed play and listen to what was being said about the guy with shot lungs.

The newscaster was saying it's taken the Metropolitan Police over two years to have gained the proof to charge and arrest the Frazer's for the brutal murder of the Dawson sisters who had left their home in Reading for a night out at the Frazer's night club.

They were then showing the earlier recording outside Scotland Yard, where the very young DCI Sandra Willis was being interviewed.

"It's taken a long while, but thanks to DNA, we are now able to prove that the Frazer Family mutilated the bodies of the young Dawson sisters. They will appear at the Old Bailey come this Friday. The CPS feels we have a watertight case against the entire family."

Glenda rewound the TV to the beginning and paused the TV again. She shot out of her bedroom and walked straight into her son's bedroom. "Wake up," she says pulling the quilt off him.

"What's your problem, Mother?" he asked pulling the quilt back over his naked body.

"We have one fewer problem to worry about; go into my bedroom and press play on the TV," Glenda said, and before her son could ask her anything, she had left his bedroom.

Five minutes later, she was back in her bedroom with two coffees. "Mother, that news deserves two glasses of champagne and not coffee," Charlie said with his quilt wrapped around him.

"One to go now, we need to find out where your father has buggered off to. I, for one, don't have bloody clue to where the shit is?" Glenda was saying drinking her coffee.

"Aren't you forgetting that Anna, the African tart—when she is back from Nairobi—still wants her payment for her silence?" Charlie said shuffling towards the door with his quilt still wrapped around him and trying not to spill his coffee.

"God willing, your father can deal with her when he shows his face in the UK," his mother said knowing he's not likely to appear in Sandhurst with the police still keeping watch on their house and movements.

Chapter 85
Colonel Jameson's Mobile

Colonel Jameson, Head of CIP, had called ahead to gain the clearance at the Downing Street Security Gate to allow DCI Willis in when she arrives with her team.

When security saw the two police cars that drove up to the gates at 2:20 am, the gates were opened. The DCI flashed the security guard her warrant card, and then both cars pulled up in front of 10 and 11 Downing Street. The door to number 10 opened and what could be the valet for the PM walked towards DCI Sandra Willis, who was already out of the police car. "If you're looking for the Prime Minister, unfortunately, you have missed him, he left a little after 1 am," even at the early hours of the morning, the smartly dressed gentleman said.

"And Mrs Davis?" she asked watching the three officers getting out of the other car parked outside number 11.

"She left just before the PM following their removal van, and I was led to believe she was going to their home in Kent with her youngest son."

The DCI was just about to ask if he knew if Graham Johnson, the chancellor, was still at home when the door to number 11 opened. "In here, officers," the recently resigned Chancellor called out to them, so the four of them walked into the Chancellor's home. He was standing in his hallway in his dressing gown and pointed to what could be his office. "Please take a seat," he said pointing to the large sofa and armchairs at the far end of his office.

Just then, Dawn Johnson appeared in a fluffy pink dressing gown. "Can I get you officers a coffee?" she asked.

"No, we are fine, thank you," DI Holmes said.

"You speak for yourself. I would love a black coffee, Mrs Johnson," DCI said sitting down on one of the armchairs with her three officers taking their seat on the sofa with the Chancellor sitting on the other armchair.

DCI was just about to speak to the Chancellor when Mrs Johnson came back into his office and handed the officer her coffee. "Thank you," she said watching Mrs Johnson sitting on the arm of the chair her husband had occupied.

"I have been ordered by the CIP to bring Simon Davis in for questioning and yes, to obtain the truth as to why he was prepared to deceive the entire population to gain the entry once again to number 10. I want you, Mr Johnson, to tell me where he has gone," the DCI said looking at his wife, who was shaking his shoulder.

"Graham, your so-called best friend would not protect you, so tell the Inspector what she needs to know."

The DCI butted in before Graham Johnson answered his wife's request. "Mr Johnson, when I brought you and Simon Davis in to be questioned by the CIP, I initially thought the two of you were guilty, and Colonel Jameson was thinking along the same lines. To a degree, I have some good news for you. I have already seen the article that will be in the Daily Mirror," the DCI said looking at her watch, "that will be read very shortly."

Graham looked at his wife knowing he was about to be arrested. "And the good news, Mr Johnson, is that there is no mention of you in the Daily Mirror, and I have been informed your name is not mentioned in the Daily Mail and once again, those two manifests, as you know, your name does not appear on those two documents."

Graham never said anything, but they could all hear him give a sigh of relief. "No doubt at some stage you are going to have to face your Peoples Unite Party to explain where you had gone wrong. So, unless I am ordered otherwise, the CIP has no interest in you whatsoever," DCI told him, and she could see the tears that started to escape from his eyes.

"Thank you, Miss Willis, but I still have to answer to my own conscience," Graham said looking at his wife, who had joined him with his flowing tears.

"Mr Johnson, I need to know if you are aware of where the PM was heading," DI Holmes asked handing Mrs Johnson his clean handkerchief.

"Before he left, he told me that he had book a flight to Paris when, in fact, he was heading to his folks' home in York, I guess, to escape you people from the Met and, of course, the vast amount of media coverage coming down the line," he said.

DCI Willis handed him her notebook. "Write down what car he is travelling in along with the registration number and, if possible, let me have his parents address."

With the information gained, she went to the far end of his office, but they could still hear her asking to put forward to Colonel Jameson's mobile.

Chapter 86
Calm Down, Jim

It was 3 am Wednesday, Graham Johnson was struggling to find sleep when he felt his wife's arm going around him. "Sleep, Graham, you have done the right thing. I don't believe Simon would have protected you if you had decided to run away." Graham squeezed her hand knowing she could be right in all the years he had known Simon, he would always put himself first.

"Dawn, if it wasn't for him, I would not have had this position in the Peoples Unite Party," he said dreading what daybreak had in store for him.

He had just dropped off to sleep when his mobile buzzed. Half asleep cursing, he picked up his mobile seeing he had a text but couldn't recognise the number. Still, he opened the message that said, "Mr Johnson, thought you would like to know that Simon Davis was picked up at the Watford Gap Service Station on the M1 and is currently being escorted to Scotland Yard. Regards, DCI Willis."

He was hoping his mobile had not woken Dawn but went straight back to sleep. Dawn came in with a tray of teas and toast that she put on the bed. She drew the curtains, and to Graham's surprise, it was daylight. "What's the time?"

"7:35, at least, you have had a few hours' sleep." Graham picked up his mobile and checked the time that message was sent, it said 4:15. He realised he had read the message and immediately dropped off to sleep again.

Handing Dawn his mobile, "Check my last text," to which she read.

"It's been on the 7 am BBC1 News," she said handing her husband his tea. Seeing Graham was going to be bombarded from his Party members, and the media are going to be on his case. And, of course, the Met might want to know why he had gone along with what Simon Davis was promising the population was, in fact, a total lie. So other than telling him she knew his friend Simon was picked up on the MI, she had decided not to tell him that every TV channel was having a field day with the PM hoodwinking those that would have voted for his Peoples Unite Party.

"Is there anything else mentioned on the BBC about the mess we have found ourselves in?"

Dawn was aware he was going to ask but thought it best at this juncture to let him find out what was being said later. "No, Graham, I just caught the end of the BBC News before coming up with your tea."

With the PM at Scotland Yard being question by the CIP with Dawn Johnson feeling relieved, Graham's name was not mentioned, but she was fully aware the

Peoples Unite Party is going to need answers from their chancellor because they knew he would have known what his friend was up to.

Back at Saints House, Jim Hat was going ape shit seeing and hearing that Simon Davis had now proven that he was a right arsehole. "Hell, Julie, now we know why the General Election was cancelled," he was saying and then added, "I always thought our PM only played lip-service to the truth."

"Calm down, Jim. Let the law get to the bottom of it as to why he was prepared to deceive the nation," Julie said.

Rob was out in the kitchen making himself a quick tea before he headed downstairs hoping Grace would be waiting with his bowl of cornflakes before they left for Premier. He would have loved to join his parents to see what was being shown on the BBC more so seeing he was responsible for what was going on, and if his mother and father knew, he would have received a mouthful from his father.

"Rob, come in here and see what's going on with our government," his father calls out.

"Can't stop, Dad. I am already late. Anyway, I can view it later on our TV in our arch at Premier."

He was just about to leave when he heard his father shout out, "Pick up the Daily Mirror and the Daily Mail, their front pages sum up what a shit he is."

"I will," he called back closing their front door heading down the stairs while knowing millions of others like his parents are going to be seeking Simon Davis's blood.

Chapter 87
Well Done, Rosie

On their way to Premier, Rob pulled round the back of Gems Supermarket, where Grace rushed in and picked up the Daily Mirror and the Daily Mail.

With the Mirrors' front page saying: Shame On You Simon Davis, and the front page of the Daily Mail had their front page in bold type with its title printed: How Dare You Hoodwink The UK's Population**.** "Rob, both papers have printed the two manifests," she said and then continued saying, "You have not said more than half a dozen words since we left Saints House."

With Rob's mobile going off. "Get that for me, Grace," he said sliding his mobile across the dashboard.

"You have three messages," and then she read them out. "George is saying mission accomplished. Your uncle is saying Happy, your name is not mentioned. Linda has written: 'No one must know you are responsible, now let the Peoples Unite Party and the Metropolitan handle it."

"Grace, I am not proud of what I have done, but I feel I have helped stop our PM from hoodwinking everyone in the UK."

Driving over Westminster Bridge, Rob started to laugh. "Not that she must ever know, but it was Rosie that brought our government down."

Grace looked at Rob in total confusion. "Why is Rosie to blame?" she asked.

"If Rosie hadn't been driving her mobility scooter down the New Kent Road attempting to overtake a bus, then she would not have finished up in an old people's home in Southampton to recover."

Grace started to chuckle and said, "I get it, and you wouldn't have visited her, meaning you would not have found yourself on the train from Southampton that the PM was on. The train crashed just passed Vauxhall Station, and you wouldn't have found the PM's red parliamentary case that he had left on the train as he was being stretchered off." Rob nodded to what she was saying.

"Yes, Grace, something like that; well done, Rosie."

"That now brings us to the end of this project of our dishonest PM being caught aiming to deceive all those in the UK able to vote. As Linda is saying, let the Peoples Unite Party and the Met sort it out. Now we need to concentrate on robbing the grave of Trevor Charles Baines this evening."

Grace was in no way excited about his uncle and George raiding a grave. "Your uncle will not thank you if the only thing they come up with is body," Grace said watching Rob getting his work gear on for their day's graft.

"You have little faith; your doubts will disperse when I share out one million pounds five ways," Rob said tossing her one of her wellington boots.

"Is that our friend Bernie, the pig, flying outside?" Grace said leaving their cabin for a busy day ahead.

Part 5

Chapter 88
Polish

Wednesday evening, Grace and Rob arrived home a little before 6 pm and seeing Linda's Mini Cooper parked up at Saints House. Rob thought Linda and Tony could be upstairs waiting for their arrival.

Leaving Grace on the fourth floor to shoot home for a quick bite to eat. "See you downstairs at 6:30," Rob called out to her just before she entered her flat.

"Don't you be late," Grace shouted back before going in.

Passing by his kitchen window on the fifth floor, he could see his brother and Linda chatting with his mother. "You two are early," he shouted out hanging his coat up in the hallway.

"Have a cup of tea, Son, and I have made you a sandwich before going to the cinema," his mum said watching him giving his sister-in-law a peck on the cheek with Rob thinking that was a good excuse for them robbing a grave.

"Oh my God," his father called out from their living room, who was watching the 6 pm BBC News. Coming into the kitchen and putting his cup in the sink, "I can't believe that a guy was in the London Eye Hospital in Harley Street having an eye test for his Diabetic disease. From all accounts, his wife had left him in the clinic seeing he would normally have a long wait, so she popped down Oxford Street to exchange a dress at M&S for a larger size.

"Unbeknown to her, her husband went straight in for his test, and 30 minutes later, he decided to leave the clinic and walk to M&S to meet her," Jim Hat said.

"So, what can't you believe Jim?" Julie Hat asked.

"With his vision still blurred from his test, he walked out and got hit immediately by a taxi seeing instead of turning left, he walked straight across Harley Street," Rob's dad said.

"Surely, the clinic should have told him he would need to wait until his vision had cleared?" Linda said.

"I guessed they thought his wife was outside in the waiting room to assist him?" Jim Hat said then added, "Other than this poor sod, all the news is about our PM facing the possibility of being charged for lying to the nation." Linda felt her face had started to burn up; she avoided making eye contact with Rob seeing he was responsible.

"Be back in an hour. I am going downstairs to speak to Jean Long about arranging about a Bingo night," Julie Hat said walking into the hallway putting her coat on.

“Before you guys shoot off, this chap being hit by a taxi brings back a memory of my father. I want to tell you a story about your grandfather when he had his own one-man car hire business.” So, with the four of them sitting at the kitchen table, Rob and Tony were always eager to hear the stories about their grandfather. Rob Glanced at the clock that said 6:15 pm. Seeing his son looking at the clock, “It’s okay, Son. It will only take a couple of minutes,” Jim Hat said.

“Rotherhithe Mini Cabs gave my dad a job to pick up two Polish seamen from the ship Maria at Surrey Docks. The job was to take one of the chaps to the London Eye Hospital that was situated back then at the Elephant Castle on the junction of Blackfriars Bridge Road. From all accounts, this guy could not speak a word of English; hence, the other sailor would assist him at the hospital seeing he could.

“Your grandfather waited an hour for the seaman to be treated. When they left the hospital, the fellow that could speak English asked my father to return the guy who had been treated to his ship Maria whilst he walked off towards Blackfriars Bridge.

“Back at the ship, the Maria, my father parked close to the ship and got out and opened the door for him. With the sailor pointing to his watch, ‘No, I don’t want to buy a watch. I have one,’ my father told the guy, but he kept on pointing to his watch, so my father repeated I have a watch and I am not interested, please bugger off. So, my father got back into his car and was about to make a turn when he saw the Polish sailor drop into the drink.”

“Is that true, Jim?” Linda asked. Jim never replied; he just shrugged his shoulders as much as to say it could be.

Chapter 89
Cheers

At 6:30 pm, the four of them were sitting in Linda's Mini Copper waiting for their uncle when George Almedia arrived with DI Jones to arrive. "Linda, that story my dad was telling us about the Polish sailor finishing up in the Thames is more than likely to be true," Tony said with Rob nodding in agreement with what his brother was telling his sister-in-law.

Just then, George and Alan Hat drove into Saints House in their Honda, followed by DS Jones in his unmarked Mondeo police car.

It was agreed that once George and Alan walked into the wooded area, his uncle would call Rob and hopefully would be able to give him a running commentary whilst they waited in the small shopping precinct.

With George and Alan being the lead car and DS Jones following with Linda's Mini Cooper at the rear, they were heading to Manor Road that ran parallel to Honour Oak Cemetery.

Thirty minutes later, the Honda parked on the opposite side on the right to Treasure House in Manor Road with the Mondeo parking behind it. They watched Linda drive pass and saw the Mini Cooper being parked up outside the small co-op supermarket facing the Honda and Mondeo.

Those in the Mini could see DS Jones putting the yellow tape across the bushes that were highlighted by George Almedia where to place them. "That's a brilliant idea," Rob said watching from inside Linda's Mini Cooper. George and Alan ducked under the tape and disappeared into the wooded area. DS Jones went to his car and took the blue light from his boot and put it on top of his Mondeo and, from his ignition, set it flashing.

Rob's mobile went off, making the four of them jump. Rob put his mobile on speaker so they could all hear what Alan and George were saying. "Over here, Alan, where my handkerchief is tied to the bush. We need to walk towards the fencing of the plot for the three graves. There must be a lever hidden on the ground to let us get under the ground," George was saying.

"Got it here, George. There's a small green lever on this tree by the fence."

"Pull it," Rob shouted down into his mobile knowing the chances were his uncle would not have heard him. George had walked over and did the honours.

"Here it goes. Rob, there's an around a 4-foot square piece of turf lifting up. Okay, if I go first, Alan?" George asked.

"There's a set of steps; follow me, Alan. Bloody hell, there's a light twitch and a further red button."

"Rob, since we are going underground, I will more than likely lose contact. I will send you photos that you can view when we are out of this grave," Alan said to his nephew, who he thought would be wishing he was with them.

George went down a dozen steps first, and Alan followed him. Alan found himself standing on a wooden floor next to George. George went up half a dozen steps and, reaching up, he pressed the red button that closed the lid. Now they were in total darkness with George taking out his lighter to enable him to locate the light switch that he saw before daylight was shut out.

"Oh my God, Alan, there's a ten by ten room down here," he said seeing the two large heavy-duty batteries in the far corner enabling them to have a large fluorescent strip lighting.

"George, there are three doors," Alan said opening the first door on his left that revealed Trevor Charles Baines's coffin that had come to rest on the soft earth where there had been trickle earth on top of the coffin that had seeped through from above.

"Lift the lid, Alan," he said handing him an all-purpose screwdriver.

"You brought the tool you bloody open it," Alan said giving him a friendly punch on his arm. George never responded to the punch seeing he was far too busy opening the other two doors.

"Jesus, Alan, you need to see what's behind the other two doors. With all the doors open, the size of this place must be 15 by 10, far bigger than I first thought," George said and sat on the last run of the steps watching Alan look into the open doors.

"Fucking hell, George, there must be millions of pounds down here," Alan said taking photographs of the two rooms stuffed with 50, 20, 10 and 5 pound notes and sent the four photos to his nephew. "This is one very large wooden engineered construction box with three separate rooms, and the only one with earth on the floor was the one with the coffin on it," Alan added. George walked over to the coffin. Kneeling and looking up, he could see a large dark wooden panel wedged in place some three to four feet above the coffin holding the earth that would have been thrown on the coffin from the mourners or had seeped through from the weight of the earth above when they filled the grave in.

So, there they were both kneeling with George using his screwdriver on the lid of the coffin. "Okay, Alan, let's lift the lid. On the count of three, George, 123…" George counted, and the lid was up, but both of them never looked directly into the coffin. They looked away at the same time, too frightened to see what they might find in the oak coffin.

George was the first to be brave and turning to face the open coffin and shouted out: "My God, I have never seen so much jewellery plus there must be 50 plus gold bars in here." George said once again sitting on the last run on the wooden steps. Alan once again was taking photos of the buried treasure in the Baines's coffin and again sent them to Rob.

Alan went through his contacts on his mobile to find DS Jones mobile number and then sent him all the photos that he would be able to view once he gained a signal once out of the grave bank.

"Alan, your nephew is one clever lucky sod," George said and then added. "Get your arse out of here, and I will make certain to leave everything as we found it," George said starting to screw the lid back on the coffin. Alan found a green button on the other side of the red one and pressed it watching the lid rise.

"George, at the top of the steps on your right, there is a further green button to lift the lid," Alan said and then climbed out. Going to the tree, he pushed the lever up and watched the large piece of turf come down.

Alan headed left to the far end of the wooded area before stepping out into Manor Road. Once out, looking to his right, he could see half a dozen people waiting to see what was going on. Alan crossed the road and walked towards the shopping precinct. Looking across to DS Jones, he held his mobile up and pointed it towards the DS. It was fifteen minutes later when George Almedia walked out of the woods with his raincoat over his arm concealing a large carrier bag and approached DS Jones. "It's all clear, Sergeant. It was a false alarm," he said and got in his car and, like Alan, he drove to the shopping precinct and parked in front of Linda's Mini Cooper. Those in the Mini were watching DS Jones taking the yellow tape off the bushes and then turning the flashing blue light off his car and taking the unit off the roof and placing it back into his boot.

It was forty minutes later that was not arranged until after the job that they were all in the bar at the Castle Palace Hotel and were sitting in the far corner with them all going through all the photographs taken.

Seeing George and Alan were back first at the Hotel, and George had ordered a bottle of their best champagne and six glasses. The young waitress walked to their table while carrying a tray and balancing a large bottle of bubbly and six flute glasses on it. "Excuse me, Mr George, but here is your drink and glasses you had ordered and was to be brought to your table when your friends had arrived," she said putting the tray on their table.

"Thank you, Susan," George said giving her a £10 pound tip.

"Just the one glass for you, Grace," Rob said knowing she struggled to hold her drink.

"Rob, I second that most of us here know that she should stick to coke," Tony said winking at his wife, who was giving Grace a hug.

George Almedia was looking at DS Jones and said, "You now have all the proof you need to go to your bosses and tell them you know where Trevor Charles Baines's stolen millions are hidden." George checked the time on his watch and then said, "If you and a team of detectives arrive at the Kenya Airways check-in desk for Kilimanjaro at terminal four Heathrow at around 11 pm, you will find the so-called Peter Goodman that the six of us know is, in fact, Trevor Charles Baines checking in for his flight to Kilimanjaro International Airport."

Alan also looked at the clock, "I gather, George, you're off to my home in Sandhurst to pick up Trevor Charles Baines? If you are, I suggest seeing it's fast approaching 8:30 pm, you better get a move on to get him to Heathrow for 11 pm."

"First things first," George said taking a glass of champagne, he raised it and said, "Here's to a job well done and, of course, here is also to the million pounds reward coming our way."

With Rob, Grace, Tony, Linda, Alan and DS Jones raising their glasses and saying at the same time, "Cheers."

Chapter 90
Total Nightmare

With George on his way to Sandhurst and DS Jones on his mobile to inform his boss DI Judy Reynolds that, thanks to George Almedia, he was able to discover where Trevor Charles Baines's hidden stolen cash was, and he forwarded the photographs to prove what he was claiming. Others round the table could hear him saying where his cash was hidden and the time and place where they could arrest the assumed dead Trevor Charles Baines.

"I am leaving to meet my DI at Honour Oak," DS Jones said.

"Go to the tree close to the Trevor Charles Baines grave; there's a green lever five feet up the bark, good luck," Alan said.

"Well done, Rob, all thanks to you that UK's notorious criminal was not dead and was, in fact, alive and well going by the name of Peter Goodman who could be arrested later tonight," Alan Hat said leaning across the table while ruffling Rob's shoulder-length hair.

"Yes, Rob, you have a habit of being in the right place when it's important. If you had not been on that train when it crashed just past Vauxhall Station, the chances are many of us would have voted for the Peoples Unite Party, and they could have won the election on total lies," Linda said with Rob sitting back with his hands on his head in fear of having his hair ruffled up again.

"Rob, I think it's strange that his chancellor, Graham Johnson, was not arrested since he must have known what his friend the PM, Simon Davis, was doing to deceive the nation. Then, he had resigned alongside the PM at the same time must mean he knew, so why else give up his career?" his brother Tony said grabbing the glass of champagne that Grace was about to pick up.

"Good move, Tony. She's already had two glasses," Linda said giving Grace a wink, who looked far from happy being stopped from drinking her third glass.

Linda took out her mobile and went to her text messages and said, "Reference to Graham Johnson, the chancellor, if I was him, I would go public on the message he had sent to Simon Davis."

"I have not seen them, Linda," Alan said with Linda handing over her mobile to him.

"You never showed me these, Rob." Rob never answered knowing he had simply forgotten.

It was Grace that butted in by telling his uncle in between burping. "Yes, we found those messages on the PM's mobile that you sent from Zanzibar to him," she said along with a further large burp. “Rob, I need the bathroom,” Grace said getting up and headed for the toilet.

Rob’s uncle never heard or noticed Grace leaving the table who was busy reading the text.

“Are you sure that you’re doing the right thing? I don’t believe you should deceive the population. Anyone other than you, I would never give this scenario the time of day. GJ.”

“Trust me, my friend, I know what I am doing; the last thing I want to do is to jeopardise your career and betray your friendship. SD.”

“You’re right, Linda, this might not save his career, but I feel it could save him from being arrested. He did warn the PM, but out of his loyalty to the PM, his close friend, he went along with it.”

“Your girlfriend, Rob, is a total nightmare when she drinks alcohol. I better go and help her in the bathroom,” Linda said leaving the table.

“Rob, you should be grateful the Daily Mirror or the Daily Mail never mentioned it was you that brought those two manifests to their attention,” Alan said with Rob nodding and knowing he cocked up being caught on CCTV outside the Daily Mirror.

Chapter 91
You Owe Me

Charlie Baines was in their lounge in Sandhurst with their 54-inch TV on, but it was on mute. There he sat staring at the TV totally bewildered as to why his father had been silent since he knew he was back in the UK for a few days now.

Just then, his mother charged in, making him jump. "Have you checked your mobile, the bastard must be somewhere?"

Charlie reached for his jacket that he had thrown off on the sofa. "Not since lunchtime," he said with his mother looking at their wall clock.

"Hell, Son, it's 9:30 pm."

Charlie looked at his mobile, "Shit, I have a text."

"From whom?" his mother shouted.

He read his text while looking up at his mother. "Shit, you're not going to like this," he said with his mother snatching his mobile off him.

"Fucking hell, Charlie, we don't need this money grabbing tart back in the UK just now with your father deciding to piss off," she said as she read out loud: "Hi Baines, earlier than expected, I am leaving Nairobi and I should be in the UK by 10 pm this evening to collect what you owe me. Anna Kajeme."

Then their gate buzzer and monitor startled them. "Hell, Charlie, we have two police cars outside."

Chapter 92
Thank You

George Almedia tiptoed into Alan Hat's home in Bracknell and removed the chair that was wedged under the doorknob and took it back into the kitchen. A few seconds later, he slid the door bolts across and opened the door. "Mr Goodman, your flight to Kilimanjaro is waiting for you," George called down the wooden stairs into the cellar.

"Three fucking days I have been stuck down here in this shit-hole," he called out. George could sense him packing his case, then he could hear him zipping up his holdall and hear him crunching over the glass as he approached the stairs and handed his captive his case.

"Judging by the crunching of glass, you have drunken all the wine in the cellar," George said.

"Yes, and smashed the bottles in fucking temper of having no means of contacting Charlie or his mother." George wanted to laugh but thought better of it knowing he had his sim card from his mobile in his pocket that he had taken out at the airport when he arrived from Kilimanjaro and popped into the toilet while leaving his mobile on the table in the coffee bar.

George locked up and put Goodman's luggage in his boot of his rented Honda and got inside the car. "You need to take me to Charlie's house first," Peter Goodman said.

"No time and no bloody point seeing Charlie is waiting to appear in court for burning down Frazer's night club. As for his mother, Mrs Baines, she is still being put under pressure daily by the Met seeing they know she knows the whereabouts of her late husband's stolen cash, and the Met feels he could still be alive."

George took out from the inside pocket of his jacket and handed him his single flight ticket to Kilimanjaro International Airport. "I need a mobile, and I don't have any cash," Goodman said.

"Let's get you checked in first, and then you can get yourself a mobile," George said.

"And cash? I don't have a bank card." George never responded. "You deaf, cash?"

"Okay, once you're checked in, I will get you a few quid that Charlie can pay me back at some stage," George said knowing that where the so-called Peter Goodman was going, he won't be in need of any cash. Perhaps a good solicitor might be handy for London's notorious criminal.

For their remaining thirty-minute drive to terminal 4 car park, not a single word was spoken.

With George Almedia wheeling in Trevor Charles Baines's case and heading for Kenya Airways desk 27, George couldn't help but notice the 7-foot DS Jones standing opposite the desk by the window with his DI Judy Reynolds standing some six feet from him. They both nodded to George at the same time whilst they went to the back of the large queue checking in for flight 256 to Kilimanjaro.

DI Reynolds was on her mobile and, within seconds, half a dozen boys in blue charged to desk 27. A few seconds later, Trevor Charles Baines was escorted out of the terminal.

DI Judy took hold of the Baines's suitcase and followed her officers and stopped wheeling it past George Almedia. "Mr Almedia, my DCI, DS Jones, along with myself, were wondering why you were back in the UK. Thanks to my DS Jones determination, we have uncovered the stolen millions you had traced to the Baines grave." George picked Trevor Charles Baines holdall up and followed her out of the terminal across the road to the car park where her old Mini was parked directly under a no waiting sign. He helped her get the case into her Mini boot and threw the holdall on her back seat.

"Miss, it's Rob Hat who you need to thank seeing he spotted his large TCB Tattoo on the back of Baines's hand whilst he was in Tanzania visiting his uncle. As for myself, I only took this project on for the million-pound reward." DI Judy Reynolds smiled and was about to ask further questions. "Don't ask, it's a very long story; perhaps you should talk to Rob Hat."

She got into her motor and, before closing the door, she said, "Mr Almedia, I will make it clear to the banks that it's your good self that should receive the reward."

"Thank you," he said and watched the DI drive out of the car park.

Chapter 93
Temper, Temper

Two weeks later, Trevor Charles Baines in Wandsworth Prison was awaiting his appearance at the Old Bailey the coming Friday. He was watching the TV in their communal area. Yes, watching but not listening to the BBC News, which was until he heard and saw George Almedia being given a cheque for one million pounds the reward from the banks for his involvement in recovering the bank's stolen cash.

Trevor Charles Baines stolen cash he had hidden in his reserved own three graves for his family over many years.

He then heard the African guy from Mwanza clearly say that the UK banks need to be grateful to young Rob Hat since he was sharp in recognising that Peter Goodman was, in fact, Trevor Charles Baines hiding in Kilimanjaro.

"That African bastard conned me," he shouted and pointed to the TV whilst the two guys playing pool totally ignored his outburst.

"Temper, temper. Baines, such an outburst from someone we all thought was dead and buried," a prison officer said passing by where he was sitting while handing him a copy of the Daily Mirror. "Have a read, Baines, and you will see what you will be missing," the prison officer added.

On the top half of the Daily Mirror front page were two photographs of his underground solid wooden box being his personal safe—that he and his late brother had constructed six feet underground some twenty years ago—at the perimeter to the Honour Oak Cemetery whilst Manor Road was being widened. With all this work being undertaken, it gave the pair the opportunity to work in the wooded area with all the machinery being used along with a huge number of labourers needed to undertake the widening of the road. This gave them the security of not being noticed.

The first photograph showed the box with the three doors closed with the two heavy-duty batteries in the right corner of the box. The second photograph showed the true size of the box with the three doors open still with his coffin in place at the first door. The second and third doors open showed all the cash stacked at least four feet deep from the floor to the ceiling.

The article highlighted that 4.3 million pounds were recovered along with four hundred pieces of high-value jewellery items had been rescued from the coffin. Also, in Mr Baines's coffin, they discovered 46-9ct 15-ounce gold bars. "Fucking thieves, I know there were 52 gold bars inside my coffin. I fucking put them in there ten years ago," he shouted out and banged both his hands down on the metal table he was sitting at. Neither of the two guys playing pool responded to him going ape shit to his lost fortune.

He then turned the paper to see what was on the bottom section where he said in a low whisper, “Oh fuck, now I know how I was recognised.” When he saw the photograph of him standing at Machame Gate before he went for his trek to the Roof of Africa. There he was standing with other climbers with his right hand over the shoulder of a young female climber standing at the end of the group. He knew now that his wife Glenda was right when she said he should have had his large TCB tattoo removed from the back of his right hand.

He remembered the young chirpy young driver that picked him up from the Tato Hotel to first drop off his girlfriend, Anna Kajeme, in Moshi Town before taking him to the Machame Gate, where the lad took a photograph to help promote the Safari Company. “So, you must be Robert Hat? Thanks for nothing, you little shit,” he said while chucking the Daily Mirror in the bin and headed to the stairs and went to his cell on the first floor, and the whole wing of the prison would have heard his cell door being slammed behind him.

Trevor was fully aware that his wife, Glenda, and son, Charlie Baines, were released on bail but had to hand over their passports in case they decided to leave the UK. Knowing Glenda and him had drifted apart; hence, he feared what she might say giving evidence. He was confident that Charlie would not say a bad word about him, but he couldn’t foresee how would help him in any shape or form.

Sitting in his cell feeling utterly depressed, he was beginning to think he would have preferred to have still been in that cellar. At least being there, he would have still been a free man.

“George Almedia and you the little shit for taking that photograph, if I ever escape, I will be coming after you two,” he said out loud that only his four walls could hear.

Chapter 94
I Am Okay, Miss

With the Frazer twins also waiting in Wandsworth Prison for their murder trial of the Dawson sisters to commence shortly. They were put in a different wing to Baines. The Metropolitan Police had advised Peter Thomas, the prison governor, to keep them apart from Baines, seeing there is bad blood between them until they could be transferred to another establishment.

Their father, Frank Frazer, was being held in the medical ward at Brixton Prison that had better facilities where he could be treated if there was a need.

There he sat beside his hospital bed with his oxygen tank beside him, knowing one of his sons had not destroyed the murder weapons they had used to slaughter the Dawson sisters with.

How stupid he was in helping his sons who had raped the Dawson sisters, and they had threatened them that they were going to report them to the police.

He knew he couldn't turn the clock back, but he had ordered his sons to drag them down into the cellar of his nightclub. He sat back in his wheelchair, taking in deep breaths through his mask and watched his twins cut and chop the teenage sisters to pieces and putting all their remains into black plastic bin liners.

He then ordered them to clean his cellar and to get rid of their bodies and to make certain the murder weapons were never found.

Frank Frazer sat there with tears rolling down his face knowing his life was fast coming to an end even if he didn't die from his lung cancer, he was never ever going to see the light of day again as a free man.

"You okay, Mr Frazer?" a nurse said who had noticed him crying.

Frank Frazer took his mask from his face and said to the young nurse, "I am okay, miss. I was just wishing I could turn my clock back and do things differently." The nurse smiled handing him a tissue, then walked down the heavily guarded ward knowing she had known many criminals in her ward thinking and saying exactly the same thing.

Chapter 95
When Is Daddy Coming Home, Mummy?

There were no tears but many regrets in the household of Judith Davis; she had filed for divorce. Her older sons had left their university simply as she thought would happen. They had been ridiculed seeing their father was now hated by the entire population.

Prime Minister, Simon Davis, had been receiving bad press more so when he received a five-year suspended sentence for attempting to lie to the population to gain the keys to stay at 10 Downing Street.

What Mrs Davis struggled with was when her younger son would ask, "When is Daddy coming home, Mummy?" Judith never had the heart to tell him that his daddy will be out of our lives for a very long while.

Simon's mother was now delighted to have her son back home in Yorkshire, but she failed to understand why he never ventured outside his family home.

Graham Johnson, the chancellor and Simon Davis's closest friend, played on the text to enable him not to be prosecuted that he had sent Simon trying to deter him from using those HOODWINK tactics. Whilst the CPI was convinced, he was not guilty, but he was guilty of choosing the wrong friend that is not a criminal offence.

The Peoples Unite Party had accepted his resignation, and he had moved out of 11 Downing Street and had joined his father in his furniture business in the North West of England.

Yorkshire was not a million miles away from Graham's father's business, but his friendship with Simon Davis was well and truly dead in the water.

Chapter 96
Big Boy

Earlier, Anna Kajeme decided not to waste her time going to the Baines family home to obtain the 500k she had demanded to stop her from going to the media and telling them that Trevor Charles Baines was living in Kilimanjaro under the name of Peter Goodman.

Within 48 hours of her arrival back in the UK, she knew she had a wasted journey from Thika in Nairobi, where she had been to bury her father.

Via the media, she was also made aware that her old enemy George Almedia had beaten her to the cash and that he was in line for a million-pound reward from the banks. Anna was also convinced that young Rob Hat had managed to get George Almedia involved, meaning the chances were that young Hat would be getting a 50% share of the reward.

Anna Kajeme decided she would stay at the Hilton Hotel until George had received his reward when she knew he would head home to Mwanza. Once George was out of the scene, she would come up with a plan to get Hat to hand over his share of the reward to her.

"This young Hat, Jim, has been a thorn in my side for a while now. A year ago, I had 750 diamonds that were stolen from Johnson Diamond in Mwanza. Yes, I was dragged off a plane in Dar-es-Salaam by the police, but I managed to push the children's bag that the diamonds I had glued on under the seat in front of me. At that stage, I had no way of knowing that Rob Hat, who was on the plane, saw me pushing the bag under the seat, and he took them.

"To cut a long story short, he managed to get a large reward from Lloyds, so I am not wrong in getting my revenge." Jim, her new minder from Thika—who had also had a run-in with George Almedia—walked to the fridge and pulled out two small Brandy's and poured them into the two cups by the teasmaid and handed her one.

"Anna, I am all for taking out George Almedia and grabbing the whole one million English pounds."

Anna was shaking her head. "Let's not be greedy. I read in the press your old enemy George took you out the last time you had robbed a bank in Mwanza that he was consulting for regarding their security," she said drinking her brandy.

"Anna, he was lucky. If my gun had not jammed, I would have killed the bastard. He took five years of my life away from me, so he owes me."

"Jim, you do whatever you like when you get back home, but whilst you work for me, you do as I say," Anna told him and watched him walk to the fridge again pulling out a beer.

"Okay, boss, but I want 50% of what we get."

Anna smiled knowing he would get sod all. "I agree. Now take me to bed and take me to heaven, big boy," she said dragging him by the hand towards the bedroom. "Yes, you can bring your beer; you're going to need it after finishing with me."

Chapter 97
Mobility Scooter

With Rob and Tony's family none the wiser to what has been going on so early Friday afternoon with Grace and Rob given a day off by Premier Supreme Car Hire. It was agreed they would all meet by Grace's mum's garage before George Almedia, Alan, Yvonne and—not forgetting—baby Grace were all going back to Tanzania. Of course, Alan Hat was also taking Rosie and her friend Pauline back with them to Machame for a holiday.

With Grace looking after her godchild, Alan and Yvonne were up on the fifth floor of Saints House saying goodbye to his brother and Julie Hat. George had joined them to say his farewells to Jim and Julie Hat. "Julie, here's a little something please I would appreciate you refraining from opening it until I am out of the country," George said handing her two boxes a little smaller than shoeboxes. "Julie, would you be so kind as to give Grace's mum, Jean, one of the boxes for me since Grace told me she was visiting her sister with her two young daughters."

Julie went to George and said with a gentle kiss on his cheek, "Thank you, my son always said you are a kind man and, of course, I will give Jean her gift. I will also tell her not to open in until you fly out of the UK."

With them going back to the ground floor to join the others who were still waiting to say their farewells, "Rob, I need to shoot off and collect my mum's prescription from Boots next to Gems Supermarket in the precinct," Grace said, who was in no rush seeing she was finding it very hard to say goodbye to the not so small godchild. Then, she was kissing everyone with tears in her eyes before she walked out of the Kings Estate.

George Almedia gave DS Jones a box and said, "Please don't open it to you know I am in the air at hopefully by 5 pm to Mwanza." Before Alan and Yvonne walked over to see if Rosie and her friend Pauline were ready for their holiday flight to Kilimanjaro. George went to his boot of his Honda and took out a box. "Alan, like our 7-foot copper, you must not open this box until your home in Machame," George said handing him the box. "Yvonne, here is a cheque for 50k that should give your daughter Grace a decent chance of a good education in Tanzania. Please give me the chance to bank my reward cheque in Mwanza Bank; otherwise, it will only bounce," George said giving her a kiss on the cheek and blowing baby Grace a huge raspberry that she found hysterical.

"Linda, I have not forgotten you guys," George said as he walked to his rented Honda again and opened the boot and came out with a further box. "No peeking until I am in the air," George said giving Linda a hug and shaking Tony's hand and handing him a cheque for 50k. "As I said, please give me the chance to bank my cheque back home being you bank it here in the UK."

George looked over to DS, "John, I have not forgotten you. There's a 50k cheque enclosed within that box."

"Thank you, George, and yes you guys were right I will be promoted to a DI next year, so thanks for getting me involved, Rob," the tall copper said.

"John, I need to get this car back to the rental company in Bayswater Road could you give me a lift to the airport?"

DS Jones nodded and said, "I would love to be your chauffeur."

"Rob, I need to make a move," George said going to his boot and taking out yet a further box. "Same again, Rob, there's a cheque inside for you for 500k," he said giving him a hug and whispered in his ear, "Thank you, my friend, for getting me to help you. Remember, Rob, I am only a phone call or an email away."

Just then, Yvonne and Alan came out of Rosie's flat carrying their luggage with the two going on holiday following them. "What time is your flight, Alan, to Kilimanjaro?" DS Jones asked.

"4.30 pm terminal four, John."

"I am taking George to the airport once he returns his rented Honda to Bayswater Road so I can help you by taking the two tourists for you," the DS said.

"Cheers John," Yvonne said knowing it was going to be a squeeze getting everyone and their luggage in their car.

With Tony, Linda and Alan standing by Rob's Morris Van were having fits of laughter watching Rosie and Pauline getting in DS Jones Mondeo unmarked police car. "Alan, can I ask who will be taking my mobility scooter to the airport?" Rosie called out struggling to get into the DS car head first.

Alan walked over to help her into the car and said, "I will rent you one in Arusha, so please there is no need for you to worry, Rosie."

Chapter 98
Hopefully, She Appears

With Anna Kajeme sitting in the driving seat of an 18cwt Ford Transit with her minder Jim Song in the passenger seat, watching Grace walking out of the Kings Estate and heading towards the Shopping Precinct. Anna could see, granted from a safe distance, it seemed with all the kissing and hugs going on plus George Almedia handing out gifts that he was about to leave the UK along with Rob's uncle and his wife and also the little brat.

"Jim, let's assume she's visiting the shops and hoping she enters the main entrance to the shops. If my memory serves me right, there's a lay by on the left, 50 yards from the entrance, where we can wait for her to come out from the Precinct." Jim sat there wondering why we should follow the very attractive Grace Long.

"What's your plan then?" the African professional criminal asked.

"Not that you will be any the wiser have rented a small very old warehouse close to the pub the Thomas Beckett off the Old Kent Road down Albany Road under two miles from here that is extremely secure for our needs. Our Rob Hat is devoted to Grace and would do whatever it takes to keep her safe."

Jim smiled and said, "So he will hand over 500k to get her back."

Anna just nodded, "Let's give it a further thirty minutes before we head to the Precinct."

Twenty minutes later, Anna and Jim ducked down in their seats as the three cars left Kings Estate. They noticed a woman and her two young children waving to the cars before the cars turned left into the slow-moving traffic in the New Kent Road heading towards the Elephant & Castle. "Those two young girls are the giveaway that woman is Grace's mum and her two younger sisters," Anna said seeing her walking into Saints House.

"Jim, when I park in the lay by, I need you to slide open the side door, and then we wait and, hopefully, she appears." She then handed him a damp tea towel. "Put it in your pocket and don't you dare sniff it."

"Why not?" he asked knowing he had no intentions or reasons to do so.

"Ether, you idiot, it will knock her out."

Chapter 99
Beautiful Grace

Linda and Tony got in their Mini Cooper. Linda said before closing the door, "I wonder what's in our boxes?"

Tony leant across and shouted, "Bars of gold!"

Rob laughed and said, "In your dreams bro," and waved them goodbye.

At 3 pm, Rob was upstairs seeing his mother shaking her box. "You're going to have to wait," his dad said.

"Mum, Jeans back home," he said watching her pick up the other box and was out the door in seconds.

At the car park at Terminal four, Alan went to Hertz and handed back his rented car. DS Jones had ten minutes earlier dropped off Rosie and Pauline with their luggage at the entrance to the terminal and was told not to wander off.

At 3 pm, Alan and Yvonne along with Rosie and Pauline were a little late at Gate 7, checking in for their flight to Kilimanjaro. With George and DS Jones saying goodbye to them and were heading for check-in desk 28 to book in for his George's flight to Mwanza.

Back at Saints House, Julie came rushing home calling out before she got into her lounge. "Boots telephoned Jean, Rob, and informed her that her prescribed medication was found outside close to the entrance to the Precinct." Rob was getting his jacket back on when his mobile went off.

Not recognising the number, "Hello."

Then there was a ten-second silcncc whcn a guy's voicc said, "Is 500 thousand pounds too much to ask for the safe return of your beautiful Grace?" Then the line went dead.

Rob had to sit down, and he was sweating and shaking. "Mum, Grace has been kidnapped." With a shaking in hand, he called George Almedia. "You said you're a phone call away; Grace has been kidnapped, please help me. Please, God, you're not on your flight home?"

Alan could hear him saying, "Sorry miss, I will not be flying today. John, I am so pleased you stayed with me until I checked in. I need a ride back to Saints House." Then George ended the call.

"Mum and Dad, we are lucky George Almedia is now on his way back here."

"Rob you need to go downstairs and tell Jean what's going on," his mother said stroking his face, and she couldn't think of anything to say that would help in what he was about to tell Grace's mum.

Rob shot into the bathroom and threw cold water over his face and put his hands through his hair and rushed out the door.

Chapter 100
Memory Stick

Rob shot down to the fourth floor for Jean who was on her way to leave her young daughters with Rob's mum whilst she went to Boots to see if she could see where Grace was and to pick up her medication. She bumped into Rob coming down. "Jean, leave Jane and Janet with my mum, and I will take you to Boots," Rob said.

"Thanks, Rob, I was on my way to leave them with her."

In their Red Morris Van and heading to the Precinct, "Do you know what's in that box George had given me?" Rob never answered; he was now fully aware she never knew what was going down with her daughter; otherwise, the gift in the box would have been the last thing she would be worried about. He was trying to figure out how the hell to tell her that her daughter Grace had been kidnapped and the kidnappers were asking for half a million pounds to get her back safely.

"Jean, this is not easy, but you need to know your daughter and the girl one day I will marry has been kidnapped." Jean's only response was to scream and Rob, like earlier, started to shake.

Jean was not known to swear that was until today, "Not my fucking darling Grace!"

Not another word was spoken other than her asking for the medication that was handed into Boots for a Mrs Jean Long.

Back at Saints House, he parked as usual at Jean's garage then DI Judy Reynolds pulled up directly behind him in her old Mini. "Rob, DS Jones called me on his way back from Heathrow with your friend George Almedia aboard. You must be Grace's mother?" the DI asked as they walked to the flats. Jean Long just nodded with her tears still streaming down her face. "Jean, I am DI Judy Reynolds as we are speaking now, I have a team in the High Street checking every CCTV to see if we can see who has taken your daughter."

Much to their amazement, the lift was working. "I gather, Rob, the kidnappers have contacted you?" Rob just nodded and opened his door, and they went straight into the lounge. Julie was in tears immediately hugging her friend Jean.

"Jean, we know DI Reynolds and DS Jones and, of course, George, Rob's friend, who had just called saying they would be here in ten minutes. They will find your daughter," Rob's mum said looking over Jean's shoulder at the DI who was nodding.

The doorbell rang, and Rob answered it. "Is DI Reynolds with you? She said that she could be at this flat." A young smartly dressed female detective showed Rob her warrant card.

"In here miss," he said as they walked down the hallway and then into the lounge.

"Boss, I have copied four CCTV on this memory stick covering 100 yards either side of the entrance to the Precinct," the DS said handing her boss the stick.

"Well down, Susie," she said watching Rob boot up his laptop.

They all heard George call out. "Your door was open," he called out as the DS and George walked into now a crowded lounge.

"Jim, come and give us a hand with the tea," Julie Hat said.

"Rob, give us your mobile," the DI caught it as Rob tossed it over to her and she called a number.

"Tony, monitor this number," she said looking at Rob, "07775 790334."

Rob shouted out, "You got that, Tony?"

"Good, do your best to trace any calls coming in on this mobile, Tony. I must stress this is fucking urgent you need the ID were any calls are coming from, cheers," she ended the call and tossed the mobile to back to Rob who was eagerly waiting for the DI to hand him the memory stick.

Chapter 101
All in Good Time

The Ford Transit was in a long queue of traffic in New Kent Road waiting to take the small flyover to the Old Kent with their captured Grace out cold with the fairies in the back. "Jim, sit in the back on the spare wheel. If she stirs, give her a further whiff off the tea towel."

He was just climbing into the back of the van when they could both hear, "Where am I?" Grace said realising she was being driven. Those were the last words she was going to be saying for a while with a big Africa guy leaning over her and forcing a large cloth over her nose and mouth.

"Jim, stay with her until we reach our destination." As she entered the Old Kent, they got onto the tail end of a further queue of traffic. It took her a further ten minutes to get to the Thomas Becket where she turned right at the pub that had a gym facility upstairs where many great UK boxers trained where chances were the heavyweight UK champion, Henry Cooper, could have trained at some time in his career.

Still, boxers were the last thing on her mind when she drove some 300 yards down Albany Road where the small warehouse on her left that still had the sign outside reading to rent.

Jumping the kerb in her Transit van, she drove round the back of the building with nothing but the waste ground and parked by the rusty old staircase. She tossed Jim a keyring, "The gold key will open the padlock while the silver key, when inside, will gain you entry to the first door on your left." Jim never answered; he just slid the side door of the van open and dragged Grace to the opening and tossed her over his shoulder and walked up the rickety rusty stairs and dropped her gently down on the small platform at the top. Thirty seconds later, Anna could see young Grace's legs disappear knowing she was being dragged into the building. She got out of the van and ran up the stairs just in time to see Jim dump Grace's body onto the dirty old mattress that she had taken in earlier along with a metal bucket and a small bottle of water that she put at the end of the rank mattress on the floor. The dirty room was eight by twelve that had seen better days. The room consisted of no windows so she could shout out to her heart's content where no bugger would be able to hear her with the only waste ground at the rear and no other building within half a mile to the small warehouse.

"Lock the door and make sure you put the padlock on the front door and let's get our arses back to the Hilton," Anna Kajeme said heading out the door.

“When are we calling Hat again?” he called out to her just as she left the room.

“All in good time,” he just managed to hear her say before she ran down the stairs.

Chapter 102
We Have to Wait

At Saints House, "Rob, this is the last CCTV copy we have regarding gaining sight of Grace coming out the Shopping Precinct," DI Judy Reynolds said who had taken charge of Rob's laptop.

"That's old Bert's Newsagents shop on the same side to the entrance to the Precinct. Bert struggles to compete with the big boys inside with a vast array of shops. There's a white Ford Transit Van parked in the lay-by," Rob said.

"Oh my God, here is my Grace!" Jean shouted out.

"Slow it down, Inspector," George asked where they all watched Grace walking in the direction as though she was heading back to Saints House carrying a Boots carrier bag. They then watched a large coloured guy come out of the side of the van grabbing hold of Grace and pushing a white cloth into her face, and she was about to fall to the ground, but her fall was stopped by the large coloured guy who threw her into the back of the transit van as though she was a sack of potatoes.

"Oh, my poor baby," Jean Long said grabbing hold of her other daughters hugging them close to her.

"Is Grace alright, Mum?" Janet asked.

"Oh, I hope so, darling," their mother said taking them to the rear of the room with the three of them sitting on the sofa.

"Miss, could you run that again for me a frame at a time?" George Almedia asked.

"Here the registration of the van is T834 LOL."

"We are not laughing out loud here," Rob shouted at the screen.

"That's a rented motor," DS Jones said looking closer at the screen.

"Can you enlarge the screen, boss?"

"That's better T&T Rentals in small print close to the bumper, sorry I can't make out the telephone number," DS Jones said looking annoyed with himself that he couldn't make out the telephone number of T&T Rentals.

"Hold it there, Miss. I know that African guy, he's Jim Song. I stopped him a while back robbing a bank in Mwanza that I was consulting for to improve their security. Mind you, I was lucky since his gun jammed otherwise yours truly would not be here today. He got five years in prison in Dar-es-Salaam."

Rob look at the driver, "I am sure that's a woman?" Rob leaned over DI Judy Reynolds's shoulder who ducked lower in her seat giving him the needed view of his laptop. "No, no it can't be Anna Kajeme, not after you George saw her off with a bloody nose earlier?" he said looking at his parents standing in the doorway looking totally confused to what was going on. George Almedia stood close to the 7-foot copper and looked up to him and shrugged his shoulder much as to say it could be. "Well is it her?" Rob asked.

"I am not sure, Rob, it fucking could be; sorry for my language," George said looking at Rob's mum and dad who would have known nothing about them robbing a grave.

Judy Reynolds pressed play again, and they could see the van heading down the New Kent Road when the CCTV stopped giving Rob's laptop a blank screen. "Give us your mobile, Rob," which he did, and she pressed send twice. "Tony, Judy here. Again a white Ford Transit van, registration T834 LOL heading down the New Kent Road towards the Old Kent Road at 5:30 pm. Name of the rented vehicle is T&T Rentals. Please see what you can pick up for me."

"Yes, I know I owe you, cheers," she said and then ended the call.

"Now what do we do, Inspector?" Jean Long called out from the sofa where she was still sitting on between her two younger daughters.

"We have to wait, Jean."

"Wait for what, Inspector?"

DS Jones answered for her boss, and told Jean, "We have to wait and see what our team at the Reading Police Station can come up with the information we have given them and yes we have to also wait for a further telephone call from those that have taken Grace."

"George, if that was Anna Kajeme, she must have known you had received that million-pound reward, and you confirmed to her on the BBC News that it was me that helped you gain that reward. I reckon she saw you leaving for the airport, giving them the freedom to get hold of Grace. Otherwise, she would give you a wide birth thinking you were still in the UK after the beating you gave her last time you two crossed swords."

George thought Rob could just be right. "Jean, if it is Anna Kajeme and we can obtain where that transit van went to and who had rented it then, fear not, your big sister will be home soon," George said ruffling Jane and Janet's hair at the same time and leaning over, giving Jean a tender kiss on her cheek.

"Rob, your father and I never saw George receiving a reward and him mentioning your name," Julie Hat said taking the cups back into the kitchen. "Jim, don't stand there with your mouth wide open. Give us a hand in the kitchen since more drinks are going to be needed seeing it looks like we are in for a long night."

"Rob, go and tell your folks what's been going on," George said and then added, "Jean, go with Rob since you deserve to know just why these low lives have taken your daughter."

After Jean followed Rob out into the kitchen, DS Jones whispered to his boss, "Once again, he's going to have to explain to his parents just how he just happened to recognise that Peter Goodman was, in fact, Trevor Charles Baines."

DI Judy Reynolds stood up and looked up to DS Jones and said, "First, he found stolen cash, granted he helped a great many with it. Let's not forget the large reward he gained from handing over those stolen diamonds from Johnson Diamond Mind in Tanzania. Nothing would surprise me if he was not involved with the collapse of the Peoples Unite Party." She said walking to the sofa to try to comfort Grace's two younger sisters who were looking scared and confused about what's going on.

Rob's mobile went off that was by the side of his laptop. Rob dashed back in to pick it up. "Put it on the loudspeaker, Rob," the DI called out from the sofa. Before Rob picked up his mobile, "Everyone, please be silent and, Rob, do not let on that I am here."

Chapter 103
It's a Large File

Jim Song just got into the passenger seat of the van and looked at Anna on Grace's mobile putting her index finger to her lips. "Hello, Rob, it's so nice to talk to you once again. Yes, I know you are standing there wishing dear old George was with you and not on his way back to Tanzania."

"Miss Kajeme, you really are pissing in the wind. For one, I don't have 500k." Anna Kajeme looked at Jim Song and smiled knowing the little shit was not being honest with her.

"Your Grace is safe and reasonably well, and you have my word, we will not hurt her. It will be you not handing over the 500k that will see her suffer. She's tucked away in a room with no windows, and all she has is a small bottle of water to last her, and that's it, and I have no intention of visiting her again. As harsh as it sounds, Rob, your darling Grace could starve to death.

"So, Thursday I will give you a place and a time that you're to bring me 500k and I promise to give you the address and the keys to release her."

Back at Saints House, DS John Jones was holding up a piece of paper saying 'keep her talking.' "Why should I trust you?"

"Because you have no other choice," Anna said and then ended the call.

"Sorry, John, she simply hung up."

Rob leaned over his laptop and handed DI Judy Reynolds his mobile knowing she would want to contact her office at Reading Police Station. "Rob, what's your email address?" the DI asked.

"Help@hotmail account."

"Is that dot com or a dot UK?"

"UK," Rob told her.

She took Rob's mobile out into the hallway, and they could just make out her talking to her office. All of four minutes later, she came back into the lounge "Rob, boot up your laptop and go into your email account." Judy took her own mobile out. "I am sending you what my office has sent me to my email," the DI said.

"I thought you were going to use my mobile?"

"I did, Rob, but for security reasons what they sent me needs to go to a police officer and not Joe public."

"I have it," and then he opens his mail.

"Shit, it's a large file, and I will have to wait for it download." With complete silence in Julie's lounge with them all waiting to see what DI Reynolds had sent to Rob. Jean Long sitting with her daughters at the far end of the lounge, failed to hear what Rob was saying.

"What is it Rob, what's going on? When are you going to get my Angel back home?"

Rob never had a clue what to say to her; it was DI Judy Reynolds who joined her on the sofa and explained what they were all waiting for.

Jim Hat came into the lounge and saw Rob tapping his fingers on the coffee table waiting for the file to open. "Rob, since you left school you have been very secretive. At no time did you mention that you saw Trevor Charles Baines in Tanzania and that you and George, along with my brother, were going to rob a grave." Rob looked around the room hoping someone was going to speak up for him, but the room was silent apart from their wall clock ticking.

"Sorry, Dad, I thought it best not to say anything."

"George, what do you know about the PM's lost red leather parliamentary case?" Jim asked George who looked at DS, who quickly turned away not wishing to get involved in the question.

"Nothing at all, Jim, only what I have heard on the TV and press."

Jim bent down at looked directly into his son's eyes, "What do you know about it, young man?" DI Judy Reynolds walked over to where Rob was sitting still tapping his fingers on the coffee table.

"Rob, you need to promise me that it was not you standing on the edge of that train after the rail crash with that large case by your side waiting for someone to give you a handoff?" Jim, like DI Reynolds, was waiting for what his son had to say.

"Yes, I was on that train, but I was not waiting on the edge of the train. I was one of the first off before the police and the ambulances along with the BBC turning up."

Rob turned his attention to the screen. "Can I now say your interrogation is over?" Then he shouted at the screen, "Please open, my Grace is far more important than Simon Davis's red bloody case."

Chapter 104
Why, Why Am I Here?

Grace, eventually, came round with not the foggiest where and why she was lying on a mattress on the floor in a room with no windows. The only light came from under the door facing her. She struggled to get up, rubbing her ribs while thinking she might have been punched or it happened when she could have been thrown into a motor. She made her way to the door and, using her left hand, found her way around the room looking for a light switch. Made her jump when she kicked over a metal object, she was pleased to know it was a bucket. "Could be handy," she said so she kept on round the room turning a sharp right a little; further she tripped over the mattress. Eventually, she got back to where the light under the door was with her hand going up the side of the door and found two switches. The first one she switched down, there was nothing. Pressing the top one on. "We have light," she shouted out as the 4-foot florescent light started to flicker for a few seconds but then came on.

Picking up the bucket, she noticed the small bottle water near the end of the filthy mattress. Picking up the water and asked, "Why am I here, Mr Water?" She noticed there was no sign of her mother's medication that she thought she must have dropped when the African guy put a stinking cloth over her nose and mouth and once again a little later inside a van but other than that, she never had a bloody clue to what was happening.

So, there she sat thinking that she should have refused Rob when he suggested taking a week's holiday from Premier to see baby Grace off along with everyone else going back to Tanzania.

Grace sat there thinking that she would have told baby Grace if only she could. "Don't you worry about me, Grace. Your godmother will get out of here soon and later in the year, I will be flying to Tanzania to take you out in Machame for long walks."

"Why, why am I here?" she screamed out hoping some bugger would hear her.

Chapter 105
London Gangster

"Charlie, life, as we know it, will never be the same again. Your father will be going away for a very long while," Glenda Baines said drinking her coffee in the kitchen.

Charlie took his coffee and said, "Mother, you're jumping the gun. His actual trial won't take place until early in 2016; all he's done so far is give his name and age to the court."

"Charlie, your old man is banged to rights if he ever gets out, he will be a very old man. Next year, when you're called for the defence, don't you dare perjure yourself; if you do, you will end up following him to prison."

"What time are the buyers for the house due today?" Glenda took her diary out of her bag.

"7 pm, Charlie. They're coming to do a few measurements and, in a perfect world, we should be out of here by the end of August."

"Mother, who is that keeping their hand on our gate the buzzer?"

Glenda turned on the gate monitor. "Shit, I never thought we would see Anna Kajeme again. She will now be fully aware she's got bugger all to threaten us with now my husband is behind bars." Anna Kajeme's driver in a BMW was sitting passionately for the gates to swing open. Glenda, simply out of curiosity to what she might want, opened the gates. Charlie met her at the door where she never waited to be invited in; she simply walked in then straight into the lounge dressed this time in a bright red leather skin tight full trouser suit. "So, what can we do for you?" Glenda asked watching her son going to their cocktail cabinet.

"Straight brandy for me," Anna called out.

"So, you're asking what I want of the Baines's family? I was in Lamberts Estate Agent in Sandhurst, and I see you have sold this glorious house for 2.2 million. Yes, I have to agree it's a fair price."

Charlie brought her drink over and leant over putting her drink on the glass coffee table and said, "And you're not getting fucking penny of it."

Anna Kajeme smiled at Charlie and turned to face his mother, "Shame on you, Charlie Baines. I have not asked for anything." Glenda walked to the cocktail cabinet and poured herself a good measure of whiskey.

Charlie then faced their unwanted guest, "So, why the hell are you here?"

Anna Kajeme finished her drink and said, "I have just come to tell you both that I have been given a book offer that will be called, 'Sleeping with the Notorious London Gangster.' The publishers feel after hearing the outlay of my true stories that I will write; they would hope it could make into not only a best seller but as the possibility of going on the large screen. I have been given a £20,000 down payment with further payments plus when it goes into print, of course, there will be generous royalties that will come my way."

Glenda looked at her son who said, "Please let us have a signed copy, now you can fuck off." Charlie said opening the lounge door and waving her out.

Driving out the Baines's Property with the gates left open after their entry into the house. "So, how did that visit go then?" Jim Song asked.

"When I send her a taster from my forthcoming book, I feel she just might change her mind with her name going into print."

"Where to now, Anna?" she smiled and squeezed his crutch.

"Bed, of course, then Thursday I have a very important call to make," she said with her hand still on his crutch.

"Yes, big boy needs a nightcap."

Chapter 106
Sorry, Big Boy

With Anna Kajeme still trying to squeeze money out of Glenda and Charlie Baines seeing she must be a strong believer that failure can't live with determination.

Back on the fifth floor at Saints House, DI Reynolds, DS Jones and George Almedia, along with Rob, were all viewing the download that the Met Office at Reading had sent through.

"This is what we viewed earlier where Grace was thrown into the back of the van," Rob said wishing he had not persuaded Grace to take this week off.

"Here we go, big guy. The van's going down New Kent Road stop starting in the slow traffic. There it goes over the small flyover New Kent Road and here it is joining the Old Kent Road getting on the tail end of the heavy traffic," DI Judy Reynolds said.

With the screen seemed to be frozen, "It's off again" George said. Eventually, the van got to the Thomas Becket where it turned right into Albany Road. The CCTV followed the van that seemed about half a mile with its indicator highlighted it's turning left.

"But, there's no road to turn left into," DS Jones said. Then they all watched the van jump the kerb and then it vanished.

The screen went blank. "Tony's added some text," the DI said watching Rob shifting closer to the screen.

"Ford Transit Van Registration T834 LOL
T&T Rentals Oxford Road Reading Telephone number 01189 63333
Proprietor Philip Right
Rented this Monday by a Jim Song
Due to be returned this Thursday by 1 pm
Judy, I hope this helps you solve your case?
Last but not least, you're taking me out to dinner this weekend."

"So, its true boss, you and our Tony Shaw, known as the brains, are fast becoming a couple," DS Jones said.

"Sorry, big boy, you're far too tall for me."

George then butted in and said, "I am all for a bit of leg-pulling but can't it wait until we get our Grace back home?"

“Right, DS Jones, we are going to use your car seeing you have the facility to plug Rob’s laptop in and we can view where that van jumped the kerb and, in a perfect world, Mrs Long, your daughter will be home within an hour or so,” DI Reynolds said putting her coat on.

“Please don’t let me down, we will be praying you are right,” Jean Long said with her younger daughters snuggling up to her looking scared having their big sister kidnapped.

“Boss, Anna Kajeme said that she would not be returning to where Grace is.”

Rob looked puzzled and asked, “Meaning what, John?”

It was DI Reynolds that said, “If she’s been locked away somewhere then the chances are, she will be alone more so since their rented vehicle needs to be back by Thursday.”

Chapter 107
Ready to Play

With Rosie and Pauline on their flight to Kilimanjaro, sitting in the row in front of Alan Yvonne with Grace sound asleep on Yvonne's lap.

Alan's curiosity was getting the better of him as he pulled out his hand luggage from under the seat in front of him and pulled out the box a little smaller than a shoebox. This being the parting gift from George Almedia had given him earlier before they departed Saints House to Heathrow. With enormous amounts of Sellotape, he started ripping it off the lid to get it open. He then placed the lid on the floor. Inside the box, he had to smile seeing whatever it was inside. It was wrapped in a Castle Palace Hotel cloth serviette. Taking off the serviette, "It's not bloody Christmas," he said seeing his gift was wrapped in cheap Christmas paper and plenty of it. Taking a set key from his pocket, he ripped a hole in the paper to see what was inside.

"Oh, shit," he said out loud putting the serviette around his gift and grabbed the lid off the floor and immediately put it back in his holdall and pushed it back under the seat in front of him.

"You okay, Alan?" Rosie asked.

"I am fine, Rosie, I had just dropped my book off my lap." Why this was going on and hearing Alan lie to Rosie seeing he didn't have a book with him.

"What's he bought us then?" his wife asked. Alan leant over and whispered in Yvonne's ear. Yvonne glanced at his holdall under the seat, "You are kidding me?"

"Refreshments, Sir?" the young Stewardess asked.

"Two coffees, please miss."

Alan looked at Yvonne and said, "I wish I was just kidding."

Alan could see Rosie, who was leaning out of her aisle seat and called out, "Two brandies here, darling."

"Alan, when your brother opens his gift, he's going to have forty-fits?" his wife said sounding annoyed. Then added, "Jean long will not have a bloody clue what to do with it and not that I do."

"George is a fantastic guy, but he's never been known for being a law-abiding citizen," Alan said noticing the warning light had come on. "You two young ladies in front, seat belts on please."

"Alan, when we go through customs at Kilimanjaro you are not putting that holdall on our trolley," Yvonne said attending to baby Grace who had woken up and was ready to play.

Chapter 108
Counting Each Tick

DS Jones was doing the driving with his boss DI Judy Reynolds on her mobile informing her DCI what DS Jones and she were doing. George and Rob were in the back with Rob looking anxious to what condition they might find Grace in. "Rob, she's going to be alright. There's no benefit to Anna Kajeme to harm her not while she believes she can gain 500k from you," George said then lowered his voice. "Okay, we get Grace back tonight and when Kajeme calls Thursday we do not say she's home safe and well. You're to tell her that you will pay to get Grace back and she's going to be in total shock when she shows her face with her latest minder, Mr Jimmy Song. I just hope this time he's not carrying a loaded gun. This piece of shit would dearly love to see me meet my maker."

"Jones, when we turn right at the Thomas Becket, you're to pull over and then forward the CCTV to the right turn into Albany Road then we drive the route to where the van jumped the kerb and vanished," his boss said.

With George in the back of the unmarked Mondeo police car telling Rob what his intentions were. At Saints House, Jim Hat was trying to keep young Jane and Janet Long from crying with their mother just staring at the ticking clock above the fireplace. Jim couldn't be sure, but he thought he heard counting each tick.

Rob's mother seeing her husband was occupied and Jean, her friend, trying to block out the doubt that she might never get Grace back, Julie took her mobile into her bedroom. Calling Tony, his brother, to let him know what was going on. Tony must have been on loudspeaker seeing it was Linda who said, "Oh my God, I bet Jean is so worried; however, Julie, if Rob's caught hold of George before he flew to Tanzania, he will not let any harm come to her. Please give Jean our love and that we are thinking of her."

Then her son came back on the telephone, "Mum, we will be with you within the hour," and then ended the call.

Chapter 109
I Am So Hungry

"Park by the bus stop and fast forward the CCVT from here," the DI said.

"Bloody hell, boss, look at all the traffic behind," DS Jones said looking in his inside rear-view mirror seeing the traffic backed up to the Thomas Becket.

"Don't you worry about them, you just keep driving slowly," she said. Then looking at Rob's screen and the placard advertising a warehouse for rent on her left, "Jump the kerb now, John," the DI shouted with George and Rob swaying from side to side as the car jumped up that could have been a high kerb.

George looked in front of him from the rear of the car. "John, 100 yards in front of us is an old building standing in what seems like a wasteland," George said with Rob sitting there with his fingers crossed. A few bumps later, DS Jones pulled around the back of what looked like a derelict building.

"John, you need to get some tools out of your box in the boot," she said as all four doors of the Mondeo opened at the same time.

The four of them went up the rickety rusty stairs; DS Jones being the last one to reach the platform at the top to the back door of the so-called warehouse. "Move over, guys," DS Jones said with a very large screwdriver and a hammer.

Rob was looking down the right side of the door and said, "I think there's a light coming from under the door on the left."

Grace had been drifting in and out of sleep, thinking it could have been what was on the cloth that was used to knock her out. It was also keeping her from staying awakc; shc was also lightheadcd. Then she heard someone banging on the outside door. "Give it to us here, John," George Almedia took the two tools and placed the screwdriver on the lock of the padlock. Wallop and the padlock shot over Rob's shoulder.

Then George heard, "Please, in here."

"It's only a key lock, John," the DI said as the four of them stood by the door with a faint light coming from under the door. "Come on, big guy, let's see just how strong your shoulder is" DI Reynolds called out.

"Stand back, Grace." George and DS Jones charged at the door, and they both finished up in the inside with the funny bit being they both lay on the floor.

Rob stepped over his two very good friends seeing Grace, sitting on a dirty old mattress waving an empty water bottle, who said, "My waters all gone, so what's kept you?"

"Let me have your mobile, Rob." Taking his mobile, she calls her mother, "Hi, Mum, I am so hungry."

Chapter 110
Lol

Needless to say, on the fifth floor of Saints House, there were a great many tears of joy knowing Grace was back safe with her only one mishap being a possible cracked rib caused from the African guy being rough with her.

DI Judy Reynolds was busy taking a statement of Grace when she was satisfied that she had gained the information Judy wanted, she gave Grace a kiss on the cheek. “Glad we could help, darling,” Judy Reynolds said.

“Thank you, Inspector,” Grace said returning the kiss.

“George, you’re not very good at whispering in the back of the Mondeo on our trip to Albany Road earlier. When this Anna Kajeme calls Rob Thursday, you’re to call me and let me or my office know where and when you are meeting her to enable me to arrest her for kidnapping,” the DI said with George and Rob both nodding. She then added, “If I know you, Rob, it’s one thing you nodding in agreement but you have a habit of forgetting and that goes for you too Mr George Almedia from Mwanza.”

“Have you finished with Grace now, Inspector?” Linda asked walking over to Grace and not waiting for the DI to answer her question she was smothering her with kisses.

“Please don’t squeeze me, Linda. Hopefully, I don’t cough or laugh for a while,” Grace said crossing her arms over her chest.

“What’s that African bitch asking Rob for her safe return?” Tony asked.

“500k, Bro, and, if we had not have rescued her, I would not have hesitated in paying for her safe return; yes, I would have coughed up.”

Grace, with her arms still crossed her chest, said, “Thank you, I love you and, in fact, that goes for all of you that got me home safe.”

“Let’s get back to our office, big guy. Grace, the next time you’re in Reading, please call in and let me introduce you to Tony since it was his knowledge that put half a dozen CCTV from different locations together that got us to you,” the DI said with DS Jones laughing.

“Spit it out, Sergeant,” she asked him kind of knowing she was about to be embarrassed.

“I have nothing say, boss. You blushing says it all,” DS Jones said giving a farewell wave as both officers left the flat.

“Come on, Grace, and you two little darlings let’s make a move to the fourth floor,” Jean Long said watching Grace hushing Jane and Janet off the sofa.

“Jim, it’s late. Let’s say goodnight to George and, of course, our son,” Julie said pulling Jim out of his armchair. Rob and George went into the kitchen with Rob filling the kettle up.

“George, ever since the Reading Police Station arrested Jim Stone, the gang leader by then it was, I believe a DI John Green for his part in the bank robbery at Clinton Green near Reading. So now whenever my name is mentioned, it’s always the Reading Station that turns up when it should be the borough boys in blue knocking at my door.” George didn’t have any idea what he was waffling on about, he just made the two teas and never made any comments.

“George, you might as well spend the night here; I still have my brothers’ single bed in my bedroom. Besides, I would rather have you here when Anna Kajeme comes calling?” George was thinking that was a good idea seeing he had checked out of the Castle Palace Hotel plus he no longer had a rented vehicle.

“That’s fine, Rob, but you will have to drop me at Heathrow that’s assuming I manage to get a flight for tomorrow,” he said making his way to the bathroom with his tea.

Rob looked at his box that George had given him tucked in the corner, “What’s in the box?”

George never answered until he called out from the bathroom before closing the door, “Please wait until I am on my way home.”

Sitting on the sofa, Rob kicked off his shoes and was drinking his tea thinking he could be a jinx seeing his life is not the norm when his mobile went indicating he had a text. Opening his mobile, he saw it was from his uncle tucking his legs up on the sofa he reads.

“Hi, Rob, we are all home safe and sound. Bernie is in with Rosie and Pauline who they have already grown attached to. I just hope they have brought more than one pair of shoes with them. (**LOL**)

Out of curiosity, I looked inside the box that George gave me whilst on our flight home. Perhaps you have done likewise; if you haven’t, good luck when you do. Love to you all, Alan xx”

Rob sat there scratching his head wondering what he was saying about George’s boxes that he had handed out like sweets. George came back from the bathroom watching him texting. “My uncle,” Rob said and then wrote.

“Hi, Uncle, yet to open it, but I will later. Nothing to worry about here but we have had one heck of a day here. Will email you Thursday and give you all the details.

Thanks for your help,

Rob xxxx”

Chapter 111
Your Latest Aftershave

9 am Thursday, Jim Hat was on his way to Gems for a day's graft with his wife who went down on the fourth floor checking on Grace after her ordeal Wednesday.

"Rob, we are going to need two dustbin bags full of rubbish," George said putting milk in his father's favourite Snap Crackle and Pop Cereal.

"No problem, we can take them out of the communal bin that's thrown down the Shute as and when we leave, but why?" Rob asked.

George smiled and said, "How else would we get 500k to Anna Kajeme since she would want to see the money."

The penny dropped, and Rob said, "Bloody fantastic idea!"

George had his ear to his bowl of cereal, "I can hear the snap and the crackle, but I am dammed if I can hear the pop."

It was now 10 am and yet to hear from Anna. "Rob, check with Grace since I would like for her to be with us when we pay her the 500k," he said giving Rob a wink that amused Rob with the thought of Kajeme getting her just rewards.

After a call from Rob with Grace in agreement and said she would wait to hear from him. "Mr Robert Hat, when the bitch calls, which she will, make sure you tell her you're waiting for the clearance of such a large amount of cash from your bank," George said who was now busy getting himself a flight to Mwanza.

"Thank you, yes it's no problem having to change at Dar-es-Salaam for my short flight to Mwanza." George put his hand over the mouthpiece, "5 pm, Rob, out of terminal four?"

"Yes, I will pick up my flight tickets from the Kenya information desk. Thank you," then he ended the call.

10:45, Rob's mobile went off. "Put it on the loudspeaker, Rob. Let it buzz a further twice."

"Hello," but there was no response.

He was about to hang up when he heard, "Good morning, Robert, I guess you have been up all night worrying about your little tart?"

"Bollocks to you, you piece of shit." Rob turned to face George who had put his two thumbs up much as to say give her as good as she's giving you.

"Now, now, young Hat. No need for such bad language. Under the circumstance, I will forgive you this one time. Anyway, Hat, that's enough of our idol chats. Seeing I am not a vindictive person, I will come to your area to receive my 500k more so seeing young Grace is very close to you that will save you a great deal of time in rescuing her."

"When and where then?" Rob put his hand again over the mouthpiece. "George, I hate this woman," he said with George nodding.

"Seeing Thursday is a relatively quieter day for the shops, how about at the top level of Gems Supermarket car park? Shall we say 1 pm, alone?" George scribbled something on the palm of his hand and put in front of Rob's face with him remembering what was agreed earlier.

"Since you're asking for such a large amount of cash, I called my bank at 9 am, and it will not be ready for collection until 1:30, so can we say 2 pm?" Kajeme never responded immediately.

"Hat, any police and I promise you will never see Grace again; she will starve to death, all alone." Then the connection was cut off by Anna Kajeme.

"Well done, my friend," George said then added, "At 1 pm, Grace and I will be in the back of your van. You will have the two bags of rubbish in front with you that you will show Anna and her minder when they arrive. When we drive to the car park…"

Rob interrupted him and said, "The top floor is in the open."

George nodded and said, "Better, still it will far quieter for us. You drive to the top; you make sure the back door is not closed. Please don't forget this, I need to come out of the back doors, and you must park up against a wall so no one can come from behind either of us." Rob never questioned his plan seeing he knew George always knew best when it comes to handing out pain.

"Your shout, George," Rob said watching his friend taking out a few plastic ties from his holdall and putting them in his inside jacket pocket.

"Rob, all you need to do is to stand there looking pretty with those two rubbish bags beside you. It will be me that gives Anna Kajeme her 500k." Once again, Rob said nothing.

At 12:30 with George's luggage in Rob's Morris Minor Van, Rob went to the rubbish Shute, and George watched him disappear into the large rubbish bin. George stood there laughing and watching two large full bin liners coming in his direction and landing at his feet. "That was not funny, young man," he said watching Rob straddling the bin and jumping down.

"True, George, but I could hear you laughing as my legs vanished into the shitty bin." George picked up the two bags and walked back to the Morris Van and placed them on the passenger's seat.

"Bloody hell, you bloody stink now you go and let Grace have a whiff of your latest aftershave."

Chapter 112
You're Friendly African

"Jim, put it back in your pants and get dressed. I want to leave sharp at 1 pm since I would like to arrive a little before 2 pm," Anna said pulling her G string up.

"Can you trust this kid?" Jim said searching for his socks.

"Yes, without George by his side, we can. Jim, Rob Hat might be young, but the little git is a clever little sod," she said watching her minder pull out a small chopper from under the bed.

"You won't need that. You can rest assured he will not want to fight. All he wants is his Grace back."

"He will not give you 500k until he gets her back," Jim said knowing he was right.

"True, big boy. Once we see the cash, he can follow us to the warehouse where we do the swop."

Whilst Anna was getting ready to leave the Hilton Hotel in Park Lane, Grace was jumping in the back of Rob's Morris Van plonking herself on the spare wheel. George jumped in sitting on the wooden floor. "Jesus, what's that bloody smell?" Grace asked.

"It's either 500k of rubbish or its lover boy's new aftershave," George said taking out his mobile and making a call.

"George, I am going to take a slow ride to Gems."

George looked at Grace and said, "Hang on a minute, Rob. I am waiting for DI Judy Reynolds to pick up."

"Good afternoon, DI Reynolds here, how can I help you?" Rob turned in his seating wanting to hear what he was telling the Inspector.

"Hi, Miss Reynolds. George Almedia here, your friendly African. Willing to help?" Rob had to smile with the word willing he said to the Inspector.

"Cut the crap out, George, what's going down?" George looked at Rob putting his fingers to his nose and then pulled his hand outward.

"Tell her the truth, George."

George shook his head, "5 pm top floor at the Gems Supermarket car park. Please don't come heavy-handed seeing you might miss the opportunity of putting her away for a long while if she sees many of your team come charging in," then he ended the call.

"George, why 5 pm?" George laughed with Grace looking confused.

"Simple, really. Rob, I should be on my way back to Mwanza around that time."

Chapter 113
Flaming June

At 1:40, Rob took his ticket out the machine at the barrier and slowly started to drive to the fifth floor of the car park.

"Change of plan. Rob, throw those two bags of rubbish back here with me," George said. The first bag he tossed over hit Grace on her arm with the second bag landing at her feet.

"Bloody hell! Rob, they stink!"

George smiled when he said, "Sorry, darling, they were meant to hit George."

"Is there a valid reason as to why you are changing your earlier scenario what you had drummed into me?" George never answered until they got to the fifth floor where Rob parked the van tight up against the wall on his left.

"It's safer for you when they arrive; they are going to ask to see the money. You then jump in the back of the van to pick up the two bags of rubbish, but you will not be getting out, it will be me following the two bags you throw out. You two need to stay by the van until it's all over."

Grace kicked the bags over to George. "Get your nose around them; you wish you had a cold!" Grace said with Rob having a chuckle upfront glad to see the back of the bags.

"Yes, Rob, you're going to be far safer staying by the van," Rob was a little disappointed seeing he could miss out on all the fireworks that are likely to be going off.

Leaving George and Grace in the back of the van, Rob walked around the top floor of the car park, but other than two cars, one was missing its front wheels while the other looked like it was burnt out. All he had on was a T-shirt and, with the strong wind blowing across the car park, it had started to rain. He wished he was better prepared for the indifferent flaming June that was fast approaching.

Chapter 114
Voice Mail

Back at the van with its front door open, he sat on the side waiting for Anna Kajeme's vehicle to arrive. The wait was only a few minutes; Rob looked to his right seeing a black BMW coming up the ramp flashing its headlights and acknowledging he had been seen along with his unmistakable 20-year-old bright Red Morris Van. The BMW drove a further 30 yards before parking up.

He was tempted to lean backwards to let George and Grace know that they had arrived, but he put his hand over his mouth still looking ahead and said, "The African is in the house."

Not inspecting an answer, "There's a further one in the back of your van."

He sat there waiting for Anna Kajeme to get out of the car before he made a move. It took a further minute before the two front doors of the BMW opened with her minder, Jim Song, walking around the back of the car while leaving his driver's door open. He joined Anna, who was leaning on the back panel of the car. Rob had no intentions of going up close to them but came forward so he could be heard and said, "Where's my Grace?" Jim Song wanted to walk forward, but Anna Kajeme stopped him in his tracks.

"All in good time, young man. Where's my cash?" she said watching a young guy that came up the ramp at high speed with the smoke coming from the back tyres of his Mini when the car shot down the ramp that displayed exit.

"Hope the silly bastard crashes!" Anna shouted at the rear of the Mini that vanished out of sight. "Okay, Hat, now you need to show me the 500k, and then you will follow us to where Grace is, and then we will do the swop—my cash for your love one." As agreed, Rob walked around the back of the van, swung the doors open, and jumped in the back.

"Told you, Jim, there would be no problem without his friend being here," she said watching the two large black dustbin sacks being tossed out of the van while waiting for Rob to follow them.

"Oh fuck," she said seeing Grace Long heave herself down from the back, followed by George Almedia who picked up the two bags and casually strolled the short distance towards the BMW.

Anna stood there with her mouth wide open in amazement to see him and Grace appear. "Jim, here's your second chance to take Almedia out who you say owes you five years of your life," she shouted at him. He was now only ten feet from the BMW when he placed the two plastic sacks down.

Jim Song pulled a small chopper cum axe from the back of his trouser belt. "Song, you can walk away now, but I guess you won't take my offer for you to run away down the ramp?" George said pointing to the exit sign and, within seconds, he was watching Song come charging the short distance towards him screaming.

"You're a dead man, Almedia!" he called out with his axe in his right hand holding it high to swipe down on George's head. George ducked low, and the moment Song's body came in contact, he immediately stood up to throw him over his shoulder with his axe flying towards the Morris Van. When Grace saw it landing, she ran forward and collected it and dashed back to the van and handed it to Rob who was now sitting on the end of the van not wanting to miss anything.

"Thank you, Grace. I am so pleased you decided to come along," George said dragging his attacker who had, unfortunately, landed on the side of his head that left a trail of blood towards the BMW. Anna Kajeme attempted to run around to the back of her car to get into the driver's seat and get away. "I will give you ten for trying, Anna," George said who had grabbed hold of her by her hair when she got to the boot of the car and dragged her back. Then, he threw her on top of Jim Song, who was trying to get up.

Pulling Anna off Song by her hair once again, he got her upright. "I did warn you the last time you tried to harm Grace that you would suffer." Using the palm of his right hand, he smashed it into her face and heard her nose crack, and he guessed Jim Song would have also heard it or, at least, seen a steady flow of blood. If he had looked up, he would have seen her nose now going to the right of her face. With the offside front door closed, he opened it and dragged her into the passenger's seat.

Then he heard Rob shout out, "Behind you!" George turned but not fast enough since Jim Song jumped on to his back and wrestled him to the floor. Song got up and was about to kick him in the head when he felt the weight of George Almedia's right foot that hit him in his crutch and doubled him over.

"Nice one, George!" Grace screamed out watching him dragging Song to the driver's side. He heaved him and sat him up. Then getting his head, George smashed it onto the dashboard, opening his damage further. Going back to the offside, he sat on Anna's lap and took two ties from his jacket. Then pulling over Song's left hand, he tied it to the steering wheel. Then, leaning further in, he grabbed Song's right hand, tugged him over and tied it again to the steering wheel.

"You are not so pretty now, Anna," he said taking a further two ties and, like with Song, tied both her hands to the steering wheel.

"Grace, and you, Rob, get over here and bring those two plastic sacks with you!" he shouted out. Within seconds, they were standing by the car holding a bag each. "Grace, now you need to pay Anna Kajeme 250k and you, Rob, give Jim Song his share."

George stood back and watched his friends shake the two bags of rubbish over them. He then went around the driver's side and sat on the back seat and, holding his nose, he wound the two rear windows down a few inches. He then took the keys out of the ignition, closed the door and then locked the car while putting the keys inside the nearside front wheel.

George checked the time and seeing it was only 3 pm. "Rob, I need to change my bloodied clothes from my case, and then I need to catch my flight from Heathrow."

At 3:20 pm, the three of them were heading for Heathrow with George sitting on the spare wheel. He took out his mobile,

"Miss Reynolds, so sorry I made a mistake with the time I should have said 3 pm and not 5 pm. You will be pleased to know the guilty parties for the kidnapping of young Grace are on the fifth floor. Oh yes, the keys to their BMW are in the inside of the nearside front wheel.

I wish you well.
George."

"What she say?" Rob asked.

George smiled, "Nothing, my call went straight into her voice mail."

Chapter 115

Never Fails to Surprise Him

With the heavy traffic back from Heathrow on the M4, they never pulled into Saints House and parked by Grace's mum's garage until after 7 pm. "That's DS Jones car parked at the far end, Grace, and just in front him, that's Linda's Mini Cooper," Rob said walking into their flats and, as always, waited for the lift that never arrives.

"You better come up with me, Grace, and see why DS Jones is here?"

Grace looked at him. "Hell, Rob, it's bloody obvious why he's here. He will want to know if we had any dealings with the two sets of hands strapped to that BMW's steering wheel," Grace was saying as Rob opened the front door and they walked into their lounge seeing his parents, Linda and Tony along with DS Jones. They were all sitting on the sofa and the two armchairs with their boxes that George Almedia had given them in front of everyone on the floor.

"What's going on?" Rob said hearing their front doorbell going off.

"I will get it. Will be Grace's mum, Jean," Julie Hat said.

Yes, it was Jean and, like the others, was holding her box. Giving Grace a hug, she sat on the corner of the sofa giving Linda a kiss on her cheek. Rob went into the corner and picked up his own gift from George and sat on the floor in front of the TV.

"This can't be passing the parcel with five boxes involved," Grace said now sitting beside Rob on the floor.

"Before we talk about these boxes, I need to tell you as I speak, Grace and Rob, both Anna Kajeme and a Jim Song are in hospital being treated for their head wounds. They will later be charged for the kidnapping of you, Grace, and will likely be serving a prison sentence."

"Rightly so," Jean Long said throwing her daughter a kiss.

"Grace, first thing in the morning, you will need to come into Reading Police Station where DI Reynolds will assist you in accusing both of them for kidnapping you," DS Jones said then added: "Of course, you two had no knowledge in how those two finished up in the hospital." Both Rob and Grace sat on the floor vigorously shaking their heads.

"Have you finished, DS Jones?" Tony asked.

"Go ahead, Tony, please tell us why we are all here like idiots with these boxes on the floor from our friend George?"

Tony took out his mobile and said, "Earlier today, I received a text from my uncle Alan in Tanzania. Please let me readout."

Rob looked at Grace and whispered, "I had a strange message from him about the box George had given us." Tony couldn't quite hear what his brother was saying to Grace, but he defiantly heard the word box.

"Okay, Rob, mind if I read this bloody message out?" he asked sounding a little angry that his brother was whispering by the TV to Grace.

"Sorry Bro," he said with Grace giving him a dig in the side.

"He wrote, 'Hi, Tony, when you open that box George gave you and Rob along with my sister-in-law and also Grace's mum and not forgetting our seven-foot friend. I managed to get mine back home to Machame knowing I could have been arrested at customs when walking through. Like us all, we love George, but his kindness could see us all facing an enormous problem if any of us were caught in possession of what's enclosed in the boxes.

Good luck,

Alan.'"

"So, what the hell has George given us?" Rob's dad called out from the far end of the lounge.

"Only one way that we can find out is to open it," Linda said ripping the enormous amounts of Sellotape holding the lid in place. Lifting the lid next, she was faced with a Castle Palace cloth serviette wrapped around whatever it was inside only to be faced with Christmas wrapping paper rolled around the item.

"Bit early for Christmas," Jean said watching Grace pulling all the paper off their gift.

Grace screamed out, "Oh, shit!" With Rob taking hold of the 500k cheque made out to him at the bottom of the box.

"On the evening when we were at Honour Oak Cemetery, George came out from the wooded area. I wondered at the time what George had in a carrier bag tucked under his arm trying to hide the bag with his topcoat over it," DS Jones said seeing Julie Hat was simply sitting there staring at her large gold bar on her lap.

"What do we do with them, they must be very valuable?" Linda asked.

"Good question, Linda, but I don't have a bloody clue," Rob said and started to laugh knowing his friend George Almedia from Mwanza never ceases to amaze him.

Don't miss the fourth in the series of Rob Hat when he once again hopes to come up smelling of roses.

Brandy Bottom 2016/2017 one not to miss.